THE LAST ROSE

TED MESSIMER

THE LAST ROSE

For Elsie
-Please just leave words, they last longer than flowers-

Ted Messimer

Act I

ACT II

ACT III

ACT I

IN THE BEGINNING
(SPRING 2014)

On a cool California morning when Andy pulled up to Marisa's house it was around 7:00. The light of the rising sun glistened in the dew of the grass. A paperboy rode his bike down the street hitting every porch with perfection as his newspapers flew through the air. Sprinklers started to nourish every yard in the neighborhood almost as if in sequence with one another. Andy sat in Marisa's driveway and waited while listening to the young and fresh country sounds of the latest country artist on his radio. One song played completely, and Andy still waited patiently. At the end of that song, he started to wonder where Marisa was. She knew he was coming at seven. It was not like her to be late. Thinking that maybe she overslept he said out loud to his phone, "Hey, call Moe." The phone answered back, "Here is the information for Marisa Lopez. Would you like me to call her?" Andy shook his head back forth as he said, "Yes, Call Moe please!" As the phone rang, Andy thought he is probably the only person in the world to use manners with artificial intelligence. 'Why do I do that?' He thought to himself as the phone rang. On the fourth ring, he heard Marisa's voicemail. "Hey, this is Marisa. Sorry, I missed you but leave a happy message and I will get back to you soon!" At the end of the message, Andy said, "Hey Moe, it's 7:13 I'm out in the driveway." He heard a tone, looked at his phone, and saw Marisa's photo come up. Fidgeting with his screen, he answered her call and said, "Hey sleepyhead, time to hit the road." Andy heard his best friend's voice say back, "I'm not sleeping. I'm just hugging Buddy goodbye and giving my friend watching him, final instructions." Andy could hear Buddy bark with excitement in the background. "I can hear him. He sounds excited. Must recognize my ringtone." Marisa said back, "Right. Give me a minute. I'll be right out. And don't have that country music on when I get out there. There is no way I am listening to that shit for twenty-five hundred miles. Hang tight baby, be right there!" There was the sound of something falling in the background as Marisa yelled, "Buddy! " The phone hung up.

Andy hit end on the phone screen and spoke to his phone that was connected to the car radio, "Please play Moe eighties mix. " Just as quickly as the country music stopped playing some uplifting pop music from the 1980's started. Marisa came out of her house lugging two bags. Behind her was her dog sitter with a couple more.

Andy got out of his car and said with a smile, "What the heck? I thought we were only returning to the islands for a wedding, not moving back there." She laughed, "No culito. We are not moving back there. This is going to be the wedding of the century though! I need to be sure I have everything! Speaking of which, you have your suit, right?"
"Of course," he replied.
"Are you sure? Because I really don't care if you forget your toothbrush or even clean underwear. But if you forget your suit, I'm going to be super upset. Let me see it."
Andy motioned to the back passenger side of the car and said in a regal manner, "There it hangs, awaiting your magical day, my queen."
"Cool. Thanks for driving me back to the islands by the way."
Andy chuckled and said with sarcasm. "Well, I mean, I am going that way and I am a fairly important part of the day, so I figured why not?"

"You know what I mean. All joking aside, thank you."

Andy tilted his head down and eyeballed her over his sunglasses as he told her in a deep and serious tone while loading her bags in the trunk, "You're welcome. Now! Are you ready for the adventure of a lifetime? All aboard the Bridezilla express!"

"I don't think you want to see Bridezilla. Let's go!"

They had been in the car for about three hours. They didn't talk much. This would be a long trip. They had to travel from California across the whole U.S. and down to the east coast of central Florida. From there they would catch a ferry to take them and the car to their place of birth, the Peeking Islands. They could have flown but they wanted some time together before the big day. There would be plenty of time for conversation. They had known each other all their lives. Comfortable silence was something they had mastered long ago.

Finally, Andy was the first to speak, "Hey Moe, tell me again why this wedding is all the way back in the islands?"

"Because Culito, that is where we are from and where most of the friends and family are still there. It's easier to make a few people travel than a couple hundred. Aren't you the least bit excited to be going back home? It has been years."

"Excited to go back? No, not really. I mean I left it all behind for a reason. But hey if you're happy. I'm happy. This will be a fun trip."

The islands they were traveling to was where Andy and Marisa had grown up. It is a semi-mountainous, five-island chain sixty miles east of Daytona, Florida in the Atlantic Ocean. They were called the Peeking Islands. The island chain was named that way because if one is traveling by boat the mountains on the islands all seem to peek out of the ocean on approach. The locals pronounce Peeking as if it were two words: "Pea-KING". There is no explanation to it other than that is the way it had always been. The two ways to get there were by boat and plane. The five islands were clustered together and average no more than a mile apart. Each has a unique and individual flavor, but the chain itself was a popular destination for families whose kids want more than a homogenized theme park or skiing vacation. It attracted people from all walks of life, both residents and visitors. The main income was fishing and tourism.

Marisa grew up in Puerto Herradura on the island of Manta Ray, which was named after the sea creature that grows to enormous size. Its location is in the southwest portion of the island chain. It is roughly seven by five miles. It has two small mountains, three wooded areas, and a river that runs through the bottom half. It is also known for its very large seaport that is almost two miles long. The seaport is a heavy tourist area. It has a carnival-like atmosphere, many shops, restaurants, and bars fill the area. It is also where the ferry to the mainland departs from. The locals simply call it Manta. There are six much smaller seaports around the island, which are used mainly by fishermen.

Andy grew up in Vista Bahia on Bear Island. Bear Island is a four-by-two-mile island at the top center of the chain. It had one large mountain at the south portion of the island and the middle was covered by vegetation. Vista Bahia was a community for the wealthy. It is at the top of the mountain and overlooks a beautiful bay that is filled with live-aboard boats. Many people who work in the service industry live on those boats below. Many of them took great pride in calling themselves "the trailer park of the sea". They loved the fact that, in their minds, they were ruining the bay view for all the "richies" in the mountains above them. Bear Island has five small seaports along the north and two in the south inside the bay. Those are used for people who live on their boats to park their dinghies.

The two had started at the same school on Manta, but Andy was later sent to a military academy located in Aullando Cala Lobo called the Rome Military Academy, on the island of Isla de Cabeza Martillo. Most of the islands were named because; to someone at least, they looked like something on a map. Isla de Cabeza Martillo, or Martillo as the locals called it, took the shape of a hammerhead shark. The northernmost point where the Rome Military Academy was located however looked like a howling wolf whose shape created a small cove. The island is the easternmost island and the longest. It is nine miles long by four miles wide. It has three small mountains, one lake, and some woodland areas. The island is where the airport is. Martillo is known for a place on the eastern side of the island called, Looking Man. On a map, it takes the shape of a man's face looking to the east. The small town at that location boasts as being the first place to see the sunrise in the United States. Technically though, the easternmost part of the United States would have been at the southernmost tip of Martillo where the part of the "hammer" sticks out. Nobody, tourists anyway, would ever go there. It was an area filled with marsh and mangroves. There is no actual town there. There are a good handful of people that do live there. Vagabond type. They are not necessarily bad people per se. If a mainlander saw them in town though they would probably walk to the other side of the street. The locals called it Shadytown, or Shady'tn. The reason being that is the phrase that the people who lived in tents out there describe it as a sunny paradise with shady people. Most of the people who live there, work at the historic seaport on Manta as buskers. All along the west side of the island are six seaports for fishing. The east side only has two that no one uses.

The island smack in the middle of the chain is Isla Sirena. Some say it got its name because it looks like a manatee and manatees are really what the sailors of the old day were talking about when they told stories of mermaid sightings. It is a four by two-mile island and the only island that has two bridges to it from two other islands. Those would be Manta and Bear Island. All the other islands have only one bridge. To get from one to another, a person may have to go through more than one island or take a boat. Isla Sirena has one mountain running through the middle and a river that runs through the mountain. All of the island's radio and television stations broadcast from this island. Other than a hospital, jail, and a few seaports, there is nothing else on the island.

Located in the Northwest section of the chain and above Manta is Isla Fantasma. Because of the location of its two small lakes, the mountain to the north of the lakes, the rest of the island being covered in thick vegetation, and its shape, from the air, it looks like a ghost. Nobody lives on that island, as it is a national park. The only way to get there is by boat. It has one small seaport. People can and do camp there often. That is the island chain where Andy and Marisa grew up. Now they were on their way back to their island home from their current home in California.

Andy had once again broken the silence. "Hey, Moe?"
"Yes?"
"Thanks for always being there for me and thanks for still being there for me."
Laughing, Marisa asked, "Where the hell did that come from?"
"Well, you know. You were always the cool and beautiful one and I was nowhere near your crowd, but you always stuck by me no matter what. Even now. I mean, we both moved out to the other coast and here you are a super successful VP of the biggest IT company on the west coast and I'm just a low-rate aspiring actor slash writer whose biggest role is playing a server in real life."

Marisa looked over to Andy with rolled eyes and said, "Oh, you know that is bullshit. Come on, when have you ever known me to be superficial or materialistic? Pinky friends for life! Remember?" She held her hand out towards him with her fist clenched and her pinky hanging out in a hook fashion. Andy smiled and said, "Pinky friends for life", as he hooked her pinky with his.

On the radio they had a shuffled mix from the eighties. Marisa exclaimed, "Oh My God! I love this song!" She leaned in to turn it up. "Really?" Andy asked, "I am surprised you remember it." She looked back to Andy confused, "Of course I remember it. This is the first song you taught me on the guitar. What's the name of it again?"
"Only in Heaven." It was by a group that I think was one of the first forms of Emo but had an upbeat and colorful sound to them. By the way, it is the only song I taught you on guitar"
"Are you sure, I thought you taught me more?"
"No, Moe. I can't believe you don't remember this clearly. About two weeks after teaching you this song you told me you met a guy, and he was teaching you guitar and showed me by playing that song. I tried to remind you that I taught you

that song and the basics of guitar, but you did not recall. It was...oh shoot. What was his name? Todd?"

"Oh yeah. Todd." She replied dryly.

"That guy ended up being a jackass."

"I remember now." Marisa interjected and continued, "You didn't talk to me for like three months. Then you ended up saving me from Todd. Yeah, he was a jackass. But it was you who taught me that song and it was the first time you seriously held my hand."

Laughing, Andy said, "I was not holding your hand, I was trying to get your weak ass fingers to form a chord."

The two sped down the highway with the cool desert air blowing through the open windows of his Charger. As the sun set down behind them the landscape appeared as it was a painting. Hundreds of different colors intertwined into one another. The car faded down the road into the distance of the mountains as clouded memories loomed ahead.

FOUR CHORDS
(SUMMER 1990)

Andy pulled into the driveway of Marisa's parent's house. He and Marisa had just finished up a game of tennis. Andy was still in his brightly colored tennis gear. It was a time when the younger tennis players were changing the image of the game. Being easily influenced by the new young rock star image making its way into the world of tennis, he followed the suit of his idols. Marisa was wearing jean shorts and a lavender polo. The two smelled of dry sweat. They did not play a full game. It was too hot of a day for that, so they had called it early. As Marisa got out of the car, she asked Andy if he wanted to come in for some sweet tea. He told her, "I don't know. I stink like a dead coon in the sewer. I should get home and shower. Plus, I have to study for a Humanities test I have when we get back from break." Marisa leaned in and grabbed his keys. "You academy boys are always showering and studying. Come on big boy. Come in for some tea." She said with a coy smile.

They walked into the house. It was a nice house for a median-income family. Marisa's mom was a special education teacher at the public school she went to, and her dad was the wrestling coach at the same school. He was the wrestling coach and had the two most beautiful girls in the county for daughters. He called it the Coach's Curse.

Her parents were not home. As she was in the kitchen making tea, Andy sat on the couch. He was looking around nervously. Her parents knew of him. His parents were well-known and successful business owners in the chain of islands. They knew she spent a lot of time with him. He did not go to the public school her parents taught at though. He went to a private Catholic military school. While they did know of Andy, they did not truly know him. He was a little nervous sitting in their house while they were not home. He did not want her parents to get any misconceptions should they walk in. He knew that they were not overly fond of him. Perhaps it was that they knew the reason he was in Catholic military school or maybe it had gone back a few years at a Christmas dinner.

Once, when Andy's parents were out of town on vacation, she invited him over for Christmas dinner. She did warn him that her mother was super close to the lord. He had tried to protest by reminding her he went to a Catholic military school so there was nothing he had not seen in the world of crazy religion. She had tried to warn him that he did not understand. She told him that after dinner her mother would bring out a cake with a candle and they would all sing happy birthday to Jesus. He thought she was joking. At dinner, though he found out she was not. It all happened just as she had described. After dinner, her mom dimmed the lights in the dining room and disappeared into the kitchen. A few minutes later she came out with a cake that had one lit candle on it. Her mother started to happily sing a birthday song to Jesus. The whole family joined in. The cake was placed at the table, and everyone admired it with big smiles on their faces. Andy was wondering why nobody was digging into the cake. Why were they all just sitting there staring at it with stupid-looking, big smiles? He had to break the silence. He had asked out loud the only thing that came to mind. Which was, "So, who blows out the candle?" Andy did not mean it in a smart-ass way. He was sincerely curious. He did, however, have a reputation for having a smart mouth and that was the way it was perceived. Ever since that day Andy was not at the top of the list Marisa's parents approve of.

While coming out of that memory, Andy was scanning the room. He noticed a guitar. Marisa walked in with a platter that had a jar of tea and two glasses. Andy asked, "Whose guitar is that?"
"Oh, that's my dad's"
"Do you know how to play? He asked.
"No. My dad does not play it much either. You play though. Do you want to play me something?" She asked with a coy smile.
"Well, I don't want to touch someone else's guitar without their permission"
As she grabbed the guitar Marisa said, "Oh, it's okay. He does not play it much anyway."

Andy took the guitar in his hands and looked back with a smirk, "Really? The badass wrestling coach uses nylon strings?"
Having no idea what he was talking about, Marisa shrugged her shoulders. "I don't know. Play me something." She told him while smiling with admiration.

Andy laughed and said, "Oh, that's how it is. I'm just a grinder monkey. Wind me up, watch me dance, and bang my symbols."
Marisa just stared at him blankly.

"Ok, let me see," Andy thought about what to play. He just rumbled a few chords together, then got into it. He started to play the intro to his favorite metal song. After a few measures, he looked to Marisa for approval. Nothing. She gave him a blank stare with a half-smile. He then started to play a very heavy riff from an older metal group that was one of his favorites. They were a group that many had considered the pioneers of heavy metal. At that time there had been rumors that the lead singer would kill and eat small animals on stage. It was not true really. It was just a slight misunderstanding of events. Andy was rocking it. This was a fun song to play. He looked at Marisa and noticed she had no idea what it was. He stopped. "What do you want to hear, Moe?"
She sat down directly next to Andy, their legs against each other and as she touched his knee with her hand said with joy, "I don't care. I'm just enjoying watching you play!"

Andy took a couple of seconds to think and broke into a happy-sounding four-chord structure followed by a lead that went upscale then back downscale. He could tell by the smile on Marisa's face she liked it and kept playing. When he finished, she asked, "What is that? I know it."

He told her, "It's called Only in Heaven. You want me to teach it to you? It is super easy."

"Oh no. There is no way I could do that. I am not musically inclined like you."

"Nonsense, it's easy. Here, I'll show you" Andy handed her the guitar and she held it awkwardly over her lap in her hands. Andy pointed on the fretboard where to put her fingers and said, "This is a D chord. Put your fingers here and strum." She did and the guitar made a very muffled sound. Andy smiled and said, "No, you have to apply some pressure with your fingers"

"But it will hurt".

"It's not going to hurt; they are nylon strings!" He said laughing. "Here, let me show you." He put his hand over hers and added some pressure. Her hand was soft to touch, and she accepted his touch with ease. Andy told her, "Just apply some pressure like this" as he pressed down on her hand. He then strummed and said, "See, easy peezy". Marisa looked at him and turned her hand over. Their hands were interlocked and for a brief second, they just looked at each other. Feeling that he had just crossed some unspoken line, Andy cleared his throat and let go of her hand. "Ok, let's do an easy one. This is a G chord."

He continued to do this with the rest of the chords of the song and decided not to show her the lead as learning four chords had taken enough time. He got her to a point that she was making a sound almost, similar to music. She played a couple of bars and asked with a prideful smile, "How was that?"
"I think the band that sang it would be very happy to hear it." He lied through his smile.

The two laughed as the faded memory had brought them back to the reality of the eastbound wedding road trip they were on.

ON THE ROAD (SPRING 2014)

The heavy beats and chilling vocals of dance music on the radio. Marisa asked, "Do you remember that British pop group you listened to in the eighties? The one that had all the screaming fans. You used to listen to them all the time."

Andy just gave a questionable, "Uh-huh" response. He was wondering where she was going with this. There was a jovial tone to her voice that he knew. She was setting him up for something. She emphasized, "I mean you really liked them! You had all of their albums, didn't you?"

I did have all of their albums, video documentaries, EP's, and who knows what else."

"I know what else. Posters. Your bedroom wall was covered in them!"

Andy sighed and replied, "And?"

"And? Dude, you had posters of other dudes on your bedroom wall. Isn't that a little, gay?" Marisa asked in a joking fashion.

A conversation like this was one of many reasons Andy loved hanging out with Marisa. Being around her was like being with the guys, only with a girl. He enjoyed having a female companion that he could have the type of conversations that one would never have with a chick. Except that she was a chick that acted like just one of the guys. She was the type of girl that would be the perfect wife. She did not want the typical wine and dine. She would rather go out go-kart racing, bowling, or just drinking. Then come home and make love. She would never start an argument regarding where her man was all night, because she would have been with him and all his tomfoolery.

Andy rolled his eyes as he said, "It does not make me gay. Not that there would be anything wrong if I were, but it does not."
"How else do you explain it then?" She asked.
"Simple. The lead singer or any of the other four members of the group for that matter were guys that every girl wanted to be with, and every guy wanted to be. So, I did not want to be with him, or them, as you imply. I wanted to be him!"
Marisa giggled and answered with just one word, "Gay."
"Whatever."
She exclaimed back, "HA! See? I got you!"
"What do you mean?" Andy asked.

"I know you. When you say the word 'whatever' that means you are lying!"

Andy shrugged and said, "No. When I say whatever, it means I think you are full of shit and have no basis for the argument you are trying to make. It means I am done with you, and I wash my hands of this pointless conversation."

She laughed, as she said, "No, it means you're lying See? I got you. Nobody knows you like me. Gay." She paused and pointed with excitement at a billboard, "Oh snap! Did you see that? There is a carnival going on in the town up ahead! I love carnivals! It's only twenty miles up the road. We should go!"

"We can't Moe. We are on a tight schedule. We need to get to, oh I don't know, a wedding?"

There was a break in conversation as the rhythmic beats and hooks of Marisa's dance music came from the speakers. Marisa broke the silence. "Hey."

"Yes?" Andy replied.

With thoughts of a carnival still fresh in her mind, Marisa asked, "Are you thinking what I am thinking?"

"If it involves us hustling carnies at their own game and walking away with prizes then yes."

"No, but you were super good at that and got me so many plush toys! What was it you always said to them as we walked away with a hand full of prizes?"

"Never hustle a hustler." He said coldly but with a small break in character as he cracked a small smile.

"Yeah, that was it. You were so awesome. But that's not what I was thinking about. I was thinking about the time we spit on the crowd from the Zipper." Taking his eyes off the road and looking over at her, Andy asked, "You mean the time that you tried to spit on the crowd from the Zipper and gave us the scare of our lives!"

"Yeah, that time." She replied with a giggle.

The car sped by a couple of lizards sitting on rocks taking in some heat leftover from the hot desert sun that faded into a nighttime sky filled with distant memories.

SHOOT THE STAR (FALL 1987)

There was something magical about the carnival for teenagers in the mid-eighties. It was a world away from the world. It was a place to be taken away to someplace other than now. Everything about it was different from the norm. The smell of farm animals and fried food punctured the air. The bright flashing lights and loud barking voices of the carnies were a stimulation overload. The sounds of laughter, screams, and music filled the humid island air at once. The two-week time span that the carnival traveled to the Peeking Islands was Andy's favorite time of year.

The midway of the carnival was alive! There was an excitement that could not be explained. Everyone was here to have fun. Nobody was thinking about the threats of war from the Soviets or what grades they got on the exams today. This was the 1980's. It was Friday night and it was all about the excess of living in the moment. People dressed in oversized shirts labeled with phrases like, "Relax" or "Go-Go". Sunglasses were worn at night and they came in all shapes and colors. Everyone was here to let go of any of his or her inhibitions.

Andy and Marisa came out of the exit of a ride called Ocean Motion. Andy felt slightly green. Ocean Motion was a giant swing in the form of a pirate ship. The ride accommodated around thirty-some people at once. It swayed back and forth getting higher and higher with each swing. While they were on the ride a deejay played loud rock music and emceed for the people on the ride. The deejay asked in a deep thundering voice, "Does everyone want to go higher?" The crowd, of course, would cheer with glee. Meanwhile, Andy would be leaning over while grabbing his stomach. He groaned, "No, mother fuckers, no." He hated that deejay with every ounce of his being every time he boomed over the microphone to go higher. There was no one in life Andy hated more than that deejay.

It was two tickets and five minutes' worth of hell on earth for Andy. He did like thrilling rides. Normally he loved this ride. But something about tonight, it just did not agree with him. Perhaps it was an overabundance of elephant ears, cotton candy, soda, and emu legs. Either way, he needed a break.

Marisa and Andy found a bench on the midway to sit down so Andy could collect his thoughts. Marisa asked what he was thinking as he seemed for a moment to be off in space. He said with a straight face, "I was thinking about the time a Roman gladiator walked into a bar." He paused and continued, "The gladiator walked to the bartender and the bartender asked him what he would like. The gladiator looked to the bartender and said in a fierce gladiator-type voice, 'Barkeep. I will have five beers!" As he said this Andy held up two fingers and laughed hysterically. Marisa looked at Andy blankly and said, "I don't get it." Still, laughing hard at his joke Andy asked, "What? What don't you get? He asked for five beer and held up two fingers!" Andy again held up two fingers and as he did, he repeated, "Five beer!" With his left hand, he pointed at the two fingers on his right hand. "He is Roman! Two fingers are in the form of, oh never mind." Still laughing Andy asked what she wanted to do next.

"I want to play a game. I want to win something!" she answered with excitement. Andy looked at her and asked, "You are going to play the game? You are going to win something?"

"No. I am going to watch you play the game and win me something!"

"Okay, let's go."

They walked around the game area and Andy asked what her pleasure was. Marisa looked around at all the different games. There were so many to choose from. The barkers all used their gift of gab to entice marks walking by to play. As the two walked with pinky fingers interlocked, one barker called out, "Hey sir, tell me, how does it feel to be the luckiest man in the world?" The man was making a clever complement to having Marisa by his side, no doubt. She smiled and said, "Oh, I like him. Let's play this." Andy looked at it and explained, "Ah, no. See the game is gaffed" She interrupted as she asked, "Gaffed? What's that?" He laughed and said, "Oh, you are so innocent and naïve. Gaffed means rigged. They are rigged so you lose. I mean they are all gaffed so to speak, and some are easier to beat than others. See; take the game you chose, for example. You must toss the softball into the milk jug. Sounds easy enough. Until you know that there is a ring welded inside the opening of the jug that is only about a quarter-inch bigger than the ball. There is a technique to win. See all those people with their balls bouncing back out? That is because they are not throwing it correctly. They should be tossing underhand, and they should have their hand on top of the ball when tossing. That will cause a backspin. Most importantly, they should be aiming for the back of the hole on the jug, not the hole itself. When the ball hits that with backspin it will bounce in". Marisa grabbed Andy's hands and exclaimed, "So you can win!" He curled his lips and said, "In theory. Now take this one over here. This is one that while gaffed, you have more control over the gaff. You get the gun loaded with one hundred BB's and are led to believe that the object is to shoot out every bit of the red star. One problem is that the guns are bent by these carnies in a way that the average person would not notice. This would throw off your aim while looking through the sight. Getting around that is easy with just a little self-zero know-how. Three quick shots at the beginning and I know exactly how to compensate. The other gaff is in the wording. See all those guys trying to shoot the star itself? They don't stand a chance. There is no way they will get rid of all the red with only one hundred BB's. Read that sign exactly as you see it, Moe."

She squinted as she leaned in and read, "All red star must be shot from card to win a prize."

A large burly man running the Shoot the Star game slapped his cane on the counter causing Marisa to jump. He wore jeans and a referee shirt. 'Clearly, he should be on the Hot Shots game. The guy that should be running this must be on a break' Andy thought to himself. The man yelled to Marisa, "All you man's gotta do is shoot the star out and you go home with something special. Is she worth a three-dollar attempt to you, sir?" Andy did not like being talked to like this. He was smarter than that. If he were not sure he knew how to win he would have walked away feeling insulted. He hated it when people patronized him. Andy looked at the guy and asked, "So all I have to do is shoot the red star out of the card and I win that big ass tiger?" The man replied, "Yes sir, all the star has to be shot out so there is no red and you have yourself a happy woman!" Andy took a step back as thought to himself, 'What a condescending asshole.' He slapped three one-dollar bills on the counter and said, "All right, give me a gun." Andy took the BB gun and leaned on the counter. He looked directly at the card with a star on it. The man leaned in and yelled, "Good luck, sir!" Andy was focused on a red star with a black circle around it. He asked one more time, "Okay, just to be sure. All I have to do is shoot the star out?" The barker, losing patience pointed his cane to the sign and said, "Just as the sign says, sir. All red star must be shot from the card to win a prize. Now you gonna talk Tex or are you gonna shoot? Cause I got people that wanna play." Andy thought to himself. 'I'll show you shooting, asshole, okay wait. Calm down. Don't let the freak get in your head. That's what he wants.' Andy took two deep breaths and aimed for the very tip of the star and took three quick shots. They all landed in the same spot just a little above and to the right of the tip of the star. Andy thought to himself, 'Okay, shoot down and left. Down and left.' The man laughed and bellowed, "Oh nice shoot'n, Tex! Just a little high. Don't worry you have ninety-seven shots left. Surely you can hit that red star!" Andy thought to himself, 'Keep talking, asshole'. He took another two deep breaths. He centered his aim on the star then moved so his sight was on a part of the circle going around the star. He lowered his aim down and a little to the left. He took seven rapid shots moving the gun down ever so slightly following the line that formed a circle around the star. All seven shots went wide between two points of the star but right along the line of the circle. The man yelled out again, "Oh nelly! Wow, my blind grandmother can shoot better than that. You're supposed to be hitting the star, kid!" Andy knew at that point the man was on to him and this game was his to win. All he had to do was focus and block this idiot out.

'Focus' Andy thought. He took three more deep breaths as he followed the circle all the way around seven shots at a time, till there was just one small stretch between two points of the star left. The man continued to heckle Andy, "Oh man. You have got to be the worst shot ever. You have not hit the star once! When are you due back in Boys Town kid?" Without looking at the man Andy took ten quick shots and the star fell out of the card. As the star hit the ground, Andy stood up straight. He put the gun on the counter and looked at the man behind the counter completely unaware that a small crowd had gathered. "Now give me my damn tiger." The man looked back at Andy trying to act confused, "Give you the tiger? You did not hit the damn star once! Why would I give you a prize? Next! Who wants to play next and show this kid how it's done?" Andy interjected. "That's not what the sign says, sir. I don't have to shoot the star. The sign clearly says to 'shoot all red star from the card'. That is exactly what I did!" The crowd started to boo at the man. Realizing this was not worth the trouble the man grabbed a giant plush tiger and handed it to Andy.

Andy and Marisa walked away from the game. She smiled as she hugged the giant tiger Andy had just won her. The carnie running the game yelled something at them as they walked away. Andy could not quite make out what he had said but he turned around anyway and yelled back to the carnie, "Never hustle a hustler, Tex!" as he formed both his hands into the shape of revolvers and shot at him once with a wicked smile on his face. The carnie grumbled to himself, "damn kids" and continued his spiel to find some new marks to take advantage of.

The two turned around and walked away, as they stumbled over their laughter. Marisa and Andy stopped, and their jaws hit the ground in awe when they noticed the ride of all rides standing before them. It was the Zipper. This was Andy's favorite ride. The ride vehicles were in the shape of a car. The car itself was nothing more than a cage. The security in the car was only a lightweight lap bar. The cars followed on a circuit that took everyone up and down in a giant oval. If there was any carnival ride that was the recipe for disaster, this was the one. This is what Andy looked forward to every year. Marisa grabbed Andy's arm with both hands tightly as she told him, "Oh my God. I hope your stomach is better. Come on, let's go."

They stuffed the tiger into a locker and went back to the Zipper. A man standing at the entrance took four tickets apiece from them. He barely noticed them as they handed him the tickets. Andy grabbed Marisa's hand and pulled her along as he smiled and said, "I'll tell you what, whatever planet he is on, it is currently not this one." As they brushed by people to get into the queue Andy said, "Man, I want some of whatever he's having". They both laughed looking back at the man, dressed in a flannel shirt and sported a beard that had gone probably five days unshaved. Andy looked at Marisa and revealed, "What a life. I want to know how to become one of these guys. How do I get a job where I get to travel the country and never have to shower?" Marisa looked at him while shaking her head and interlocking their arms, "You're stupid, culito." She smiled as she added, "I love you though. Now come on! Let's go!"

They sat in the car with only a lap bar strapped over their laps. The attendant came by and checked the door to make sure it was locked into place. They both heard the reassuring sound of the click. They pulled up and down on the lap bar to be assured it was locked. The car moved up a few feet as the next car was loaded. As they waited for the ride to get completely loaded and start Marisa spoke. "You didn't mean all that stuff you said back there, right?"
"About wanting to be in the carnival?" Andy asked. "Hell yeah dude. Have you ever seen the movies depicting the life of a carny? It's so raw and adult-like. It seems so...free!"

"I mean the stuff you said about the guys running this place. It was kind of mean."

Andy looked at her and said, "Mean? I was just joking around."

"I know. But sometimes you take it too far. Someday when we are grown up, you're going to have to learn tact. I mean I can take it because I know you. But not everyone else will be able to take it. I worry that someday karma will come back and bite you in the ass."

"Well, as long as karma is a five-foot, one hundred twenty-pound stripper with a bag of coke, she can bite me anywhere she wants."

She tried to stifle a laugh and lightly slap him as she said, "I'm serious. I don't want to see you bring anything bad on yourself."

"Ok. Sometime when I grow up, I will learn tact. But for now, tonight, I'm going to be a young punk-ass teenager. Care to join me?" He asked with a smile.

"Of course", She smiled and held on to him as the ride started and the music pumped up.

They felt themselves shoot upwards as they left their stomachs behind, only to catch their stomachs again as they were flipped over the top and hurled back towards earth and they watched the ground quickly approach them. The ride vehicles were designed to flip around with the inertia of the motion the circuit provided. At some points, it would be hard to tell which way was up and which was down. The ride continued to lift them and throw them down and spin them all around. Marisa screamed a delightful fear with each rotating motion. She had a python-like grip on Andy's arm. She was laughing hysterically. Andy smiled. He was not screaming as she was. It was not in his disposition. He was thoroughly enjoying this moment. He had a different way of showing it. He was not quite as extroverted as she was. The ride continued to toss the two up and down and they were both enjoying the moment in their way. The view was a blur in the nighttime sky as the world spun by. The music was only a mash of noise and beats. Nothing else existed in the universe for this moment except the two people on this one particular ride called the Zipper at this one particular carnival currently located in the Peeking Islands.

The ride came to a quick coasting halt. Marisa and Andy's car had just crested over the top and they sat overlooking the view of the carnival. In the distance, they could see a highway filled with flickering headlights and taillights. Further out in the distance they could see the lights of boats on the water. Marisa asked, "Do you wonder where they are going?" Still feeling a rush from the ride Andy asked in a heavy breath, "Who?"

"The people in all those cars. Are they on their way home to a loving family? A third shift job? Are they on their way here? Or is it someone running away from this God-forsaken small ass town forever?"

The conversation between the two was interrupted by an announcement over a speaker. They heard in a thick southern drawl, "Hey carnival-goers, we apologize to all y'all for this inconvenience. We are having some problems with the ride. Give us a few minutes as the maintenance crew makes a few adjustments and we will be fixin' to have all y'all down in a jiffy."

Marisa looked to Andy and just laughed as she grabbed him tight and asked, "Oh well, what now my prince?" She put her hand to her forehead and asked in her best movie-like Southern voice, "Whatever shall we do?" Andy looked at her and replied, "Frankly my dear, I don't give a damn." He loved it when their minds were linked. She caught her breath in between her giggles and said, "Seriously, what are we going to do?" Andy shrugged his shoulders and answered with a sheepish smile, "We could make out." Marisa smiled and said, "I have a better idea, help me out." She started to throw herself into a quick forward momentum and just as quickly threw herself back and forward again. She instructed Andy to do the same, "Come on, I'm bored with this view. I want to look straight down" Andy started to mirror her motions and in seconds the ride vehicle was pointing straight down as they could view the midway below them. Everyone looked like mice scurrying in every direction. Every person below them was on a mission to the next point of fun. Marisa asked, "Think you could hit them with spit from here?" Andy laughed, "You're not serious?" He worked up a little saliva in his mouth and spat it down. It was too little to tell if it even hit the ground. Marisa said, "Oh come on, that was weak."

"I suppose you can do better. Oh, show me your devious ways, spit master Moe."

She took a few seconds to work up a thick amount of saliva with a churning of her throat.

Andy chimed in, "Nothing but class from you." As she continued to work up the mucus he spoke again. "That is absolutely disgusting. Is that what they teach in public school these days?" At that moment she released a giant lougee from her mouth. It missed the hole in front of them completely and instead landed on the gate in front of their faces. Andy laughed as he said, 'Oh my God, it is totally going to suck for someone if that thing releases. It is so thick!" It just stuck there and hung in place from the gate that was only about eight inches in front of them. At that moment an announcement came again from the speaker, "All right, everyone. We got things fixed here and be get'n all y'all off directly. Sit tight."

The Zipper started to move the ride vehicles around the circuit very slowly. As their ride vehicle came over the top and into descent the car started to tilt in a way that their backs were facing the ground. They were looking straight up. The giant lougee, working with gravity started to stretch and hang over them. Andy's eyes went wide with anticipation. "Oh my God! Fucking really? Dude, if that thing lands on me I am going to be super upset!" Marisa just laughed hysterically and screamed, "It's going to land on us!" She tried to say but was laughing too hard. Tears were forming in her eyes.

"Oh, come on Moe, this is not even funny!" He said, trying to sound angry but was laughing.

The car slowly moved to the ground as it would stop and go to let other riders off. Each time the ride moved the lougee hung above them swaying back and forth a little. With each sway, it taunted them with the threat of releasing itself directly onto their faces. Marisa continued to point and laugh at it. Andy shook his head back and forth with a squeamish look of disgust on his face. As their car approached planet earth they started to level out. They finally approached terra firma and Andy let out a sigh of relief and started to laugh. The ride attendant opened the gate to their car and they quickly both stepped out laughing. Andy felt guilty and felt the ride attendant somehow knew the mischief they had been up to with his secret carny psychic powers. He grabbed Marisa's hand while avoiding eye contact with the ride attendant and they briskly walked away, laughing while wiping their watery eyes as they faded into the darkness of memory lane.

EL RANCHO I (SPRING 2014)

The two wedding-bound road trippers moved across the desert at a speed meant only for those who choose to live dangerously. The sky above the carnival in the distance was overcast as they continued their quest to the east from the west.

The ambient light from the carnival that they had seen the billboards before lit up the cloudy nighttime sky above. Marisa sat in the car admiring the view and wondered if a couple sitting high atop a Ferris wheel, leaning on each other while holding hands, could see her and Andy driving down the road? Did they contemplate the destination of the car? Did they wonder if perhaps they were bound for a wedding? She smiled as she dosed off into a light sleep.

Marisa awoke as she felt a nudge from Andy. The car was silent. She outstretched her arms and asked with heavy eyes, "Where are we?"
"Somewhere in either Texas or Louisiana. I am not quite sure. I stopped paying attention a long time ago."
"Oh. Well, that's comforting to hear from the person behind the wheel. Do you want to stop?"

"Yeah, I'm sorry. But I think this is as far as we're going today. I'm going to pull off at the next exit and hope we can find a place. Otherwise, we may be sleeping in the car."

Marisa gave a light laugh and said, "It wouldn't be the first time we've done that."

Andy looked over to Marisa with admiration of her trooper attitude and replied, "True. But my body now is not as adaptable to that type of punishment as it was ten years ago."

"Twenty-five", Marissa stated.

"What?"

"You lost a decade there somewhere old man. High school was more like twenty-five years ago."

Andy said under a chuckle, "You have your memories the way you want them, I'll have mine."

"Okay, have it your way, old man." She said as she jabbed his ribs.

The road-weary travelers pulled into a motel parking lot. The large sign on the side of the road was white with large red letters that said El Rancho. The sign was illuminated by bright light bulbs overlaying the letters. Upon parking, it was easy for Andy to tell this is what he would refer to as a no-tell motel. Marisa looked over at Andy as he said, "Hey, as long as there is not a dead hooker under the bed and needles in the nightstand, I am happy"

Marisa shook her head and laughed, "You're stupid, culito. Where do you come up with this stuff?"

They walked into the main office, which appeared to require maid service. It looked very old. The walls had a slight yellow hue to them. At one time they were probably white. As they approached the counter, they noticed what looked like a logbook. There was also a dinner plate that earlier had spaghetti on it and a coffee mug that was half full and marked with a variety of stain marks on it. Behind the counter, there was a pegboard with hooks on it. Only one hook had a key on it. On the shelf below the pegboard were a variety of magazines piled on top of paperwork, a crumpled fast-food bag, there was an ashtray overfilled with butts, and a bottle of liquor labeled Night Train. A small radio on the shelf was playing some old country twang. Andy rang the service bell. A big smile hit his face as he anticipated who was going to walk out to greet them. Marisa just looked at him and lightly said, "Stop." Andy rang the service bell again with an eager ear-to-ear grin on his face.

They heard a raspy voice come from the back room. "I'm coming, I'm coming," it said in a slow but slightly agitated manner. His accent was thicker than even the music on the radio. Andy was giddy with excitement and Marisa could tell. She grabbed his hand tightly, which was a silent way to tell him to contain himself.

Into the reception area walked an elderly man. Andy guessed he must have been in his seventies. He was dressed in dirty khaki work pants, a white muscle shirt decorated with dried spaghetti sauce. His grey chest hair peeked out over the top of his shirt. Grey hair stubbles covered his face. The shirt was about two sizes too small, as it could not cover his entire belly. He wore a dirty red cap. Andy smiled and quickly covered his mouth with his hand and forced a laugh into a faux cough as he rang the bell one more time. Marisa put her foot on top of Andy's and applied pressure.

The old man stepped to the desk as he put his hand on the bell, "Yep, it works. Now how can I help you fine folks this evening?"

Andy regained his composure and said, "Yes, sir. We are looking for a room tonight."

"Well, you don't say." Said the man slowly looking at the two as if looking at a puzzle with one missing piece.

"Yes, sir. I notice there is one set of keys hanging there. Does that mean you have a vacancy?"

"Where are y'all from?" The man asked. Andy told him, "We are from LA. We are from out of town."

"Oh, well no shit, isn't that nice? I see not too much gets past you city slickers. You're pretty bright," The old man said. He paused as he looked slowly over his shoulder towards the pegboard then ruffled through the guest book. "Turns out it is your lucky night. I do have one room available."

Marisa could tell that Andy was trying this poor guy's patience. He did not mean to. It is just how he was. He could not help it. She said, "We live in LA, sir. We are originally from Florida and on our way back there for my wedding."

The old man took a step back and said, "Well, don't you two make a fine couple? Congratulations. You are in luck. The one-room I have left happens to be the honeymoon suite. All y'all lovebirds can get an early honeymoon." He looked at Andy and winked while curling his lips to grin. Andy started to speak, "Well, actually" and was interrupted by Marisa as she said, "That will be fine, sir. Thank you". She then grabbed Andy's arm, put her head on his shoulder, and smiled as she said, "Pay the man, honey."

They stepped to the door of their room. The honeymoon suite. Andy, grasping the white oval key chain in his hand that was labeled only with the room number turned to Marisa and asked with the apprehensive tone of someone about to take a leap of faith into a canyon gorge, "Ready for this?"

As the key entered the hole each bump connected with its counterpart. Each click could be felt as the key entered further just as the memory of another road trip leading to another hotel in a time not yet forgotten entered the

heads of the two about to enter the honeymoon
suite.

DEZZI AND THE CASINO
(SUMMER 1997)

Marisa sat in the lobby of Moore Broadcasting, waiting for Andy to get out of work. Moore Broadcasting was a conglomerate of five different radio stations. The flagship station, Q95, was playing over the speakers in the lobby. A receptionist sat at her desk answering phones while working on a computer workstation. Marisa was sitting patiently on a couch as a popular boy band faded out and an instrumental music bed with heavy beats took over and she heard her best friend's voice take over the airwaves. "Q95! Your hit music channel! That song was for Rebecca and the crew working at Seaport Subs on Manta. My name is Andy Chelios and the clock on the clubhouse wall says it's time for me to go! The wild child, Trevor Wilde is ready to take the controls next. I just saw him walking around the building with a giant mug of coffee and he is ready to take you into the night. Hey Ann, from Isla de Cabeza Martillo, you like listening to Trevor, right?" A female voice on the phone answered back, "Yeah, but I like you better!"

"Awe, thank you, baby, I love you too. But what could Trevor play next to make you really like him?"

"Sonic Ploy"

"I'll make sure Trev gets to Sonic Ploy next! Hey Nina, what station along with Peeking Dodge is giving you a chance all summer long to drive away in brand new Dodge Challenger?"

The excited voice on the phone yelled," Q95!" It was followed by a heavy stream of laser sound effects and over-modulated radio static. Then a choir sang to a beat, "Today's hit music channel, Q95!" As the jingle echoed the station went straight to commercials.

There was a door about ten feet in front of Marisa. Above it was a sign that said, "Production suite B". Without warning, the door flung open and outran a man with headphones draped around his neck. He was carrying a hand full of CDs, a couple of reels, a sweatshirt over his shoulder, and some paperwork. He rushed to the receptionist as he put everything but the headphones and sweatshirt on her desk. He said in a deep pleasant voice, "Hi Mary, would you please put these in my mailbox? I need to get to the air studio." Mary looked up and replied, "Sure thing, Andy's already introduced you and in his final spot." He thanked her as he turned with a bright smile and said, "Hey Marisa". Before she could even finish saying, "Hi Trev." He had already rushed through a glass door and down a long hallway while putting his sweatshirt on. The door slowly closed shut on its own. On the door was a sign that said, "Our on-air personalities are delivering our product. Please be quiet."

Marisa continued to sit on the couch. The receptionist continued to type and answer phones. On the radio just as a commercial ended a choir sang, "Q95 weather!" A heavy beat music bed followed it. She could hear Andy deliver the weather and current temperatures. As he finished, he said, "and on your radio, it is always Q95! Trevor Wilde is up next and standing directly to my left. How are you doing buddy? You look as if your glowing, what's up?"
Trevor answered, "I am doing splendid Andy."
Andy laughed and replied, "That's awesome, my friend. What do you have lined up for tonight?"
"Well Andy Chelios, of course, we have the hot eight at eight and hit music for all of the islands all night long. But more importantly, I have something else."

"Oh, don't be a tease, Trevor Wilde, tell us what you got what you really, really got!"

"You know Q95 has been giving away the Dezzi prize package all day today."

Andy said, "Oh don't I know it! Don and Amanda gave away two Dezzi concert packages this morning, Blaze gave away two pair's during the all-request lunch hour, and I gave away a pair on the drive at five! Wait, don't tell me you have another pair to give away as well?"

Trevor quickly replied, "Oh no Andy Chelios, not a pair but two pairs of tickets!"

Andy added, "Just so everyone is clear. You are getting so much more than just concert tickets to see Dezzi. In addition to the tickets, you get backstage passes, and you get to meet Dezzi and join her and the crew for a pre-show dinner, and Q95 will put you up in a super sketchy hotel in downtown Miami!"

Laughing Trevor said, "That's right Andy, plus the seats are on the stage!"

"Oh my gosh, Trevor, that's close enough to catch her boob sweat! How do I win?"

Trevor answered, "Be listening to Q95 tonight, and when you hear the Q-tones be caller 95!"

Andy followed up, "So get your speed dial set and be ready for the wild child, Trevor Wilde to play the boob tones, I mean Q-tones, I'm outta here, Trevor Wilde is on your radio next! It's Q95!" There was an influx of lasers and other sound effects. A choir sang, "The beat continues!" a deeply modulated voice bellowed, "Your hit music channel! WEIR, Serving Isla Sirena, Isla de Cabeza Martillo, Manta Ray, and all the fishies in the sea!" followed by the choir singing, "Q95!" as it segued with the current music of the 1990s perfectly.

Four minutes later an eighties throwback song could be heard on the speaker in the lobby as Marisa awaited Andy. The phone on the reception desk rang and Mary answered, "Q95, your hit music channel. How may I direct your call?" There was a pause as she continued, "No ma'am, he has not come out of the studio yet. No, I don't know what he was thinking ma'am. Yes ma'am I will tell him to come to see you before he leaves. Thank you. Goodbye."

Andy came out through the glass door. As he walked out a salesperson walked by and said,

"Great show today Andy, you were hilarious." Andy just grumbled, "Ah, no Chuck. It sucked. It was horrible" Andy was dressed in jeans and a Q95 sweatshirt with headphones hanging around his neck. He smiled immediately when he saw Marisa. She liked that his face always lit up when he saw her. It made her feel special in a way. As he walked to the reception desk, he looked at Marisa with a smile and winked. He held one finger in the air and mouthed, "one minute". He looked to Mary and said, "Hey Mary. Any messages?"

Mary put a stack of reels on the counter and said, "These Peeking Dodge spots need to be dubbed before tomorrow." Andy asked, "Are they just dubs or actual voice-overs? If they are only dubs have my board opp, Danny, do them, please. He should be out shortly. Anything else?" Mary thought and said, "Michael from Venus Records called. He wants to know if you heard the CD from the new rapper and when you are going to play it."
Andy laughed, "The new white rapper? Since the last white rapper over a decade ago worked out so well let me get right on it. If he calls back

today, tell him I have not listened to it yet, but I will this weekend and I'll call him Monday. Is that all?"

"No. Mrs. Moore-Harper wants to see you in her office ASAP. She said not to let you leave without seeing her"

Andy sighed and looked down at the floor. He knew what was coming. He looked back to Marisa and said, "This will only be a few minutes. I'm sorry." Marisa just shrugged her shoulders, smiled, and continued to sit on the couch. "Go get the car ready Moe, this won't take long, I know."

Marisa was sitting in her car with the air conditioning blasting when she saw Andy come out of the building with a backpack over his shoulder. She could see he was talking to himself, and it must have been quite the conversation as he was slamming one hand into the other. 'What a weirdo', she thought as she laughed. He got to the car and before getting in he took off his sweatshirt and replaced it with a Q95 polo. He took off his shoes and jeans, reached into his backpack, pulled out some cargo shorts, and put those on. Then he stuffed his jeans, sweatshirt, and shoes in the backpack. He sat down in the passenger seat of Marisa's car and sighed. She looked at him and said, "You know they have a thing called bathrooms you can do that in. You don't have to do it out in front of the whole world." Andy just shook his head. "Whatever. Yeah. Man, I just wanted to get out of there. Thanks for picking me up today. Sorry about the wait."

As she pulled into the flow of traffic Marisa asked, "Yeah, what was that about? What did your GM want?"
"Oh, just to give me a red ass. She was mad about the boob comment, and she was upset about me saying we are putting our winners in a sketchy hotel when actually it is a high-end place that she is paying a lot of money for. Which is bullshit since she is not even paying the money. It's Waterloo Records that is flipping the bill. But whatever."
Marisa asked, "Red ass huh? What is a red ass?"
"Huh? Oh. You know, red ass. Your boss, who is a bitch, chews you out so bad that your butt

cheeks clench up super tight and they feel like they are on fire. Red ass." Andy explained.

Marisa replied, "I see."

Andy spoke, "But hey, thanks for picking me up, I lost my license."

"I know," Marisa said.

"How do you know?" Andy asked, "I haven't had a chance to talk to you in a few days."

"Well maybe it was you bitching about it on the air the entire shift or maybe it was that hour of calls you took having people tell you about their run-ins with the law."

Andy laughed, "Oh you heard that. I did not know you listen that much."

"I listen to you all the time, culito! Or should I call you Mario? Varoom, Varoom!"

"Hey, be nice", Andy said with a laugh, "It was just a speeding ticket on top of a few unpaid speeding tickets."

Marisa asked, "What were you doing speeding in a car that you're supposed to be giving away on the radio?"

"Come on. Really? When else am I going to have the chance to drive a car like that and see what it has?"

Marisa pulled into the parking lot of the apartment complex where Andy lived and pulled up to his apartment.

There was a pause and Andy continued, "But hey, you want to hear some really good news?"

Marisa smiled and said, "I'm always up for good news from you."

"Right. Do you know those two pairs of Dezzi tickets Blaze gave away today? Well, I possess one of those pairs."

Marisa's eyebrows went up, "Do I detect contest rigging, Mr. Chelios?"

Andy rolled his eyes and asked, "Do you want to go or not?"

Marisa said, "Well since you asked so nicely, how can I turn down an offer like that?"

Andy asked, "So that is a yes? Cool. Pick me up at I guess eight tomorrow morning."

"Why so early?" she asked.

Andy told her, "Well Moe, we have to get on the Ferry and then to drive all the way down to Miami for one. For two, who knows what traffic will be like? Then there is the meet and greet with Dezzi and the dinner. Both happen early."

Marisa asked, "Just one thing first." She looked at him with a mock inquisitive glance, "Why do you always choose me to take to all these concerts?" She changed her tone to an overly exaggerated sarcastic tone; "Surly Andy Chelios of Q95 can get a date with any girl in the islands." Andy breathed out heavy making a flapping sound with his lips, "Because I don't want to go to a concert with just anyone, Moe. I want to go with you. Plus, you have proven you know how to handle yourself backstage around all the celebrities. You don't act all star-struck and stupid."

Marisa jabbed him in the side and asked, "Even after the Sister Scott incident?"

"Oh yeah," Andy remembered, "You told the guitarist he looked like one of the kid groups popular that year. I don't think he knew what you were talking about. It's all good. Just one thing, I am not supposed to have these tickets. So, this time, we will not be representatives of the station. Nobody there can even know I work with the station, or in radio for that matter."

Marisa responded with another teasing tone, "You mean I don't get to hang out with Andy Chelios of Q95? I have to hang out with just Andy?" She went back to herself as she said, "I would prefer it no other way."

Andy got out of the car and said, "You're one in a million, Moe. One in a million." He was about to shut the door and she asked, "No kiss?"

He laughed as he leaned back into the car and said, "I suppose that is ample payment for the ride." As he leaned back into the car, he kissed the tip of her pinky as he put his hand to her mouth. She kissed it back. He backed out and shut the car door, flung his backpack over his shoulder, and walked to his apartment.

It was around 2:00 PM when Marisa and Andy reached Miami. Marisa had asked him if he wanted to go check into the hotel and unload their bags before going to the arena. He was excited to get to the show and meet Dezzi. He had said that they should go straight to the arena.

They pulled into the parking lot of the arena. Once parked, Andy shuffled through a large manila envelope. It had everything they needed. Concert tickets and a variety of laminated passes to get them through different checkpoints. It also had a promotions sheet of different up-and-coming Waterloo Records artists and a one-page biography on Dezzi highlighting her rise to fame. Andy sorted through all of it and handed Marisa her laminates and tickets. They both hung them all around their necks. With a sarcastic tone to his voice, Andy looked to Marisa and said, "Well, don't I just feel like king shit of fuck mountain."

The info on the first laminate said entry to gate 43 open at 4:15 PM. Andy looked toward the building and saw they were at gate 1A. He looked at his watch and noticed it was 3:20 PM.

They still had some time. The two sat in the car conveniently parked under the shade of a tree. The air conditioning was almost on full. Andy was so excited. He had met a lot of pop stars in his time. To him, they were all normal people. He had even hung out with a few. Meeting these big-name pop stars was not a big deal to him. He did it all the time. With Dezzi, it was different. He was enamored with her music. He thought of her as the most beautiful girl on the planet. He did not normally fall for white girls with blond hair. But she had a surfer girl look to her that was almost a forbidden mystery and there was something about her eyes. The look in her eyes was something he could not put into words. Then there was her voice. Andy loved listening to Dezzi for her voice. He would have married her if not for any other reason, just her voice. He would always joke around at the station when talking about Dezzi. He would say she was his future wife. She just did not know it yet.

Andy had been to a lot of concerts in his lifetime. Some were through the radio station and some were through personal means. The concerts that were through the station were so-

so. He did not care about most of the music they played. He always thought that he got paid really good money, to play really bad music. He could not stand the current pop music of the 1990s. But there were some artists, like Dezzi, that he appreciated. He was very much looking forward to meeting someone he truly admired, if not a little nervous at the same time.

It was 4:30 and they were at gate 43 waiting to be let in. There was a small crowd that was already gathered. Marisa looked to Andy and made mention of how many people were there. Andy said, "This is the only show in the state that Waterloo is giving tickets to radio stations for. I am sure there are prize pigs from all over Florida here. Plus, a lot of these people are probably friends and family from the corporate sponsors and Waterloo Records." Andy and Marisa looked up toward the front of the crowd as a man in dark pants and a white button-up short sleeve collared shirt spoke up. "May I have everyone's attention please?" He had to say this a few times before the crowd was looking at him. He continued with his spiel, "I need everyone's attention, please! We are going to start letting you in. He started to stress his words as he spoke loudly, "Please have your credentials ready. All we are checking at this point is your concert tickets. When you make your way to me, please go to one of the attendants with scanners so they can scan your concert ticket. Once again, all we are looking at right now is your ticket for concert entry. Please have that ready. After you have your ticket scanned, please go to the security checkpoint. Have your bags open and ready for inspection. You should not have camcorders or other recording devices, weapons, drugs, or alcohol. Once you are through you will go into the building and be given further instructions! Now everyone please start to move through in an orderly fashion!" The crowd started to move forward. It was a pleasant experience. Nobody was pushing or shoving too much.

Once inside the building, they were all ushered into a large room. The same crowd of about seventy people that were outside was all now inside this large room. Nobody had any more clue what was going on than the person next to him or her. There was the sound of seventy conversations all going on at once.

Marisa looked around at all the people. They were all from different walks of life, yet they were all similar, like-minded people with the same thing on their minds. 'What's next? What are we supposed to be doing and where is Dezzi?'

The sound of feedback came from a speaker at one end of the room. It was the sound of someone turning on a microphone too close to a speaker. Everyone looked in the direction and saw a man holding a microphone stepping away from the speaker. "Good afternoon! How are you guys doing?" He asked. There was the sound of seventy people all saying good in their way at once. He asked again, "I said, how are you guys doing? Are you ready to meet Dezzi?" The crowd cheered a little louder this time. "That's great! My name is Sirius, and I am with Waterloo Records." Sirius was dressed in pressed khaki dress pants and a blue polo that had the Waterloo label on it. Sirius continued to speak. "On behalf of Dezzi and Waterloo Records, we thank you very much for your support. Now, in about twenty minutes Dezzi is going to come out and sign autographs. What I need everyone to do right now is this. Please form a line that starts directly in front of me. We are going to have someone come down the line to quickly check your credentials. Please have out the green laminate that says, meet and greet. Have that ready as our people walk by. Now a couple more things before we bring Dezzi out. We know a lot of you have brought personal items to get signed. We ask that you have her sign only one item. Also, in the interest of getting this done quickly please do not try to engage in conversation with Dezzi or take a picture. Please also do not ask her to personalize anything or write a long note. Dezzi has a lot to do today, and we want to keep this moving so that everyone is happy. Thank you. Now start forming that line starting with you two," He pointed at two people in the front as Marisa and Andy formed in behind with the rest.

As the line moved forward Andy watched as Dezzi smiled and thanked everyone who approached her with humble sincerity. Andy was nervous. What was he going to say? There was so much he wanted to tell her. There was only one person now between himself and Dezzi. He wiped his sweaty palms on his jeans and tried to take a couple of deep breaths, but they were short and quick at best. His heart raced like a jackhammer. He walked towards Dezzi as she smiled and warmly said "Hi." He tried to smile back and all he could get out of his mouth was a quick and quiet, "Hi." He handed her a book that was a songbook for piano from her most recent album. As she took the book from his hands, he noticed how tall she was. Dezzi had at least four or five inches on Andy. She was a lot taller than she appeared in videos. He was thinking, 'Say something. Say something.' Now yelling at himself in his head, 'Come on, idiot! Say something to her'. She signed the book as she handed it back to him, she smiled and said, "Thank you." He looked down and quickly said, "Thanks." as he walked away finally able to find some air to breathe into his lungs.

Marisa came to Andy from behind and grabbed him by the hips. She was smiling big. "Hey, wasn't that cool? You got to meet Dezzi!" He answered back. "Yeah." She laughed and said, "Yeah? That's it? What did she say to you?" "Umm. Nothing really. She just said hi."

"Did she sign your book?"

"Yeah, but it's not for me. It's for my neighbor, Jason. I told him I would get it signed for him."

Marisa looked at him and asked, "You didn't get anything signed for yourself?'

Andy just shrugged his shoulders and said, "Well, I'm here. That's good enough for me. Jason is a cool neighbor, so why not?"

Dezzi was ushered away by some staff and Sirius came back out and said, "Everyone give it up for Dezzi as she exits!" Everyone clapped. A lady yelled, "I love you, Dezzi!" Before exiting through a door Dezzi turned, smiled, and gave a showy curtsy.

Sirius started to talk through the microphone again. "All right guys. At this point, if anyone does not have an orange pass, we are going to ask you to exit through the doors behind you. Rachael will help you out. A girl in an usher suit waved and smiled. As those without the orange passes left Sirius said, "Thank you all for coming, enjoy the show." He waited for the door to shut and then continued talking again. "Back to you guys still here. You are going to walk through the door over in that direction, marked DD, and follow the hall to the end. There will be another usher there to guide you to the next room where you will see tables set for ten apiece. Please walk into the room and pick a table. Any questions? No? Good. See you guys in there."

They walked into a large room filled with tables that sat ten. At each table, there were two chairs with a red ribbon tied to them. They had been told to not sit in a chair with a red ribbon. Everyone started to find a seat at the tables. Of course, every single person asked which table Dezzi would be at. They were all told just to go grab a seat. Once everyone was seated, they were all instructed to get back up and make their way through a buffet line. The buffet was typical. There were a few types of meat to choose from along with a variety of starches, and of course deserts. Wings, finger food, and salad filled out the other options.

After everyone had their food and was sitting down eating, more people started to enter the makeshift dining area. Some were dressed in a manner that indicated they worked with

Waterloo Records. Others appeared to be part of the stage crew. Marisa noticed Dezzi walking in with a man dressed in a suit. She asked Andy if he knew who he was. He started to explain as the man walked with Dezzi to the table behind them. Andy stopped talking, looked down, and nonchalantly put his hand over his face. Marisa asked, "What's up with that?" Andy said, "That's Michael Anthony. He is one of the A and R reps."

"Oh. Does he know you or something?"

Andy answered, "Well, he would for sure recognize my voice. We talk on the phone at least twice a week. But I doubt he would recognize me physically. We have only met in person once. Then again, he may know what I look like. For all I know, he has a profile of me on his desk and knows everything about me."

Puzzled, Marisa inquired why a record rep would care about him. Andy replied, "Because it's his job. He must convince me to play his artists on my radio station. So, knowing everything about me helps, I'm sure. I mean, look at the way he greets people. When he shakes hands, he is using his other hand to either touch a person's shoulder, grab his arm, or the ever so crowd-pleasing, two-handed handshake. It's his job to make people like him. These guys are the sleaze of the music industry. If not in this job, he would probably be in car sales or politics and very good at it." He paused, then he continued, "Anyway, remember I am not supposed to be here. These tickets were meant for radio station winners only. So, I am doing my best to maintain a low profile."

Everyone was eating and conversing. Andy could not help but glance over at Dezzi. It was not in a creepy stalker way. Or maybe it was. He was only curious as to what she was eating. He noticed that all she had in front of her was a salad and she was only picking away at it like a rabbit.

Andy felt a nudge from Marisa. "Andy," She said, "this nice lady was asking you a question." Some lady a few seats away had been trying to make conversation and had asked Andy his name. The whole table was conversing in a small talk way, the same way people on a cruise ship do when they are forced to sit with strangers at dinner. Andy was not good at this. He could talk to millions through a microphone in a radio studio and share his deepest secrets or make a very tongue-in-cheek remark. He could stand on a stage and emcee to thousands with ease. He enjoyed that. It was the one-on-one interaction with actual humans he did not feel comfortable with. Some close friends might describe him as shy or reserved. He knew though, he just did not know the right things to say. He felt out of place and was unable to relate when put in social interactions. He dreaded talking with people without his celebrity mask on. If given the choice, he would rather have a root canal.

An overly obese lady in a loud dress and even louder voice that screamed Long Island said again, "I'm Sally from Boca. What's your name?" Andy looked down at his shirt and said, "Well, the sticker here says that it is Andy, so I guess that is it." In his head, Andy was making a clever joke. But no one at the table had laughed. Another man at the table that seemed overly dressed for a concert asked, "And what do you do for work, Andy?" Remembering he was not there as radio talent Andy quickly said the first thing that came to mind, "What do I do? Oh, I am in marketing." Someone else asked what he marketed. He said, "Ah, whatever people pay me to market, I guess. I help people with big ideas live out their dreams. So maybe I am a consultant as well." All he could think of was how much he was failing at this. Thankfully Marisa was a mind reader or at least knew Andy well enough to know he was not enjoying this, and she took the conversation over. Andy continued to look around the room with his hands tightly clasped and silently judge people.

The dinner was finished, and it was time to get ready for the show. All the crew had left, as had Dezzi. One of the representatives from Waterloo stood up and announced that they would be ushered out to their front row seats soon. Andy was wondering what they were talking about. He thought he had stage seats. He wanted to speak up and ask about it but he did not want to rock the boat either. Thankfully, the annoying obese lady in the loud dress also had stage seats and had no qualms in addressing the question. They were told to go out in the main corridor with everyone else and it would be sorted out there.

The group was gathered off to the side of a busy concourse and told to wait. The other thirty thousand people to see the show filled the area. All of them rushing to their seats or lined up at the concession stands. A young girl had walked by with a bag hung over her shoulder and was selling roses. She kept yelling out, "Roses! Buy roses for Dezzi!" Andy thought that was weird. He had never been to a concert where the audience throws roses at the performer. Plenty of Broadway shows, but never a concert. He got the girl's attention and purchased a single rose. As Sally, the obese lady with the loud dress invaded Andy's space she asked, "Are you going to give that to Dezzi?" It was fairly loud in the concourse, so Andy had to raise his voice a little as he said, "No, Sally, right? I had something a little different in mind for later. But since you were observant enough to bring it up now." He paused and turned to Marisa, "Thank you for sharing so many great moments like this with me. It means the world to me that you do this. I appreciate you so much and I am so happy to have you in my life." He handed Marisa the rose and she blushed as she smiled and took the rose in both hands. She did not know what to say or do except to thank him. Sally yelled out, "That is so cute! You two make a great couple!" Andy started to say, "Well, we are actually..." He was interrupted when Marisa grabbed his hand, smiled, pulled Andy toward her, and said, "Thank you, Sally."

Andy did not like this type of attention and was praying for it to be over. His prayers were answered when a tall and lanky man in glasses approached the group. He was wearing jeans and a blue t-shirt, and some sort of headset with a mouthpiece. He yelled out, "Twelve of you have pink passes that say 'stage'. You are going to be following me." He then pointed to a girl next to him, she was dressed the same and also had a headset with a mouthpiece as he said, "This is Anna. The rest of you are going to follow her to your front row seats."

Andy and Marisa followed the man in the blue shirt and ten others through a door and through what seemed like a maze. When they stopped it was easy to tell where they were. They were backstage. They could see crew scurrying around. Some of them were stagehands and some were sound technicians. They all had a job to do and were doing it. It was like controlled chaos. The man in the blue shirt gathered the group of twelve. He said in a very matter-of-fact tone, "Hey guys, my name is Chris, and I am the stage manager. Welcome to the show. You guys have the best seats in the house! I need you to listen close now." He started to stress his tone and speak slowly. "These seats are literally on the stage. That means that if you have to go to the bathroom, you need to go right now. Once the show starts, Dezzi is not allowed to leave for a bathroom break, so neither are you. Who needs to go?"

Sally said, "Oh Peter, Mary, and Joseph. Where do we go, Chris?" Chris asked again if anyone else needed to go because now was the time. A couple of people took Chris up on his offer and came back. The small group of twelve was taken to their seats and once again instructed that from this point forward they were not allowed to leave. As Chris continued down his list of do's and do not's Andy lost focus. He was looking out at the crowd. He really was on stage. It was not in the center or anything like that. It was more of an off-to-the-side position. Those in the front tiers of the audience that were observant may have noticed them. For the most part though, they were on the stage. The seats were in line with the drum set. They could see all the tape markings on the stage and if Dezzi had ever used setlists, they probably could have seen those as well.

The house lights went out. There was excitement in the air. People cheered and yelled out Dezzi's name. Marisa grabbed her rose tightly as she looked down at it. Andy looked at the faces in the crowd filled with anticipation. A voice said over the PA system, "Ladies and gentlemen please welcome Waterloo Recording artist, Dezzi." Thirty thousand people screamed out at once as their hearts sizzled with electricity.

The two concertgoers left the venue in excited delirium. They were still on a high of an emotional show. As they got in the car and drove to the hotel Marisa asked, "Oh my God! Wasn't that amazing? You haven't said anything since we left the show. Didn't you like it?"

Andy said, "Oh, I loved it. Sorry, I'm just in awe. That is probably one of the best concerts I have been to. She sang her heart out, she played many of her unknown songs to keep music aficionados like me happy and many of her hits to keep the fair-weathers happy. She played for so long. And all the stories she told in between were great. Who knew that Dezzi was also a stand-up comic? She was hilarious."
"What was your favorite part?"
"Oh, without a doubt when she encored with her yodeling. Near the end, I was getting a little scared that she was not going to do it. But when she came out for her encore and yodeled my heart sank."
"Yeah, I thought so. I know you were looking forward to that. I looked over at you and for a second it appeared as if someone nearby was cutting onions." Marisa said as she teased him.

Andy just looked back at her and laughed as he said, "Whatever."

They pulled into the hotel valet. This hotel was something he had booked on his own and not part of the Dezzi prize package from the radio station. Andy did not want to be staying in the same hotel with a group of what he referred to as prize pigs. A man came and handed them a ticket and pulled away in their car. Andy never did like valet. He understood the concept and appreciated it. But he always felt he was being controlled by the business that offered it. He felt that if he wanted to go anywhere, he had to get permission to leave. Not having access to his car was a situation that left him out of control.

They approached the front desk for check-in. It was a very loud area. Above them on the second floor was obviously a bar. There was a live Cuban band playing. The music was good. Andy enjoyed Cuban music. It was just too loud. The way the curvature of the high ceiling above was designed did nothing for acoustics but amplify them to an annoying level. Andy felt sorry for the front desk staff if this was their permanent working condition. He would have a headache if he had to hear that noise eight hours a day, every day. The noise to the right was just as bad. The constant ring, beeps, and jingles of slot machines were a bit overwhelming. The smell of smoke in the air permeated the entire building. It was repulsive. It had the smell of a large brush fire that filled the lungs and made it hard to breathe. One could taste the cigarettes in the back of their throat by simply breathing.

They approached the front desk as a bellhop had put their bags next to them. It was a very well-staffed establishment. At least seven people were working at the desk, and it must have been around midnight. A large Hispanic woman called up Andy. He greeted her and asked how she was doing. She told him fine and asked how she could help him.

Andy spoke up. "We are checking in. Reservation for a double queen, last name Chelios." The lady typed and looked at her computer and after a few seconds said, "I'm sorry. I don't have that listed. Is it under a different name perhaps sir?"

"No ma'am." he said, then spelling out his last name, "I made the booking a month ago. Two queen beds, one non-smoking balcony room."

The woman appeared to be looking at her computer screen, as she said, "No, I'm sorry sir, I don't have that." She paused. "Oh, you know what? Here it is. You made a reservation for tomorrow night."

Andy said, "No. I am positive I made it for tonight."

Marisa interjected, "Ma'am, is there a chance that you can find something available tonight?"

The woman shook her head back and forth and apologized that the hotel was completely booked because there was a concert in town. Andy rolled his eyes.

Andy sighed and asked, "Would you look again, please? There has to be at least one room we can have."

Marisa spoke up, "Ma'am, we are so far from home. Would you please check again for us? We can give you some time if you need it. We will go check out some games and come back in twenty minutes or so if that helps."

The woman behind the counter said, "Let me check with a manager and see what I can do. We can hold your bags back here in the meantime if you want to go out on the casino floor." Marisa thanked the woman as she grabbed Andy by the arm and walked him away from the desk. They looked at the hundreds of slot machines before them.

Andy watched as crowds of people walked from one place to the next. He had never been in a casino before and this was nothing like he pictured it. It was not like the movies anyway. No guys were walking around in suits with a beautiful girl next to them. He saw a lot of people dressed as if they had just stepped out of the trailer park. In their hands were drinks and cigarettes. There were a lot of Native Americans walking around as well. As they observed the casino floor it was like an information overload for Andy. There were so many noises and flashing lights he did not know where to look or where to go. He could not focus. Two parents walked in front of him with their adolescent kids walking behind them. Andy was perplexed. It was past midnight. 'Who takes their kids to a casino this time of night? Who takes their kids to a casino at all for that matter?' Andy wondered as he said to

Marisa, "Now that is class right there. Come along junior, watch as me and Mommy wash away your college tuition."

Marisa just looked at him and said, "Stop."
"Why are we doing this again? Shouldn't we be up at the front desk waiting to see if they can get us a room? What if someone else walks in and snags it from us? We should be up there waiting."
"We are more likely to get a room if they see we are here to spend some money. That is the whole purpose of this place."
"Whatever. Okay, Moe, where do we go? Lead the way."
Marisa smiled and said, "I don't know. We will have to walk around the floor and find a machine that speaks to us! Come on poo-poo head!"

Andy walked around feeling nervous. He felt that he was being watched and judged. He was thinking they probably don't want someone just walking around the floor. It makes one look suspicious. In order to get attention off him, he grabbed Marisa and sat down at a bank of six slot machines. They sat down and Andy looked at the machine in front of him. There was a large colorful digital display that explained the payouts and how the game was played but it might as well have been written in Chinese. Andy could make no sense of it.

He looked at a little vending machine-like slot for money. It had labels indicating the money it accepted. It went from twenty-five cents to twenty dollars. Marisa was already putting in money twenty dollars at a time. There would be a lot of bleeps and music from the machine. Andy watched her screen as four columns of animated symbols scrolled by. After a few seconds, it would all stop, and nothing would happen. Then she would do it again.

Andy asked, "So I just put money in and press this button?"
Marisa affirmed with a head nod yes.
"How much do I put in?"
"That's up to you."
"Well, you are putting in twenty dollars. Do I put in twenty dollars?"

She smiled and said as she pressed the green button, "If you want to win big, you have to spend big."

Andy laughed and said, "Yeah, whatever. Fuck that. If it's meant to be, it is meant to be. No matter what I spend."

He put in a quarter. As he pressed a green button, he closed his eyes and moved his lips as if silently speaking to God. He reopened his eyes and watched as the digitally animated avatars scrolled before him. Arcade-like music played along with a bunch of bleeps as they slowed and stopped there was the sudden sound of cling, cling, cling, cling.

Andy perked up and yelled. "Winner, winner, chicken dinner! Hey! I won! Moe, look I fucking won!" as the machine continued to make a digital sound of change hitting a metal rack and the animated numbers added up on the screen. It stopped at fourteen dollars.

"What the fuck? That's it? Fourteen dollars?"

Marisa laughed hysterically and said, "I told you, culito. If you want to win big you have to spend big. Don't be a cheapskate."

"Whatever. I just fucking won. First pull on a slot machine ever in my life and I just won!" He was so excited. "So where is my money? Isn't it supposed to come out of here or something?"

Marisa continued to press buttons and watch her screen as she laughed at him and said, "No. If you want the money you have to press the button that says cash out. It spits out a ticket and you take it to a cashier to give you money."

"So, I won. I should cash out, right? I beat the casino. I should take my fourteen dollars and go buy a drink, right?"

"It's up to you. You can do that, or you can continue playing on credit"

"What's credit?"

"It's the fourteen dollars you won. You can use that to keep playing."

"But I could lose all of what I just won if I continue playing right? I mean that is how they get you?"

Marisa turned to him and said, "You can do whatever you want. As long as you are having fun."

Andy thought about it and started to silently justify to himself. 'If I continue to play, I could win more. I had never touched one of these things in my life and I just won on my first try. Maybe I have that natural luck I've heard gamblers talk about. But I could lose it all. But if I lose, I am only losing money I did not have to begin with. So really it is not a loss.' He smiled and pressed a button labeled 'credit'. He chose the option of twenty-five cents. He watched the screen scroll by and make its sounds. It came to a stop and nothing happened. He lost. He tried again the same thing happened. He started to think that maybe he should quit while he was ahead. He kept pressing the credit button and kept losing as he watched his winnings of fourteen dollars dwindle to ten dollars.

Marisa looked over to Andy and could tell he was enjoying himself. To the average passerby, he may have looked very serious and focused. But that is just how her friend was. He did not openly show emotion. Just because he was not smiling did not mean he was not doing cartwheels inside. She knew this about Andy; she knew he was currently happy. If he was happy, she was happy. She continued to play her game.

Andy was at a credit of eight dollars. He was getting a little frustrated at not winning like he did the first time. He really expected to win again. The first time was so easy. All he did was hit a button and he won fourteen dollars. He had to get another win. He changed the credit to one dollar per play. Six plays later, the avatars scrolled by. The machine made its noises. It was followed by a cling, cling, cling noise. Andy was excited. He just won again. It was twenty dollars this time. He thought to himself that maybe now he should cash out. He won back his original winnings plus four dollars and seventy-five cents. At this point, he had officially beat the casino. Granted, it was only by four dollars and seventy-five cents, but a win was a win in his book. Then he thought to himself that he is still playing on money he did not have in the first place. He wanted to walk out a millionaire. Thinking of what Marisa had told him to play big to win big he continued one-dollar credits instead of only twenty-five cents. He did this until the very end. Till his credit was zero.

In his mind, Andy replayed the events that just took place. Why did he not just cash out the first time? He could be upstairs enjoying the live Cuban music and having a drink. He thought that he should walk away now. But he was plagued by the thought that the casino had just beaten him. His ego had been damaged. He had to win something. At this point, it was not even about the money. It was all about principle. He had to get back what he lost. There was no way around that. Determined to win back his losses, Andy took out his wallet and looked through his money. He took out a twenty-dollar bill and inserted it into the machine. He played at two-dollar credits per play. Two minutes later, Andy had twenty dollars less in his pocket. He repeated the process with the same results. He could not believe he had just spent all that money so quickly just pressing buttons. He had to win. He pulled out another twenty and felt Marisa grab him. She said, "Hey, these machines have become cold. Let's go get a drink."

She pressed her cash-out button, and a ticket came out.

"How much did you win?" He asked.

"Seventy-five dollars."

"Wow. How much did you put in?"

She shrugged her shoulders and said, "A few hundred or so."

Andy's eyes bulged as he shook his head and laughed, "Wow. So really you lost like one hundred some."

She looked back to him with a smile feeling thankful that math was not his strong suit and said, "It's all about perspective. I had fun so I won. Come on", she said grabbing his arm, "Let's go have a drink, I'm buying."

They were at the bar and listening to the Cuban band play and enjoying Corona by the bottle. The musicians were amazing to listen to. The Latin beats filled the air along with the sounds of horns and the hot vocals of a female lead singer. They infused a little bit of jazz into the music and it was all improvisation. It was amazing to be so close to God-given talent.

Marisa turned to Andy and asked, "So what do you think?"

Andy smiled and said with excitement, "Oh man, they are fucking awesome! They are probably a family and have been playing with each other all of their lives. I mean, you can tell. The way they play off each other so well. They were probably born with instruments in their hands. I love them!"

"I meant gambling. What do you think of gambling?"

"Oh that. I guess I can see how some people think it is fun. I mean, the losing sucks. But I felt really good when I won."

"So now you see why people do it?"

"Well, no. I mean." Andy paused as he tried to think of what he wanted to say. "I guess I can understand why people do it. I mean, I put my money in, I won and I felt good. I wanted to win more. But then I started to lose and I just wanted to get my money back. I felt like shit losing my hard-earned money, so I had to get it back. I kept losing but I had to keep playing because what if the next pull was the big winner? I would be devastated if I had lost money and walked away. Then some schlep comes up and wins big on what would have been my next pull. I would simply die if that happened. So, you keep playing with that thought process. Then you win a little again and hope is restored. Then you lose twice as much as you put into it and you feel the need

to get it back. I don't see what people enjoy about it, but I do see how they get addicted. It's like these people, the casino. They dangle this little carrot over your head and you keep reaching for it in hopes that you get just one bite of the tasty carrot. Not to mention, I expected a little more. I expected a machine that I get to pull on a giant arm rather than pressing a little button. I expected a little more fanfare even if I lost. Looking around, I don't think all these people are here to have fun. I think some of them are spending what little they have so they can afford to keep their lights on. They have hopes of solving their problems here at the casino when, really, they are just digging themselves into a deeper hole. They are grabbing desperately at the carrot." Marisa looked at Andy and said, "Wow, you are looking way too deep into this."
"Yeah, I know. So short answer? Yeah, I had fun, I guess. But I wouldn't do it again."

Marisa and Andy walked down the wide spiral staircase to the front desk to check on the results of finding a room. The woman at the desk smiled as she greeted them and informed them that she was able to find a room for them. It was a single queen room with no balcony, but there was a window. They thanked the lady for making it happen. She called out to a bellboy for him to take their bags to their room.

They got to the room and tipped the bellboy as he left them alone. For the first time in a long time, they heard something they had not heard all day. Silence. Andy looked to Marisa with a smile and asked, "Do you hear that?"
She inquired, "What?"
He nodded his head and said, "Exactly." Andy then lifted the bottom of his shirt to his face and took a quick whiff. "Wow, I smell like a ham sandwich served on a dirty ashtray. I really need to shower." Marisa just laughed as she said, "You are such a weirdo. Go wash, dirty man."

Marisa stood by the window overlooking the parking lot. She could hear Andy in the shower as she twiddled her hair in her finger. He was singing. She could hear his voice. "I love you, baby, because you're quite all right with me baby!" She laughed to herself as he literally continued with, "blah, blah, yadda, yadda, doo doo, blah baby! Bah dah, bah dah, dah-duh-dah-

dah!" What a goofball she thought. They had known each other since they were just little kids. He had always been there for her no questions asked. He was funny, in his unique way. He made her laugh anyway. Like now for example, he was singing way off-key and making up words to a song that every person on the planet knew. It was either because he did not know the words, or he was just being silly. He would do that sometimes. He would make up words to a song he knew she liked just to try and ruin the song. He pressed buttons that way occasionally. She knew he did not mean ill of it. To him, it was fun. It was his way of showing affection. He really was a great guy and she wished he would let more people in as he did her so they could see it. She said out loud to herself as she stared out the window, "You're such a silly ass. Whatever am I going to do with you, culito?" The words silly ass and culito were pretty much interchangeable. Culito was her slang way of calling him a silly ass.

Andy stepped out of the bathroom as he slammed the door open to the side. He was wearing navy blue boxers and a white undershirt. He said in a bellowing voice, "Behold the greatness that is me! I smell of—"He paused as he sniffed his armpit and continued, "Value Store soap!"

Marisa laughed and just shook her head and said, "I guess I will take advantage of that myself now if you're done in there."

Andy just looked at her playfully while crossing his arms as he said in a bellowing voice, "Unless you want your stink ass to be sleeping on the floor you had better. By order of Captain Clean, only people who shower regularly may grace the sheets of this bed!"

She brushed past him and shut the door. A minute later he heard the water in the shower start. He bellowed out again, "If you need help with your back or, whatever, just call for Captain Clean!"

Andy threw himself down on the bed. He thought to himself, 'what did I just say? Oh, Andy, the alcohol is still in your system. You need to gain control and slow your roll. You can't be talking to her like that.' He lay on the bed looking at the ceiling. He continued his thoughts, 'Moe is an awesome and sexy girl, but you need to rein yourself in man. She does not think of you that way and you should not think of her that way. So you're just going to be nice and share a bed like a gentleman tonight. Stay on your side of the bed. Don't let the drinks make you try something you'll regret in the morning. You are just friends, remember that.'

Marisa stood in front of the mirror and looked herself in the eyes. She was about to sleep with Andy. They had slept together many times before. When they were kids, they would sleep next to each other all the time. Even though high school and college they shared a bed on occasion. They never had sex. It was just two people sharing a bed. But this was different. They were both adults well into their twenties now. This was different she thought to herself. Even this concert was different than the rest they had gone to. Then there was the rose she thought. She wondered how he thought of her. He treated her like a sister. Sometimes though the comments he made led her to believe he had feelings of a different nature for her. There was no man in her life she was closer to. Sometimes she would catch him looking at her in a particular way. Other times she was sure he had caught her looking at him the same.

She walked out of the bathroom and Andy looked at her as he asked with a smile, "What is that?"
"It is my negligee."
"So, it's like your pajamas? That is what you wear to bed?"
"Yes, and what are you wearing? Boxers and a shirt? Sexy." She said with sarcasm.
"Hey, normally I wear nothing, but considering the circumstance, this is my nightwear, yes. Try to contain yourself," he said with a smile.

She walked toward the bed and looked down at the nightstand. The rose Andy had given her was on it. She picked it up and said, "Thank you for the rose, Andy. I love it. It was so unexpected."
He just looked at her and said very blasé, "Don't mention it. I guess it just seemed like the thing to do. You drove me here, I guess it's the least I can do."
"Don't be a moment killer, culito."

"Oh. This was a moment?" he laughed, "What I meant to say was that I knew it would make you smile and so I enjoy going the extra mile."

She said, "That's more like it" as she went toward the mini-fridge and grabbed a bottle of water, opened it, and put the rose in. She placed it back on the nightstand as she sighed out loud and smiled. She had felt warmness in her as she thought about the Rose.

She looked on the counter by the TV and noticed some candy wrappers. "Where did you get the candy?" She asked.

"It was in a basket by the TV." He answered.

"You know they charge you for that right?"

"What do you mean?"

"They keep an inventory and charge you for the candy." She lifted a sheet of paper off the counter and continued, "It says right here. It lists everything. That was a five-dollar chocolate bar you ate. I hope it was good."

Andy laughed, "Well maybe they should put a sign up or something."

She told him, "They did. It's this menu and price list that was sitting on top of the candy."

"Yeah, but I did not read that. I just figured that was a sign like any other I don't read, like 'please don't take bath towels to pool' or something like that."

"They have a pool here?" She asked.

Laughing, Andy said, "No. I mean, I don't know. But you know, a sign that says something like that. Nobody really reads them. If anything, they should not put it in something that looks like a gift basket if it is not a gift. Oh well. They already took a lot of money from me, so what is a few more bucks? Plus, dude. I was starving. So yes, I guess it was a five-dollar chocolate bar."

Marisa lay down on the bed next to Andy. They were both on their backs lying side by side. They spoke of the concert and all the parts they enjoyed. Marisa asked, "So did you check if this place is Gideon approved?"

"What?" Andy asked off guard by the sudden change in subject.

"Isn't there supposed to be a Gideon Bible in every hotel room across the country? Come on, you're the one who went to a private school and should know this stuff." She teased.

"Well, actually. You know it's not a different kind of bible, right? It is the King James Bible and the Gideons are the group of people that drop it off. It started near the early 1900s when two strangers had to share a hotel room. They found they had a common trait in their faith and thought it would be a good idea to start a club of Christian businessmen. So, they got a club together and named it after Gideon. He was some guy that I think was a judge and had led a small band of men against a much larger army. So anyway, they tried to think of a good way to spread their word of God and came up with the idea of leaving Bibles in hotel rooms for others traveling on the road to read."

Marisa laughed out loud as she said, "What-ever!"

"What, that's really what happened."

"I think you're making it up. You always make stuff up."

Laughing, Andy said, "I swear to you I am not making this up."

"See, you're laughing. That means you are pulling my leg. Where do you come up with this stuff?"

He looked over to her with his hands pressed together palm to palm in front of his chest and smugly said, "Private school!"

Marisa paused and said, "So you still have not answered my question."
"Which was?"
"Is this room Gideon approved?"
He looked at her as he laughed, "How the fuck should I know?"
"You check the nightstand, culito!"

Marisa rolled over the top of Andy to get to the other side of the bed. As she rolled over him, he could feel the bare skin of her sleek legs rub his. He had only starred at her legs a billion times before so he knew how sexy they looked. In this second, their skin was sharing the same space in the universe. He could feel her weight on top of him as he felt a sense of security from that. He caught a whiff of the perfume she was wearing. He did not know what it was, but the scent had excited him. It was a wonderful smell. He took a deep breath. As she maneuvered over him Andy caught a glimpse of her breasts peeking through her negligee. They were the perfect, size, shape, and form. They looked so soft.

She had reached the other side of the bed. She reached to the nightstand, opened the drawer, and pulled out a bible. She opened to the front as she pointed to the stamp on the inside cover, "See. Gideon approved."
Andy just laughed as he said, "That's great."

She put the bible back in the drawer and turned off the lamp. They both lay in bed next to each other looking at the ceiling. Andy was hoping she would stay on that side of the bed and not roll over him again. He was worried that if she did, this time she would feel that the first time had caused a little swelling in his lower regions. He would feel so embarrassed if she knew.

A few seconds had passed. Silence. Deep silence. They lay in bed next to each other. Andy tried to think of what to say or do. It was Marisa that spoke up. "I don't like this side of the bed. I want that side." She said as she started to roll over him again. Andy just closed his eyes and thought to himself, 'baseball, baseball, baseball.' He once again felt her weight on top of him. He felt the skin of her legs rub on his. He could smell the sweet smell of her perfume as if it were the only smell in the world. Marisa had completed her roll over and they were lying next to each other. On their backs, side-by-side, their legs were touching.

Andy spoke up, "What is that you are wearing?"
"What do you mean? I told you earlier, my negligee."
"No, I mean the perfume."
"Oh, this. It's just something I picked up from the lotion store. Don't you like it?"
Andy smiled to himself in the dark, "Ah. I am not going to lie to you, quite the contrary. I love it. It kind of drives me insane." Marisa said thanks.

Marisa laid in silence looking in the darkness at the ceiling. She was wondering what was about to happen if anything at all. He did just compliment the perfume that she had put on before coming to bed. He did not just compliment it. He said something that indicated that he liked it. Was that a signal from him? She could have sworn on that second roll over him she felt from his body that had excited him. So at least he was physically receptive to her. Or maybe she was only imagining it. She could swear she could feel some sort of electricity between them. But she could not be sure.

While lying on his back, Andy looked into the darkness at the ceiling. He was so uncomfortable. He was not an on his back type of sleeper. He preferred to be on his side with a pillow in his arms and another pillow supporting his back. He wanted to be on his side though. He could not roll over towards Marisa though. They were so close to each other that she would for sure feel him. That last rollover she did, caused him to gain a full erection that he had not yet lost, no matter how much baseball he thought about. The thoughts that came with it also caused him to gain a tiny wet spot in his boxers. This would be extremely embarrassing if she felt that and her current thought process was not in line with his. He could not roll over away from her because then if she had been thinking the same as him, she would feel rejected.

With his heart pounding rapidly, Andy took a deep breath and leaned in toward Marisa. She rolled on her side facing him. The two looked into one another's eyes without saying a word. Andy put his arm around Marisa and stroked her back with his arm. She smiled and touched his chest. He then leaned in and pressed his lips gently to hers. She reciprocated by returning his kiss and while putting her arm around the small of his back and pulling him in tight. Both of their hearts were pounding wildly. Neither of them could believe this was about to happen. Both were unaware the other was thinking the same exact thing. The intense vibe in the air sure indicated otherwise. All of these years of being so close and this was finally going to happen. These two friends that were clearly designed for one another were about to connect in a way that was more than metaphysical. The passion both of them felt at the moment was so intense. With each kiss, the mutual feeling of passion grew stronger and deeper. Each contact of the lips and rub of a hand inspired a manic-like need to keep going deeper into this abyss. At that moment, Andy had a strong feeling of passion. He pulled back slightly and just looked at Marisa. She looked back at him with a slight smile and small laugh as she asked, "Oh-kay. What, exactly was that?"

"I am not sure. Just one of those things that happen I think." Andy replied.

Marisa said, "I'm not sure those things just happen. That was something."

"That was weird," Andy said back.

Marisa could only agree by slowly responding. "Weird."

Andy told her, "Yeah, but not like kissing your sister weird. Just unexpected, weird."

"Right." She said.

"Well. Night Moe!" He paused as he took a breath. He put his hand on her cheek and kissed her forehead before rolling off her onto his side briefly as she slapped his ass and said, "Night Culito!" He reverted to being on his back while staring at the ceiling. Shortly after, both had gone to sleep while staring up into the darkness wondering what the other was thinking.

EL RANCHO II (SPRING 2014)

Back in the present time and at a seedy roadside motel, an anole clung to the stucco wall at the El Rancho Motel. Its head abruptly jerked up and down, as it smelled the new scents the air brought in from the unfamiliar intruders. They stood outside the door to a room and one of the strangers jammed a jagged metal object into the door handle.

Andy took one deep breath as he stuck the key attached to a white plastic key chain. He could feel the key make its connection and before turning he turned to Marisa and asked, "You ready for this?" She turned to him and smiled, "Always ready for anything with you." He turned the key and opened the door. She asked, "Are you going to carry me in?" Andy looked to Marisa and told her, "I don't think this is the time for that just yet." He gestured with his hand for her to enter the door. The two entered the room and Andy was in awe. The carpet was red shag. There was a small kitchenette. The cupboard doors were painted white with red trim. The counters were red. In the back middle of the room was a large bed on a raised platform. It was in the shape of a heart. It had red sheets and a white comforter. It was covered in pillows that came in a variety of shapes and sizes. They were all either white or red. There was a flat-screen TV with a DVD player connected. A small pile of movies was stacked next to the DVD. Andy grabbed a movie at random from the stack he exclaimed, "Oh look! They have Raiders of the Hairy Hole! I've always wanted to see this one!" Marisa laughed and said, "Well this must be your lucky day because there it sits in your hand." Andy put the movie down and said, "Mm no. I don't think so. Why would they have these movies? I mean this is the honeymoon suite, right? Why would a couple on their honeymoon need these movies to get in the mood? Shouldn't they already be in the mood since they are on, you know? Their honeymoon? And look at this kitchen. Holy freaking Christmas! Everything is red and white! Oh, there is the bathroom! Let me guess the color scheme in there is--" He paused as he walked into the bathroom and yelled out, "Hey Moe! You are not going to believe this! The bathroom is painted red and white!" He looked down into the sink that had had not been cleaned since the last tenant had been in. Shavings covered the sink bowl and there were a few dried markings of a rough night and cheap wine around the toilet.

Andy came out of the bathroom and said, "You know Moe, I'll be honest with you. I'm not sure I want to shower in there. I think I may leave dirtier than I am." She looked at him and replied, "You such a prim donna drama queen. It can't be that bad. This is the honeymoon suite, culito!" He smiled and said, "Have at it, my queen." She grabbed her toiletries from her suitcase and entered the bathroom. Andy lay on the bed and heard her turn the water on. He heard her yell, "Oh my God! Why does the water look yellow?" Andy laughed and yelled back, "Quit being such a drama queen and wash your stinky ass!"

Ten minutes later, Andy heard the water stop. One minute later the door to the bathroom door opened. Still a little wet, Marisa stepped out with only a towel around her toned body. "How was it?" he asked.
"Just close your eyes before turning the water on and you will be fine. I think the pipes in this old ass building may be the original."

"Oh, it can't be that bad." He said with sarcasm as he rolled his eyes.

Marisa walked over to her suitcase and pulled out a negligee. She unwrapped her towel and stood in front of Andy completely naked as she started to change. He turned his head and covered his eyes with one hand. She laughed and asked, "Never seen a grown woman naked before? Oh wait, I know for a fact you have."
"I have seen many grown women naked and yes, one of them has been you. A few times perhaps. But that was different. Right now we are only days before the wedding and I probably should not be seeing you like this right now."
She laughed and said, "You are such a weirdo at times. Go take your shower smelly man and bring back, oh what is his name? Captain Clean."
"Whatever," Andy said as he went in to take his shower.

Marisa could hear the water of the shower start up. She got up off the bed and from her suitcase pulled out a bottle of perfume. She sprayed the sheets and pillowcases and rolled back into the bed.

Andy came out of the bathroom in boxers and a T-shirt. Marisa looked at him and said, "Some things never change." He looked at her and laughed as he replied, "What? I'm a guy. Simple things, simple pleasures. I don't need all that frill just for bed wear. I mean I'm going to bed. Who do I need to impress?"

"It's okay", She said, "I think your choice of pajamas is just fine. You look great. At least it's not like you are wearing Monkey Beans pajamas to bed."

"Oh, those are at the cleaners." He joked. "And since you like pajamas so much I hope you like this little song I wrote for you. Are you ready to be serenaded?"

She giggled as she sat up with excitement and said, "Oh sing away, Valentino."

Andy stood at the foot of the bed and cleared his throat. He took a long hit from an imaginary joint and said in a thick Jamaican accent. "Dis one go out to all de people across de lan dat like der pajamas as mush as I do." He paused as he moved some imaginary long dreads from in front of his face and took another hit from his imaginary joint. "Pajamas...Pajamas, I hope do

like pajamas like me! Pajamas, I like de way de make me feel free." Andy then started to heavily sway his head back and forth as he continued to sing. "Pajamas, pajamas, pajamas, pajamas. Pajamas, pajamas, pajamas, pajamas.
I hope you like pajamas like me!" he bowed and took another hit off his imaginary joint. Marisa clapped her hands and laughed hysterically. She said, "Oh my lord. I wonder if maybe you have been really smoking something. You always make me laugh."
He looked at Marisa as he shrugged his shoulders, "It's what I do. I live to serve."

Andy walked to the bed and grabbed a pillow and went to an all-white couch that was off to the side of the bed. Marisa just looked at him and asked, "Really? You're not going to sleep with me tonight?"
"I told you earlier babe, the big day is coming up very soon and it does not feel right."
"You and I have slept together many times Mr. Chelios."
"In fact, there have been many times when..."
"Bow chica chica bow bow" Andy chimed in.
"Exactly!" Marisa said as she pointed at him.

"Well, there was that time at the Dezzi concert. Other than that, what are you talking about?"

"Fourth grade," she said.

"Fourth grade? He asked.

"Fourth grade." She repeated

He inquired, "What happened in fourth grade?"

Marisa looked to Andy and said, "How do you not remember? It's what our pinky friends for life is based on!! In fact, our whole relationship is based on the pinky swear and that happened because of fourth grade! Oh my God. Tell me you remember! Tell me you remember the day that cemented us together forever!"

A fly on the wall buzzed momentarily as it stuck to its current spot and Andy squinted his eyes and looked directly at Marisa as he slowly said, "Oh yeah, that day."

PINKY SWEAR (FALL 1979)

Little Marisa and Andy stood facing each other surrounded by trees in a far back corner of the playground. They hung out here a lot. A lot of the kids would hang out in this spot. It was out of view of the teachers watching over the playground. It was where kids would go to sneak a smoke or just be outside of adult supervision. Today it was just Andy and Marisa hanging out in the area. They enjoyed spending time together away from everyone else on occasion. Today was a little different from the rest. They were not out there to swap dirty jokes or answer keys for a test. They were not there to share a cigarette. Today it was curiosity that would be sparked. Marisa had brought up a recent health class. They had been learning about the human body. She asked, "Did you see those pictures in Mr. Allen's class?"

"Which ones? Do you mean the ones of the lungs and lips after tobacco use?" He asked.

"No", she replied. "The ones of our bodies and how they are different."

"Oh, those. Yeah, that was kind of strange. Your body is kind of funny looking"

"Mine? What about you? At least I don't have a thing hanging from mine"

There was a pause in the conversation between the two kids. Marisa broke the silence. "Aren't you curious?"

"About what?" Andy asked.

"About what it all really looks like. I mean, we were just shown cartoon-like pictures. Not even real pictures. I want to see what it all really looks like, don't you?"

Andy shrugged his shoulders as he put his hands in his pockets, "I guess, my dad has some magazines in his closet with real pictures. I've seen those, but it is all just girls. No boys."

Marisa put her hands on Andy's shoulders and said, "But those magazines are not the real thing. Aren't you curious to see what it all really looks like?"

"I am, but Mr. Allen said we would one day when we are grown-ups and married."

"That is a long time to wait. Don't you want to know sooner?"

Andy nervously said, "I guess, but how am I supposed to do that."

"Well, if you show me yours, I will show you mine."

"Um okay. So who goes first?"

"Well, you do of course" Marisa replied.

Andy stammered, "Um, you go first."

Marisa said, "How about we go at the same time? On the count of three, we both pull down our pants."

Andy agreed. They both loosened their pants and looked at each other in the eyes. Marisa started to count to three. When she said three nothing happened. Andy said, "You did not pull down your pants!" Marisa exclaimed, "Well neither did you!"

"Now what?" Andy asked.

Marisa explained a new idea. "Okay. On the count of three, we will pull down each other's pants."

Andy agreed and they both grabbed each other's pants by the waistline. Marisa counted to three and they both pulled down each other's pants. For a moment, they just stared at each other's different parts in wonderment. Andy asked, "Where do you pee from?" Marisa answered, "From here."

"From where? I don't see anything."

"From here," She said, pointing to the location on her body. Then she asked Andy, "Can I touch it?"

There was a large crack sound. It was the sound of someone stepping on a branch. They heard a voice. It said, "Who is back there? You know you are out of bounds!"

Andy and Marisa quickly pulled up their pants. Marisa looked at Andy and said, "You can't say nothing to no one. We will be in a lot of trouble."
"I won't," Andy said.
"No seriously Andy, you can't say anything. I know you don't like to lie. But you can't say a thing. Pinky swear it to me, you won't say anything!"
"I swear, I won't say anything."
"No Andy," Marisa said with urgency, "pinky swear it!" She held out her hand with a clenched fist and her pinky outstretched to a curve. Andy grabbed wrapped his pinky around hers and said, "I swear."
She said, "Good. Remember, that is pinkies swear so now you can't say nothing ever. To no one."

At that moment, Mrs. Greeger, the playground monitor appeared before them through the trees. She said in a serious tone,

"Mr. Chelios, Ms. Lopez. You know you are not supposed to be out here. What pray tell are you two doing? You are out of bounds."

Andy looked at her blankly. He could not think of what to say. He was not ever good at fibbing. He just stood there like a deer in headlights. It was Marisa that spoke up first as she nervously said, "We wasn't doing nothing, Mrs. Greeger. We was just talking."

"You were not doing anything", Mrs. Greeger said as she corrected Marisa. "And I know that is not true. What were you two doing back here? Don't you know this is out of bounds?"

Marisa glanced back to Andy quickly and back to the adult in charge. "I swear, Mrs. Greeger, we were just talking. We wanted to be away from the other kids because they pick on Andy."

Mrs. Greeger looked at Andy and asked, "What say you Andy, is that true?"

Andy looked at Marisa and she itched her lip with her pinky as her eyes narrowed in on his. She was subtly reminding him of the pinky swear he had just made. It was pinkies swear. He could not fib, but he could not break a pinky swear either. He paused and stammered. "Um, yes mam. The other kids pick on me and I um, wanted to hide from them. Marisa was keeping me company um, so I am not alone."

Mrs. Greeger looked at Andy and said, "Well, we have had this conversation before Mr. Chelios. Someday you are going to have to learn to stand up for yourself. Maybe the other kids don't like you because you have a smart-mouth, and you think you can get away with it because of who your father is."

Andy said, "No Mrs. Greeger, they all pick on me because they don't like me. They want to beat me up. Why don't you ever believe me?"

Mrs. Greeger looked down at Andy and sternly said, "Because kids like you have it all, Mr. Chelios. You have everything handed to you on a silver platter. You think you can have it your way all the time."

"No, Mrs. Greeger, that isn't true! I don't think I deserve anything! Why are you taking their side all the time?"

Marisa interrupted, "Why are you picking on him now?"

Mrs. Greeger looked to Marisa and snapped, "That will be enough from you, young lady. Let him stand up for himself or he will never learn."

Another playground monitor, Mrs. Angleton had shown up at that moment. She asked, "Is everything okay Mrs. Greeger? Do you need assistance?"

Mrs. Greeger said, "We have two hooligans here up to no good Mrs. Angleton. Take them to Dr. Kilion's office and call their parents. We don't know what they were doing. They claim they were just talking. But we will get to the bottom of this. Mrs. Angleton grabbed both kid's hands and took them to the principal's office as instructed. They both waited in silence on a bench outside of Dr. Kilion's office till their parents had come in. When they did come in it was a meeting that lasted around thirty minutes.

Later that night both Marisa and Andy had snuck out of their houses to meet up and discuss what had happened and make sure their stories had matched since they had been separated.

Marisa asked Andy, "So what happened to you when you got home? Are you grounded? I am. No TV, no friends, and I'm only allowed to come out of my room for meals and to go to school. For two whole weeks! What happened to you? Did you get in trouble?"

Andy took a deep breath as a tear came down from his eye. Marisa looked at him and asked, what's wrong? Did your parents beat you up again?" Andy just shook his head back and forth. "Well, are you grounded? What happened?" Andy looked at Marisa with a hardened stare as he wiped a tear off his cheek and coldly said, "Worse." Marisa asked him what he meant by worse. He said, "I'm being sent away to private school."

Marisa yelled out, "What? Well, what did you tell them? You did not tell them the truth, did you?"

"No Moe, I told them just what you said to Mrs. Greeger on the playground. I told them how the other kids pick on me and the teachers don't do anything about it. They pick on me too. So my parents are sending me away to a place where they say that won't happen. I am so sad Moe. I'm never going to see you again. You are the only one that is here for me and my only friend."

Marisa said, "We'll see each other still. You will be home for summer, right? I will always be around for you. Pinky friends for life!" She held out her hand with her pinky outstretched and curved, he grabbed it with his pinky and said, "Pinky friends for life."

In the hotel room, the fly had removed itself from its place on the wall and flew away as it buzzed to a place on the counter. Andy stared down Marisa on the bed and said, "Yes, I remember it well. I got sent away for that. But I never did tell a soul. I pinky swore on it. He held up his hand as he leaned towards Marisa and said, "Pinky friends for life," as they interlocked their pinkies.

Andy stepped away from the bed with a pillow in hand and said, "Regardless, pinky friends or not. I cannot sleep with you only days before the wedding. It almost seems sinful."
Marisa laughed. "You silly Catholic boys. Always worrying about sinning. We are not sinning. We are just sleeping next to each other. But suit yourself. If you want to sleep on the ugly couch be my guest. As long as your soul feels clean, I guess."
Andy laughed and said, "Well, cleaner than whatever is on that bed probably. Good thing we do not have a black light."
"You're gross."
"That may be true, but I am not the one sleeping on a jizz bed." He said as he lay out on the couch.

She laughed and said, "You're stupid, culito. I don't know where you come up with this stuff. But I love you, good night."

Andy smiled and said, "Night Moe. Love you too." She leaned over to the nightstand and turned out the light and they both took their separate trips to dreamland. Somewhere in the darkness of the room, a fly on the wall witnessed it all.

WELCOME HOME
(SPRING 2014)

They had been traveling on the road for more than a few hours. They had gotten an early start on the day to reach their final destination with no more overnight stops. When they crossed the Florida / Georgia line, Andy said, "Welcome home, Moe! Hey, do you know how to tell the difference between an alligator and a crocodile?" Marisa answered dryly, "The alligator will see you later and the crocodile will see you in a while."

"Oh. I guess you do. Okay. Here is one. A man is walking around the carnival with a parrot on his shoulder-"Marisa stopped him as she said, "Hit a black top and win a prize."

"I see. You heard that one too? It appears I have run out of material."

Marisa laughed, you got jokes, and I have heard them all."

"All right. Here is one you have not heard. Do you know the difference between a pack of wild pygmies and an all-girls track team? The wild pygmies' are a bunch of cunning runts and the all-girls track team are- "

Marisa interjected, "Think very carefully about the words you use in this punch line culito."

Andy said, "Ah. Yes. Of course, the all-girls track team just run really fast."

Marisa slapped Andy on the shoulder and shook her head.

They finally reached Daytona and made it just in time for the ferry to the Peeking Islands. They were in their hometown after disappearing for so many years. Everything around them had looked so different. What were once empty fields were now mega shopping centers or apartment complexes. They all looked the same too. There were palm trees that were not native but were in perfect health and gave the area a tropical look. Every complex had large fountains by the gated entrance. They all had names like 'Fair Harbor' or 'Hidden Garden'. This island had become extremely superficial at some point in the past twenty years. There was nothing from the past left. Even some of the road names had changed. Then there was the traffic. They both silently wondered where all this traffic had come from. Why are there so many cars on a freaking island? Andy slowed the car as the light changed yellow and then came to a stop when it changed to red. A car behind him slammed on the breaks. There was the loud sound of the driver leaning on their horn. They could hear someone in the car behind them yelling something but could not make out the words. Andy looked to Marisa and said, "I guess yellow now means go really fast, and red means jam on through." Marisa just smiled and nodded. She was tired from the road and just ready to be home. Andy starred up to the clouds in the sky. He felt a jab in his ribs as Marisa said, "Green light."

"What?"

"Green light. Green means go."

"Oh. Yeah. Sorry."

The sound of a long horn behind him was heard as Andy dropped into gear, floored it, and smoked the tires.

They had approached another red light. Marisa sat up in excitement. She yelled, "That's it!"

"What?" Andy asked in excitement.

"The church! That is where the wedding is! Pull into the parking lot. I want to see inside."

Andy pulled into the parking lot of the church and there were a lot of cars that had filled it up.

It was Thursday, Marisa aksed, "What church runs a service now?" As they got out of the car and sat on the hood while observing the church, Andy said, "Maybe it is another wedding. You may find this hard to believe Moe, but there might be other bridezilla's out there."

Marisa nodded as she said, "True, but I am the one that matters."

Andy agreed, "You are the only bridezilla that matters to me if that counts for anything."

"Oh no," she said. It's not a wedding. Look."

Andy looked to where she was pointing and a hearse was pulling in.

"I'm sorry, Moe" Andy said, as he knew what she was thinking.

Marisa was silent as some tears trickled down her face. Andy leaned over and wiped the tears from her cheeks and eyes. "He was a great man," Andy said. "He would be very proud of what you have become today. You are a strong business leader at the top of her field. You have made a very good life for yourself and 'ol Chuck would be very proud of you."

She tried to talk through tears, "I loved him so much. I miss him so much. It's not fair. He was taken far too early."

"He loved you very much."

"I know, Andy, but I never got the chance to tell him how much I loved him. I thought I'd have more time."

"Cancer is a bitch, Moe. Sometimes it is slow and sometimes it creeps up super quick before we know what is going on."

"But why him? Why my dad? He was such a strong man! He should have beaten it!" She continued to cry as she leaned into Andy, put her arms around him, and buried her face in his shoulders.

Andy continued to comfort her as best as he could. She looked at him as she wiped her face and asked, "I look a mess, don't I?"

"No Moe, you look fine."

"No. I've been crying. I know my makeup is running. I look a mess."

"You look fine."

She took out her phone and put it in selfie mode. Andy could not tell if it was a laugh or a cry as she said, "Oh man, look at me. I look like a clown that got caught in a rainstorm." Andy, still trying to comfort her said, "Well, not really. Clowns are more colorful and smell like manure. You just look like someone who had a rough afternoon and smell like a person that has been on the road all day." Andy smiled when he was at least able to get a small giggle from her. She looked at him and said, "Thank you so much."

"For what?"

"For being you. You have treated me so well our whole lives. You have always been there to make me laugh."

Andy said, "Well, you know me. I live to serve. I am your personal grinder monkey. Crank me up and let me entertain you by crashing my cymbals together."

She laughed and replied, "Not like that. You always know how to pick me up when I am down. We have shared a whole life. And now? Now it's going to be different. Everything is going to change. I feel like I am going to be losing a best friend."

Andy spoke and said, "This, this wedding will not change anything, Moe. We will always be best friends. Nothing has ever changed us in the past and nothing will now or in the future. I will always be your pinky friend for life." He smiled and held out his pinky as she grabbed it with hers. They moved their hands together down by their sides as Marisa leaned into Andy once again and said, "Oh my God. I am such a hot mess."

Andy grabbed her face with both hands and lightly leaned away. He looked at her and said, "You're fine. Let me take you to your friend's house and y'all can get that bachelorette party going. I think being around your girlfriends would be really great for you. Plus, it's a bachelorette party. One thing I have learned working in a restaurant is that bachelorette parties are super fun. Well, not for anyone in the near vicinity of said party, but for the gaggle of the women involved it is fun."

She laughed and asked, "Gaggle? What exactly is a gaggle?"

Andy answered, "A gaggle is a group of middle-aged drunken women out to tear up the town. Gaggle."

She shook her head and said, "you and your made-up words. Yeah, take me to Ally's house. I think that is where they all probably are. Where are you going to go?"

"Well, I am going to go check into my hotel then head out to the bachelor party, of course. Because I hear those are kind of fun as well."

She looked at him and asked, "Promise?"

"Yes, of course. What else would I do?"

"You would sit around at the hotel by yourself and mope around. I know you. I got you. Pinky swear that is not what you are going to do?"

"Well, I won't pinky swear on that, but I promise I will do my best to have a good time at the bachelor party without you."

"Ugh. You're too much. Take me away to the party please." They both got back into Andy's red Charger.

NINA (SPRING 2014)

The bachelor party was in full effect. The whole crew was there. Johnny, Ron, Rob, David, Chet, Bill, and Keith. They were all old friends of Andy. Everyone but Andy was there. The drinks were flowing, girls were dancing, and the music was playing loudly. Chet's phone rang and he walked out of the room to answer it. When he came back Johnny asked who it was. Keith told Johnny it was Ally and that Andy and Marisa had made it back to town.

Johnny asked, "Well, where the hell is Andy? How long have they been back?"

"I don't know," Keith said, "But Marisa has been there over at Ally's for a couple of hours now."

With a stripper on his lap, Johnny yelled out, "Well, call that boy up! Tell him to get his ass over here! He is missing the party of the century!"

Keith attempted to call Andy, but he did not answer. Keith left a message and hung up.

Andy sat at the bar alone. In front of him on the bar was a glass of scotch on the rocks sitting on a napkin, a pack of cigarettes, a book of matches, and an ashtray with a couple of butts in it. He looked at his phone lying on the bar top as it lit up and started to vibrate. He looked over at the caller ID that said 'K-ROCK'. He took a deep breath, rolled his eyes, and hit ignore. The bartender stopped and asked, "You doing okay, Andy? You need anything?" Andy just waved his hand back and forth across the bar and said, "No, thanks, Zach." As he stared at the bottles on the shelves in front of him, Zach grabbed the ashtray and emptied it before putting it back in front of Andy on the bar. Andy looked at his phone and picked it up. He listened to the voicemail that Keith had left. It said, "Yo-yo Andy man! Heard you're back in town. The bachelor party is going on now. We got brewski flowing and hot chicks dancing. All we need now is you! Get yo ass over here now, mister!" Andy just smiled, set his phone to 'do not disturb', and put it in his pocket.

A girl approached the bar and sat next to Andy. She was approximately 5'1 with a beautiful figure. She had long straight black hair. Her skin had a naturally tan complexion to it. She looked at Andy and said, "Hi there." Looking up from his glass of scotch and looked at the girl and said, "Hi." He looked back down at the glass. The woman had paused and put out her hand as she said, "I'm Nina, nice to meet you." Taking the napkin from under the glass and putting it on top of the glass Andy turned to her and said, "Nice to meet you, Nina. I'm Andy" She looked at the napkin he had put on top of the glass, smiled, and said, "I'm not going to bite. I was sitting over there with my friends, and you looked like you could use some company." Andy looked over his shoulder to a table that he assumed was the friends she was talking about. He feigned a smile and said, "Listen, Nina, right? You are a beautiful woman no doubt and I am sure you are a wonderful and fun person to be around. It's just that right now, I may not be the company you are looking for. Thanks though." He started to get up and Nina asked, "Aren't you going to drink that?" Andy looked at her and said, "Oh this? No. I don't drink." He reached for his wallet and took out a twenty and a ten. Andy yelled out to the bartender, "Hey Zach! The ten is for you and whatever is left is for Nina here." He put the money under a coaster and walked out of the smoke-filled bar.

As Zach approached to take the money Andy left behind the woman asked, "Do you know that guy?" The bartender said, "That's someone who used to live around here. His name is Andy. Andy Chelios." The woman looked back to Zach in shock. "I use to listen to a guy named Andy Chelios on the old Q95 all the time!" While wiping off the bar with a damp rag Zach said, "That would be the one." Nina asked, "Well, that was a long time ago. What happened to him? I mean I don't hear him on the radio anymore."

Zach answered, "Nobody is sure. He was here one day and gone the next. Some say the life of the limelight was too much for him to handle. He started hanging out in the mangroves with the shady'tnrs and got overly addicted to drugs. I hear one day he snapped and wanted to distance himself as far away from here as possible. Others say he left for a girl. Nobody knew for sure. Rumor has it he moved out to California."
"Do you know how long is he here? Where is he staying?" Nina asked. Zach shrugged his shoulders and said, "Not sure, but that hotel matchbook might provide some answers. I do know this. He did not have a drip to drop, he did not have a ring on his finger, and he bought you a few drinks. So, what'll it be?"

ONLY IN HEAVEN
(SPRING 2014)

A quartet sat off to the side of the front of the church and played softly as people sat in mostly silence. Some people shuffled through the program for lack of anything better to do. Others admired the wedding party standing at the front all beautifully dressed and matched. Some people spoke softly with one another. Kids fidgeted in their seats uncomfortable in the suits and dresses they were forced to wear. It was a fairly large crowd of around two hundred. It was two hundred and forty-seven to be exact. The church was beautifully adorned. Over one thousand flowers were decorating the stage and pews. Purple streamers and other fanfare hung from the ceiling and walls. There was even a horse-drawn carriage complete with all white horses waiting out front. This was a princess' wedding.

As the quartet finished their last song there was a slight pause. The church was silent except for a few people shuffling in their seats with the anticipation of a kid at Christmas. The organ struck its first chord and the crowd all stood to their feet, turned, and looked to the ornate doors of the church to watch the woman of the hour enter the room.

Andy stood next to Marisa and turned his head to catch a quick look at her. He was dressed in a black and grey zoot suit with two-tone alligator shoes. As he gazed upon the bride, he could not help but smile. She was absolutely beautiful. Her brunette hair was perfectly straightened out and the tips slightly touched her shoulders. Her dress was all white and hug tightly to her body. She carried a beautiful bouquet.

The entire audience was in awe. Although she looked slightly nervous, Andy could tell that Marisa was in complete control and enjoying what was the happiest moment of her life. The corners of his mouth lifted as he felt his eyes start to water up. In a second's time, he remembered a lifetime of happy moments that they had together. She had been such a great friend to him over the years and he to her. They had seen each other through the worst and best. He had often thought about what kind of man would marry her. Being married to her would be like trying to tame a wild horse. It would take a special kind of guy. He was elated that she finally found that guy. Just looking at her, he could tell that her happiness had been fulfilled. In one teardrop rolling down his cheek, a lifetime of memories filled his heart.   Andy was snapped out of those memories as he felt a nudge. He shook his head quickly and heard the pastor say, "I ask again, who gives this girl away to be wed?" Andy cleared his throat and said, "I do. I give this girl away to be wed."

As he released the interlock on their arms, he formed a fist with his right hand and used his pinky outreached in a hook fashion to make a subtle itch to his lip and smiled and winked. Marissa smiled back. Andy motioned with his right arm towards Johnny, who had been anxiously awaiting his new bride to join him at the altar.

Johnny stood tall and proud with a special look of affection to his soul. His especially dark hair complimented his light and airy eyes. His jawline sculpted around his smile filled with confidence perfectly as he faced Marisa and the two conjoined hands.

There was not a dry eye in the house as the newlyweds were presented to the audience. The pastor said with pride, "Ladies and Gentlemen, on this day of May the fifth, 2014, I present to you, Mr. and Mrs. Johnny Smith." The world's newest couple faced the crowd, each with joyful smiles. As they walked together to exit the church, friends and family cheered them on with congratulations. It was at this moment, life seemed to move in perfect slow-motion meant to be seen only on a movie screen. Everyone applauded the couple as they walked by with a grace only achieved in true happiness.

It was a ceremony for the record books. It is possible that perfection like this may only be compared to something found only in Heaven.

It is at this point in the story that you, the reader, must be thinking, "What a wonderful happy story. He was so sweet! She was so fun! But why did they not end up together? They seemed so perfect for one another! That is what you would think if this were the end of the story. You may have noticed there are many more pages behind your right thumb. That was only act one...
This is not the story you thought it was.

ACT II

HER STORY
(DECEMBER 25TH, 2016)

It was Christmas day in 2016 as Nina sat alone in her car and except for her uncontrollable sobbing, it was completely quiet. Her hands were shaking as she thought about the day that got her to this place in her head. It had been a long messed-up day. It had been harder than most. Her mind was foggy, and she had a hard time piecing the day together. It had started early in the morning when she had taken to the bottle earlier than usual. By noon she was pretty lit. Then, there was her ex-husband, Leo. He was a mean soulless man that always tried to get in her head. He had left many voicemails in the past telling her what a bitch she was. He even told her repeatedly to kill herself. He did not help with their kids and he was constantly stalking her. Today he had taken it to a new level. Today he broke into her apartment and let his friend rape her.

He had broken into her apartment many times before and beaten her. Despite having a restraining order, the police never did anything. Leo's parents were influential and rich with Mafia money. His family took very good care of him even though he was a grown man. He still lived at home with his mother. He was a total man-child that enjoyed beating on women. Especially his ex-wife, Nina.

That day he had done more than just beat her. He knew she was drinking and this time after he beat her, he let his friend rape her. She had been violated in every fashion of the word. She played that scene over and over in her head. She could not block it out. She did not even bother to report it. She knew the police would blow it off just as they have the previous beatings.

As she sat alone in her car sprinkles of rain covered the windshield and only a shimmer of light from her cell phone illuminated the car. She was alone. Not just in a physical sense, but she felt alone in the world. She had her kids. She tried her best to raise her four kids on her own. But it was not easy. She struggled a lot. For whenever she was able to take one step forward it would seem as if she took three steps back.

Nina sat in the car writing letters. She wrote to her kids, she wrote to her mom, and she wrote to Andy. She was not completely alone in the world. She did have Andy. He had taken really good care of her and her kids. He often helped with her bills and rent. She did not even have to ask. There had been many times she would protest, but he did anyway. She knew he adored her. She really did love him. In fact, as of two days prior they were engaged. She had surprised him with a proposal of marriage in a parking lot. It was not the most romantic way perhaps. But she could tell he did not need an extravagant presentation. She fondly remembered the look of shock and surprise on his face. The woman he loved with all of his heart just proposed to him and he was happy. As was she, in fact, it was the happiest she had been in a long time. She smiled as she briefly thought of that moment only forty-eight hours ago.

Which brought her back to where she was now. She was alone in her car on Christmas evening. A small stack of handwritten good-bye letters sat next to a Bible on the passenger seat. She grabbed her phone and sent a text to Andy. It said, "I'm going to kill myself. Please forgive me."

Within seconds she got a reply back that said, "Please don't?" She had texted him back saying that she loved him. She asked him to tell her kids that she loved them and wanted him to take care of them for her. She got another immediate text back begging her not to do it. He had text how much he loved her and could not live without her. Nina then tried to call Andy. There was no answer. It was 9 PM and he would be at work. She knew this. But she was hopeful. She tried calling one more time and it went to voicemail. She did get a text back. It was Andy telling her that he was at work and could not talk on the phone but he would call her as soon as he was done. She sent one more text back. It simply said, "G'Bye."

TINO (SPRING 2017)

There was a loud bang and Andy shot up out of sleep. His eyes popped wide open with the sudden noise and he sat up looking around the room. He heard the pitter-patter of four tiny paws attached to a Siamese cat run out of the bedroom. He yelled out, "Tino!" Andy vigorously shook his head back and forth trying to fully shake the sleep from his brain. 'What a horrible dream' He thought to himself. In the dream, he had images of what it must have been like in that car for Nina. These were images that plagued even his awakened mind. These were thoughts he could not shake. He wondered what it was like for her on that final day. Knowing Nina's battle with depression and how hard she was on herself he liked to think he might have a slight idea of her mindset at that moment. He thought the act of suicide might be like a sneeze. Perhaps when a person is depressed, the urge to take one's life was like the body's involuntary reaction to sneeze. The impulse to react can be so strong that a person in that state has no choice but to react as their body tells them to. Just as when a person is about to sneeze they feel certain that anything short of sneezing will not relieve the sensation. Though, he knew he had no clue. He cringed hard as he tightened his fist and let out a loud sigh. He wiped his hands over his face to try to stimulate some blood flow or just wipe away the sleepy feeling his face still had. As his hands rubbed over his cheeks, he could tell it was a day to shave.

Before getting out of bed Andy scanned the room trying to figure out what Tino had knocked over that woke him with a loud bang from his horrific dream. He looked at the top of his dresser and noticed it was only a small speaker. Almost on cue Tino walked back into the bedroom and made his usual morning sounds. Tino was a displaced pet that Andy had taken in during his California days. Tino was from an earthquake that had one day followed Andy home and kind of just stayed. He was very big and extremely talkative. Tino jumped up on the bed next to Andy. The Seal Point Siamese with blue eyes started to kneed on the part of the bed where Nina would occasionally sleep and with his luminescent eyes looked up to Andy and purred. Andy stroked Tino and said, "I know buddy. I miss her as well."

Andy got up and started to take a shower. He could hear Tino meowing just outside the shower non-stop. He yelled out, "Hold on Tino! I'm almost done!" He laughed to himself as he said, "Silly cat!" After the shower, he went into the kitchen with Tino at his feet. He said to his furry friend, "Well I can't get there and feed you if you trip me now can I?"

Andy prepared breakfast for Tino and himself. They sat on the lanai of Andy's small home on Isla Sirena in the Peeking Islands. As they ate breakfast, they would watch the boats go by in the channel between Bear Island and Isla Sirena. Tino had a bowl of warmed-up tuna and Andy made some waffles topped with strawberries and bacon on the side. As he ate breakfast he zoned out and he thought about the day when love walked into his life. He remembered it clearly. It was the day after his best friend's wedding.

From atop a counter just above his grill sat a radio at Sal's Street Meat. Sal's was a street cart located in the center block of Water Street in the historic seaport of Manta Ray. Sal's was the cart that those in the know would go to for food. A song faded out on the radio and a voice said, "It is 102.7 WVCX and it is I, Jake Robison! You know we are the station that plays all the current hits. But for now, let's take a step back, shall we? Let's go back in time for the all-cool, all request, retro power hour!" A jingle played singing the station's name and a throwback song started.

INQUIZITIVE INQUIRIES
(SPRING 2014)

Andy woke in his room at the Silver Tree Suites, a hotel tucked away in the town of David on Manta Ray. It was only yesterday that he had given away his best friend in marriage. Her name was Marisa and they had known each other for decades. They were friends since they had been kids and continued their close relationship into adulthood. There really was no one else she had been closer to. Since her dad had passed away, it seemed only fitting that he be the one to give her away. It was such a magnificent wedding and reminisces of the reception lay amiss around his suite. His pin-striped zoot suit was flung over a chair. A few confetti poppers lay on a table. Glitter was all over his pillow. He stretched out and smiled as memories of the wedding passed before his eyes. Marisa was so happy and her new husband was a very lucky man. At the ceremony, it was easy to tell by the way they looked at each other it was a match to last. She had finally found the man capable of keeping up with her and taking care of her and that made Andy very happy.

He had gotten out of bed and cleaned up for the day. He started to tidy the room a little. Andy always tried to stay in luxury hotels, despite there being housekeeping with a specific job to do, he still felt bad leaving the place in a mess for them. He did what he could. It was never anything too extreme. More so simple stuff like not leaving clothing or trash lying around and he would make the bed. Even though he knew housekeeping would make it look a hundred times better anyway. In his mind, he felt good about it though.

Andy scrolled through his phone as he sipped on some coffee. He had a couple more days left in town before he had to drive back to the west coast. He was going to see if there were any old friends who wanted to hang out. As he was doing this the phone in the hotel room rang. After looking at it for about three rings he picked it up and questionably said, "Hello?"

A voice on the other end responded. It was a female voice. It said, "Hello. Is this Andy?"

Andy said, "Erm, yes. Who is this?"

The soft voice on the other end said, "You don't know me but my name is Nina."

Andy vividly remembered two days ago when he was sitting in a bar avoiding the bachelor party.

He was not drinking as he did not drink anymore. An old friend of his was a bartender there so he was there in trusted company. Plus, at the time he knew a bar would be the last place any of the wedding party would expect to find him.   While at that bar, a girl had approached him and tried to strike up a conversation. She was drop-dead gorgeous. She stood at maybe just an inch over five feet. She had light brown skin and probably did not weigh more than ninety and that was guessing high. Her hair was black and long. It went down to about her ass. She wore tiny, tight shorts with a sleeveless shirt that advertised her breasts that were large for Andy's preference. From her ears dangled extra-large hoop earrings. She did not smile big. She had a rather serious look on her face. She was about as close to flawless as it could get for Andy. He heard the voice on the other end of the phone ask, "Hello? Are you still there?"

Andy shook his head to zap himself out of his memory and said, "What? Yes, I'm still here, Nina. From the bar, two days ago, right?"

"Yes." The voice said back.

"I remember you. Listen, I'm sorry if I was rude. I did not mean to blow you off. I really was not in the mood for company that's all. But I am glad you called. Speaking of which, how did you get this number? How did you know to find me here?"

"The bartender pointed out a matchbook from the hotel you left behind and I figured that being my best chance, my only chance I would give it shot."

Andy responded, "Well I am glad you did, I guess, I think. I mean, it's kind of weird but I'm glad you did. Sorry I am rambling."

Andy heard Nina laugh as she said, "You're funny. Would you like to meet up? How long are you in town?"

Andy said, "I'm in town for about three more days, I think. I would love to meet up."

Nina asked, "Back at the bar where we met, or do you have something else in mind?"

"Well, when I lived here a while back there used to be a pizza joint sharing a parking lot with a gas station on Tawassie Road on Manta. It's right by the historic seaport. Do you know if it is still there?"

She said, "It's still there. It's where I work."

"Oh really? I don't suppose you want to go there if you work there."

Nina laughed and said, "I'm joking. I don't work there. I don't even live here. I'm from Daytona. I'm in town for a few days. Is that where you want to go? I'm sure I'll find it on my GPS"

Andy told her, yes and they agreed on about an hour.

Andy walked into Mac's Pizzeria. It was just as he remembered it. For the first time in a long time, he felt as if he were at home. When he used to live nearby, he would come here at least once a week. If he had friends or family in town visiting it was his go-to place. The feel of the restaurant did not have the typical corporate feel to it that a lot of restaurants in town had. The servers were not in silly brightly colored uniforms covered in flair. Instead, they looked as if they dressed themselves. The staff wore whatever jeans and T-shirt they had pulled out of the dresser that day. In this aspect, they were like normal people rather than someone with a required over the top cheery attitude. They did not have that forced good time smile. The friendliness was real and sincere. The décor was simple. It was not overboard with ketch. There were booths all along the walls and tables filled out the middle. Family-friendly pop rock music filled the air. The food was perfect. It was all made to order so it was fresh. It may have taken longer to get but the wait was worth it. The pizza was served exceptionally hot. So much so that while one could pick it up by the slice, it slid directly down the throat. Almost no chewing required. It had been cooked and melted to perfection.

Nina and Andy had a marvelous time over pizza. Andy had enjoyed it. Since moving to LA from the islands he had not had any good pizza. Californians did everything so weird. Especially food. Which was a shame to him, as he loved pizza. This was really a special treat to him.

Nina asked, "So what brings you back here?"

"A wedding" Andy answered as he swallowed a mouthful of pizza.

"A wedding?" Nina asked.

"Yeah, my best friend Moe, erm, Marisa was getting married and since her father had passed away from cancer a while ago, she wanted me to be the one to give her away. So, we drove out here together. It was a fun trip. We shared a lot of memories."

Nina said, "I'm sorry to hear about her father."

Andy said, "Thanks. It was a while ago, but thanks. But why do people always do that?"

She asked, "Do what?"

"Say I'm sorry when they are told someone they don't even know has died. I mean, I'm not ragging on you specifically. But overall, people seem to do that with ease. I feel so uncomfortable when I am told someone I don't know dies. I know I am supposed to say I am sorry, but I don't feel the compassion I am supposed to. Does that make sense?"

Nina plainly looked at Andy and said, "I guess. You have a weird way of putting things."

Realizing his lack of social skills was not getting him anywhere he grasped to change the subject. "So Nina, what do you do in Daytona?"

She replied, "You mean for work? I race cars."

Andy's eyes widened as he said with excitement, "No shit? Really? I am totally into racing. Any kind of racing. If there is a start-finish line I am all over it!"

"Well, that is what I do."

He asked, "Do you mean street racing or for real circuit and drag racing?"

She told him with a prideful smile. "I do it all."

Andy was really into her now. He thought to himself, 'Not only is this girl beautiful but also she is into racing like he is. Not only that but she is an actual driver!' He was starting to think that if he played his cards right that he could have a girlfriend that is an actual racecar driver. He asked, "Do you have your own car?"

She told him she had two. They were both Challengers and she loved her cars more than life itself." Wiping his mouth with a napkin he asked, "What color?"

"They are both red."

"Both of them? Why is that?"

"Why not?"

"Fair enough," he said as he wiped his hands with a napkin and took a drink of tea. She then proceeded to give him the entire history of the Dodge company and the Challenger cars along with details of Mopar. He was trying to listen. It was a little hard. He loved racing, but he was not really a mechanical guy and was not really into the specifics of cars. He was impressed with the knowledge she had about the cars. He told her, "You should sell these for a living. You know so much. I have an old Charger myself. I don't know near as much about it as you do. I know how to fill it with gas. Erm, I know it is super-fast and expensive to insure. That's about it."

She asked him, "What do you do out in California Andy?"

Andy told her, "I'm an actor."

She asked with excitement, "Oh really! That is cool. What would I have seen you in?"

Andy said, "Nothing really. I've been in a few commercials and I did one television pilot that did not go very far."

"So how do you make your money? I hear it's expensive out there?"

"It is. I wait tables to pay the rent."

"Oh. So, you're a waiter?"

Andy rubbed the back of his neck with his hand, "Yeah, but I am going for the acting thing. That and I like to write. I write poetry and I'm trying to get that published."

She asked if he had any of his writing picked up. He said, "No, but there were a few bands I wrote songs for. Nobody you would have heard of yet. But they may make it someday and to be honest, I don't care if they make it. I got paid for the songs either way."

She laughed and said, "I am just busting your balls, Andy. I don't care what you do. I'm just making conversation. But tell me about your writing. I love to read."

Andy was taken back a little bit. Nobody had ever asked about his writing. Other than bands looking for music nobody ever seemed to care.

Andy started to tell Nina all about writing. He said, "It's like this. Ever since I was a kid I loved to write. I never had support though. Even later in my high school creative writing courses, my teacher failed me. But that was a personal thing. She did not like me for whatever reason. Plus, I think my stuff was a little too dark for the school I was in. Despite the destructive criticism I continued to keep on keeping on. I love to write. Not just poetry but short stories, songs, whatever. If I am writing I'm in a happy place. You know what else? These days' people tell me they love my writing. Some have told me I have a gift."

"Who told you that?" Nina asked.

"Most people that read my blogs."

She inquired, "You write blogs? You did not mention that."

He said, "Yeah I do that too. There is not a lot of money in it, only what I can get from people who advertise on my page and whatnot. To be honest though I don't really make a lot of money doing that. I'm not so good."

"What about this gift you said people say you have?" She playfully asked.

"The writing I am good at. It is the business aspect. I'm not good at selling my blogs, or myself, plus this whole Internet thing has me puzzled. I mean the getting yourself out there part. I don't know how the kids these days are making millions by just sharing pictures or videos of themselves pulling stupid pranks on the internet. I just don't get it. I mean how they, get out there?"

They continued to ask inquisitive inquiries about each other trying to learn a little bit more. To an onlooker, it would appear that two people sitting at a table were highly interested in one another. Each clinging on to the next words out of the mouth of the other with anticipation. There was a mutual feeling of attraction between the two. It was a breath of fresh air or more like lying down in new sheets fresh out of the dryer. Andy pondered the look he got from Nina. He wondered if his mind was playing tricks on him. The way this girl looked at him was different. She seemed sincerely interested in everything he had to say. He was not accustomed to this and was not sure how to take it. Was it even possible that a girl would take this much interest in him?

Especially one that was as beautiful as Nina? She appeared to be hanging on to every word that came from his mouth with great interest. Girls this beautiful and smart never hit on him back in L.A. He was reminded of something a friend had told him on a trip to Vegas long ago which was, "If hot chicks do not hit on you at home, they are not going to hit on you anywhere else. Caveat emptor; buyer beware." Andy digested that thought for a minute and wondered if he was being played.

They continued their conversation and after some time, they received and paid their bill. The two did exchange phone numbers and made plans to meet the next day in the afternoon to go ride go-karts. Andy went back to his suite feeling excited about a new lease on life.

RED, YELLOW, GREEN, GO!
(SPRING 2014)

Andy's phone rang from the nightstand. He could tell from the light breaking in through a slit between two curtains it was still early in the morning. He smiled as he saw the caller ID said, 'Nina'. He answered in a quiet hello as he cleared his throat. A straight-toned voice asked back. "Hey what are you doing?"

Andy asked, "What time is it?"

"It's 7:30. What are you doing?"

"I was sleeping. What's up?"

"I'm awake. This is normally the time of day I drop my kids off at school. My body is kind of on this set clock. Since I am up, I thought you would want to meet up for breakfast." She sounded so chipper and excited for 7:30 AM.

Andy said back, "7:30 you say? Meet up for breakfast? That is a little ahead of our date schedule but for you, I think I might make an exception."

Nina said, "Great. Do you want me to pick you up or meet somewhere?"

"Meet me in the lobby of my hotel. We will have breakfast here. It is actually pretty good."

She agreed and said she was on her way over to his hotel.

The breakfast at the Silver Tree Suites came with the package. It was more than the average continental breakfast. There was a warm food line filled with choices like pancakes, waffles, scrambled eggs, sausage, bacon, and grits. Or one could have a made-to-order omelet made anyway way they wanted it. There was a large selection of cold cereal, muffins, and fruit. The two got their food and sat down at a table outside with a view of the downtown area.

Andy said, "I have to be upfront with you. Last night in my hotel I was thinking about my time with you. You made me feel really good. You have me on an emotional high. You have truly elevated my spirits. It's not that I was down. I have a happy life. It is pretty awesome to be me. You just elevated my flight to a new level. Like if I entered an eternal spring day, came across a winning lotto ticket, or had a chocolate shake."
She looked at him puzzled and asked, "So you put winning a lotto ticket and having a chocolate shake on the same level?"
He smiled and said, "Yeah, I guess. I'm a simple guy with simple pleasures."
"I'm a simple pleasure?"

"No!" Andy laughed and put his hands up in the air. "You are amazing. Oh, what am I trying to say? You make me feel fantastic when I'm with you. I feel unstoppable after spending time with you. I think you're pretty awesome."

She told him, "Thank you. You are one of the few people that appreciate my awesomeness. Most people take advantage of my kindness and some people can be really cruel. You're pretty awesome yourself. You make me feel special." She said this all with such a straight face and tone of seriousness. He still could not figure out if she was for real.

Andy smiled and said, "Wow. Thanks for telling me that. But my awesomeness is only a mirrored humble reflection of yours. Tell me, when you are not being awesome what else do you like to do?"

She told him one of her favorite things to do was get in her car and drive while listening to music. She expressed her love for her cars and how much she loved being in them. Trying to figure out a little bit more of this puzzle named Nina he had asked what type of music she liked to listen to. She simply answered, "All kinds."

Laughing and poking fun at her response he asked, "Could you be a little more vague?"

She had told him that she liked dance music. What she meant more specifically was EDM. It was not the dance music Andy was familiar with. To Andy, if someone said dance music, he thought of the stuff that was played in the clubs during the 1990s or maybe even the early 2000s. This music now. The kind the millennial generation listened to; it was a whole new breed of music. He enjoyed it though and he learned more about it as Nina had texted him artists he should be listening to. Later down the road, it was all he was listening to, and he even set up a special music folder of music he downloaded because of her.

They sat and talked about the club scene for a little while longer as the patio started to fill up with more people. They decided to head to the go-kart park.

The park they had chosen was called Fun World. The locals called it Fun Whirl as an inside joke since the "D" had been missing from the sign for as long as anyone could remember. It was a small sidetrack adventure to all the watersports offered on the historic seaport. There were midway games, small rides, and of course a go-kart track. It is what the place was known for.

They went through a small queue to get in their first race. While waiting in line Andy said, "You know, you might know everything there is to know about cars and racing, but you are about to be publicly humiliated, just say'n."
Nina gave him her staple serious look, which was masking a smile, and said, "I do this for a living. Do you know about money-shifts? Do you know how to hit an apex?"
With his chin up in the air full of confidence Andy told her, "I know that I am going to put your gully ass in the wall and make you take the turn of shame."
"Do you even know what you are saying?" she asked.
"Of course. The turn of shame is what you do when I put you in my review. I turn right into

victory lane and you turn left into obscurity. And gully is what you are. It is a chonga, only on the racetrack instead of in the hood."

Nina shook her head back and forth. "I am going to show you what I do. You have no idea how badly I am going to beat you now." Then she started to whip out facts about the Dodge Challenger as she always did to show just how much she knew about cars and racing. Andy interrupted her. She asked, "What?"

Andy smiled and said, "You gonna bark all day little dog?"

She stared at him blankly.

He said, "Okay, not a fan of movies. It's our turn. Go. You're holding up the line."

The two got into their go-karts and got comfortable as they made seat adjustments and put on the seatbelts. They were positioned in the back of the pack of eight. Andy liked it that way, as it would be fun to pass all those people. He looked over at Nina and yelled, "When that light hits green I hope you are ready to go. Because from here on out it signifies the rest of your life!" She looked over to him and looked back forward without saying a word. Her fingers were wrapped tightly over the steering wheel. The look on her face was determined and serious. She took this very seriously. This is what she did. She was not about to be beaten by this smart-ass she is on a date with or any of these other weekend warriors on the track today. Besides, she raced real cars against professional drivers. These were only karts driven by average Joe's. This was child's play. Regardless, she was still going to put Andy in his place and shut his little smug mouth. She slowly tapped her fingers as she gripped the steering wheel.

A man in jeans and a black T-shirt stood in front of the two lead cars as another man dressed similarly went down the line of cars and checked the seatbelts of everyone. The man in the front yelled, "Listen up! This race is three laps! There is no rubbing or bumping allowed. If you see us wave a black flag directly at you then you slow down and come into the pits immediately. If you see us point a wrapped yellow flag at you that means you are doing something wrong, and we are watching. There are yellow lights all over the track. If you see a yellow light, slow down and hold your position in line till you see green. And of course, green means GO! Let's have fun, keep it clean, and good luck. Give me a thumbs up if you're ready!" Everybody's thumb went up in the air. The man in the front yelled, "Drivers! Start your engines!" Andy looked around his car confused. 'My engine is already started, what the hell is he talking about? As the man was giving the command a tall signal light about twenty feet in front of the pack lit up. It went yellow three times to green. Another man standing off to the side waved a green flag and Andy pushed the accelerator to the floor. The kart had a lot more jump to it as he anticipated. Which was fine. At least the person in front of him was paying attention and took off as well.

Over on Nina's side when the light hit green it did not go as well. From the last yellow, she anticipated the timing and hit the gas just as the next light turned green. The person in front of her did not react as quickly and felt a hard bump from behind as Nina ran into their rear.

As the race started Andy noticed, from the corner of his eye, Nina took a jarring hit as she nailed the person in front of her and did not get the start he knew she was hoping for. He chuckled to himself as he pressed forward and maneuvered himself into position. While coming down the first small stretch out of the pits the pack all vied for position into turn one. All the karts fell into place and Andy snuggled into 6th with Nina still in the back in 8th. Turn one was almost right out of the gate and it was a fairly tight left turn that brought them back 180 degrees.

Everyone came out of turn one successfully and was quickly eyeing turn two which was a wide and flat 180-degree turn to the right. The cars scrambled for position and Andy still found himself in 6th, Nina had moved up to 7th. They came out of the turn and had a quick jaunt to turn three which was a tight and flat hairpin turn to the right and would have them facing the direction they had come from. All of the tires squealed as everyone took that turn way too hard. Nina drifted through it and was right on Andy's rear. After coming out the turn they had a straight section of track that took them up a bridge going over turn two. Andy hit the gas and veered to the left to pass the kart in front of him. At the same time, he had unknowingly blocked Nina who was planning on doing the same move to him. She made a sudden adjustment to the right and lost a little position as she felt a bump from behind. They went up and over the bridge. The pack was still running tight as they approached turn four.

Turn four was a ninety-degree banked turn to the right. Seeing that it was banked he kept a good speed. Nina was right back on Andy's tail and keeping an eye on what this wild man was about to do. She knew what he should do. She was a race driver. This was her thing. But he was so haphazard it was anyone's guess what he or any of these other amateurs would do. As the turn approached, she watched Andy cut across the turn into the apex and while doing so passed two cars. She was pleased he did the right thing and followed right behind. They were now in 3rd and 4th respectfully.

Directly coming out of turn four was a 360-degree helix that led them into a tunnel going under the area between turn four and five. This allowed a long straight section of track that was out of view of the track attendants. The front of Nina's car was almost touching the back of Andy's. They were fast approaching turn six. It was a hairpin turn to the left. Just as they came out of turn six, they were geared up for a long straight section of track. Nina pulled up to Andy just to his left rear and matched his speed. She started to touch his left rear with her front right and lightly applied pressure.

Andy had just come out of the hairpin of turn six. He knew Nina was somewhere close behind him just not sure where. He did know that he saw nothing but straight track and two cars in front of him. He had hit the gas and was gaining on a car getting ready to pass. With no warning, he felt that he lost control of the car as it started to spin rear up and front down. His tires made a hard rubber on cement rubbing sound as he went sideways across the track. The steering wheel vibrated as he came to a stop and in a flash of light saw Nina tuck under and pass him. He could have sworn he saw a smile come from her. "Fucking, cock-sucking whore", he cursed as he thought out loud. Then his eyes opened wide as every car in the pack came straight at him. Some slammed on the brakes, others went into a wall and one hit him right in the side. The good news was he was still in fourth if he could get his car out of this mess first. The bad news was Nina was gaining a good amount of ground.

A smile hit Nina's face as three words went through her mind: touch, turn, and accelerate. Those are the steps she took to run a successful PIT maneuver on Andy. She laughed at the look of shock and surprise on his face as he lost control of his car. She was just passing the car in the second position as the lights on the track went yellow. "Fuck!" she thought as she continued her pass as the car in front of her followed direction and slowed. She snuggled herself into 2nd place.

As Andy got his car moving forward again his spirits lifted as he was first to get going and he noticed the yellow lights were yellow. He gunned it to turn seven to catch up with the three lead cars leading the caution. Turn seven was a hard banked ninety-degree turn to the left. It led to another straight section of track that he led everyone behind him to till they approached turn eight which was a flat ninety-degree turn to the left that would lead to the start/ finish line or the pits to the right. It was in turn eight that Andy caught the leaders. He noticed Nina was in 2nd and a smile hit his face as they came down the front stretch and one of the attendants pointed a yellow flag wrapped around its pole at her. He spoke out to himself as he said, "That's what you get bitch."

All the cars were lined up and traveling at quarter speed as they came down the front stretch. An attendant waved a green flag at them and they all took off. They all held position till turn two when Andy took over position three. He was right on Nina's tail. He was confident he could pass her going over the bridge and into turn four. But he had something else in mind. He stuck to her like glue through the helix of turn five and as they entered the tunnel he floored it and rammed her hard from behind. It gave her a good jolt and she flipped a middle finger high up in the air.

Nina felt a bump from behind and felt her head get thrown back and forward. She knew it was Andy, so she just threw a middle finger in the air and barreled to the hairpin of turn six. She took it hard and used her experience in drifting to take the corner with a little more speed than Andy. One could not really drift in these karts, but what she did was something close. They came out turn six and she gunned it. She started to draft the lead car on the backstretch and could feel Andy right behind her. She was just about to pull out and pass the lead car when Andy had beat her to the punch and was now even with her. He had a huge victorious smile on his face then it disappeared when he did not fly by her.

She shook her head back and forth, as she knew exactly what his thought process was. She yelled out to him, "You can't slingshot past me like the pros, dumbass!"

He yelled back with confusion, "What?"

She yelled louder, "We are not going fast enough to slingshot!"

He yelled something she could not understand as he leaned his body forward. As if doing that would give his car more speed to pass her. Nothing happened and they both maintained a battle for second place neck and neck. He then looked over to her and yelled, "You're going down!" With that, he swerved the side of his kart into hers and ran Nina into the wall. The two karts stayed together as he applied more pressure from his steering wheel and held her into the wall. Both karts slowed dramatically and were overpassed by everyone behind them.

Slightly shaken up, Andy pulled out slowly with Nina right behind him. They went around turn seven and as they approached turn eight a man was standing on the wall waving a black flag at both of them and pointing them into the pits. They slowed their cars down made the tight turn number eight and drove their karts into the pits.

Andy led the way into the pits as another man was waving with his hands and motioning him to come forward to the front of the pit. Andy drove through the pits to the front with the caution of someone who was suddenly, a safe driver. He came to a stop. The man in jeans and a black T-shirt put his foot on the front of the car to prevent Andy from going anywhere else. He walked around to the rear of the car and cut the engine, as he said, "All right there, buddy. That will be enough racing for you." The same thing happened to Nina and they both got out of their Karts. As they walked out of the pits toward the track exit one of the attendants came toward them. He held up a cell phone took both of their pictures. Andy smiled for his picture as he did this. The man looked at Andy and said, "You think your funny boy? The two of you are now banned for one year. I don't want to see any one of your faces around here for a year. Capeesh?"

Andy said, "Yes sir, sorry sir." Andy used all of his might not to roll his eyes. Nina gave the man the same stoic look she always had on her face.

The two found a food court and stepped to the counter to order their food. Andy looked at Nina and said, "You got this right?"

She looked at him with shock and said, "I don't have any money. I am behind on bills and have to feed my kids."

He looked back to her and said, "yeah but you lost. That was the wager. Loser buys food."

"I don't remember a wager."

He laughed and said, "Oh there was a wager. You don't remember?" he playfully asked. He then said, "Okay. Ill spot this one time."

She said, "Besides, you did not win. We were both disqualified."

Andy responded, "Maybe. But I pulled into the pits first. Therefore, I am the winner, winner. Chicken dinner. "

Andy paid for the food and grabbed both of their trays.

They found a table to sit at with their food. The courtyard was a perfect spot for lunch. It was close to the water on the seaport. The smells of the saltwater filled the air. The sounds of boats coming in and out could be heard. If one were not careful, they may lose some food to a seagull swooping in or a fearless pelican strutting by. It was crowded enough to the point there was no awkward silence, yet still allow everyone there to enjoy their own space. The tables and chairs were white and metal. Although freshly painted, they looked antique. Kind of like something a person might expect to find in their grandmother's yard. Over the eating area, sails from sailboats were strung up to protect those eating from both the sun and anything that may drop from the sky. There was a musician on a stage that played steel pan drums.

Nina had a steak sandwich and Andy had two Coney dogs and fries. As she picked at her steak sandwich he asked, "Do you always eat so much?"
She looked back at him with zero emotion and asked, "Are you always so judgmental?"
Andy's heart had dropped, as he knew he was joking around with her but she may not be picking up on that. For Andy, this was his way of flirting. He tried to redirect before this went bad. He did not want to screw this up. He had a strong interest in this mysterious and hard-to-read girl. He said, "No. I was just trying to joke around.

Sorry. I was not saying your fat. I hope you don't think your fat. You are not. In fact, I am wondering where do you put all of that? You weigh, what? Eighty-six pounds soaking wet?"

She answered, "I weigh 105."

Andy leaned back slightly and said, "Boob weight does not count."

She grabbed her chest and said, "I love my tits actually."

Andy asked, "Hey! You know what kind of bees make milk?" He paused and said, "Boobies!"

Nina smiled and lightly laughed.

"What did the bra say to the hat?" he asked.

Nina shrugged her shoulders as she snagged one of his fries.

"You keep on a-head, I'll give these two a lift."

Nina gave another light chuckle and added a slow, "okay. That's about enough."

"What do boobs and friends have in common? Some are big, some are small, some are real and some are fake."

She laughed and said, "All right."

He thought he was on a roll. He asked, "Why don't nuns wear bras? Because God supports everything."

Nina put her hand in the air and said, "Okay. Stop. You took it too far."

Andy quickly apologized, "I'm sorry. You were smiling and almost laughing. I thought it was okay."

She told him. "It was funny. I was enjoying it. Then you ran it into the ground. I notice you do that sometimes. You have a weird way of saying things and sometimes you take it too far.

Andy then said, "Thank you."

Nina looked back at him and asked, "For what?'

He paused, as he appeared to be in deep thought then he spoke. "My entire life I've been seen to others as offensive. I knew this. Not because anyone ever told me. I could just tell. But no one ever stepped up and told me when to stop. They would just let me keep going to the point that they were offended by my mere presence then walk out of my life forever. I appreciate you stepping up with the intestinal fortitude and letting me know my fault. You're really special. I like you. So, if I offend you, please let me know. I don't want to do that."

Nina asked, "Intestinal fortitude? What's that?"

He smiled and said, "Balls Nina, it is balls. I appreciate you have the balls to tell me what is wrong with me."

She said, "It's not like there is something wrong with you. It's just sometimes you take a joke too far. But if you want me to let you know, I'll let you know. I can't believe no one has been straightforward with you. It's just the way I was raised."

"Me too. That's why I appreciate you. As long as we are being straightforward." Andy paused. Nina looked at him and asked, "and?"

Andy set down his Coney dog and wiped his mouth with a napkin. He said, "I'll be straightforward with you. I like you. I know it's only our second date, but I enjoy hanging around you. I hope you are having a good time as well." He paused for a second waiting for a response. She only looked at him with anticipation. This is a hard girl to get a read on, he thought. He continued though, "I hope that maybe we can keep in touch and see where this leads maybe. But I have to tell you a few things about myself. I must know first, am I pushing too hard? Is it too much too soon? Should I go on? Is there maybe a chance for a third date?"

She just nodded her head, "I like you."
Her sandwich was almost three-quarters done and it looked as if he had barely started his. Except for his fries, which she had kept eating.

"Nina, I'll be upfront and honest with you. I am not the guy that is going to remember important dates. Especially when it comes to goofy anniversaries. Your birthday, your kid's birthdays, and maybe your mother's birthdays. I will be able to remember those. But anything beyond that is lost on me. I don't like PDA's. I think they are disgusting. I don't even like to hold hands in public. But kissing in public? No way. I hate when I am forced look at couples do that. It is so gross. So why would I infringe that on others myself and be a hypocrite? I will not surprise you with special just because gifts, especially overpriced purses that are five hundred dollars just because of a name. I don't do things like that. It is not how I am made. Sometimes I'm cold and distant. I am not the type to freak out because I don't hear from you every ten minutes. It is not because I'm uninterested, it's just who I am. I don't always need to be 'doing'. Sometimes I like to just... 'be'. I am not the sappy type so please don't take it the wrong way. I won't do any of that sappy stuff. But I will write for you as if you are a muse. I love to write. Even more when I have a beautiful muse such as you to write for. I will write you poems every day. Oh! Flowers. I will never surprise you with flowers on the dresser."

Realizing he had just spewed out a small novel he stopped. He looked to her for a response.

She looked at him and said, "Okay", as she took a bite from her sandwich and snagged another one of his fries.

In his mind, Andy laughed slightly. After all of that, is that all he gets? This was one tough cookie to crack.

"Just bring your words, they last longer than flowers." She said, as she took a drink of soda and wiped her mouth with a napkin.

Andy smiled and said, "Thank you."

That was all he needed to hear. This girl was a genius. He just spit out an entire manifesto and she said everything that needed to be said in one sentence. The two continued their lunch.

EXCLUSTIVITY (SPRING 2015)

Over the next year or so, this would be their relationship. Much like the race, it would be filled with twists and turns. Wins and losses. They would have their good moments and they would have their bad moments. The bad moments were never really that bad though. They both knew how to communicate with honesty and show appreciation for one another. Those attributes in both would save this relationship and keep them growing stronger together. The relationship would continue to grow with constant communication and weekend trips to see Nina and her kids. He would grow to love her kids as much as he loved her. Nina did continue to be a challenge to read at times. Unless she was talking about her cars, her boobs, her kids, or how much she hated her ex-husband she was a woman of few words. She was more of a listener. Which would work out in the long run since Andy did not mind being the talker. He was happy that he had a captive audience that had stuck around for so long. Over the next year, the lights may have changed color many times. At the end of the day, they always went back to green.

Andy was nervous as he sat on the bed in his humble Los Angles apartment looking at his phone screen at Nina. He had been waiting for this video chat all day. Talking or video chatting was nothing new to them. It was something that had occurred every day. On most days it would be multiple calls. He had built up strong feelings for her. It had been a year since they first met when he was back home on the islands for his best friend's wedding. He could remember taking laps on that go-kart track with her as if it were yesterday. The two had really gotten to know each other well. She was different from the rest of the girls he had been in his life. She had been extremely appreciative of everything he had done for her. She seemed to enjoy conversations with him. She laughed at his corny jokes and made him laugh himself. He had a desire to ask her out for quite some time. But he wanted to do it in person and not over some video chat. At the same time, he did not want to wait until they saw each other face to face again. He could wait no longer. He had to make his move before she moved on. He could feel his heart in the bottom of his gut as it beat a thousand beats per minute. He was pretty sure that she would say yes if he asked her out, but in his mind, there is always that chance she could say no. They lived on opposite sides of the country. She lived in Daytona, Florida and he lived in Los Angeles, California. Why would she want to be involved in a long-distance relationship? Those never work out. He did have a plan to solve that, however. The first step was to get her to agree to a relationship. Otherwise, there would be no point in putting his plan into action. He took a deep breath and said, "So." He paused as she looked at him with her large curious eyes as she asked, "Yes?"

"The past year we have been devoting much of our time together. You have made my life a happier one in many ways. I enjoy talking to you. I think the conversations we have are never-ending. It's like we never run out of stuff to talk about." He paused again as he clasped his hands under the table and bit the bottom of his lip. She looked at him and said, 'Uh-huh." Andy continued, "So I guess what I am trying to say or ask is would you be willing to?" He paused again and she just looked at him. He took a big breath and asked, "Would you want to, or I mean, could you take what we have to the next level? I mean, make this exclusive? Or I mean?" He paused again and put his head down as he looked up at her over his glasses and spoke softly, "Would you want to be my girlfriend?"

She looked back at him blankly for a few seconds and laughed. He squinted his eyes as he said, "Not exactly the response I was hoping for. "She shook her head back and forth as she smiled and said, "No. I'm sorry. It is just that I kind of assumed we were already dating."

Andy had a glazed or maybe stunned look to his face for a moment as he asked still unsure of himself, "Oh. So then, I guess that is a yes?"

Laughing very hard now Nina said, "Of course!" Andy's face lit up with a big smile as he asked, "So, I am your boyfriend? We are exclusive?"

She rolled her eyes and reassured him with a resounding yes.

Then he asked, "So wait a minute. All this time you knew we were already dating and you let me go through the nervous act of asking you out anyway?" She laughed and nodded her head up and down. "Why would you do that?" He inquired. "It was fun, I guess. You looked so cute."

A radio sat on a counter of Sal's Street Meats on the historic seaport. As always, Sal had a long line of customers waiting for their chance at a quick grab-and-go lunch. As Sal traded food for money, a song could be heard fading out on the radio. There was a sudden burst of laser shot sound effect as an overly modulated voice announced, "You are smack dab in the middle of the all-request, all cool, all retro power hour! More of your favorite retro hits are on the way! It is 102.7, WVCX!

RETURN TO PEEKING
(SPRING 2015)

A plan had been set in motion. Andy was set to move back to the Peeking Islands to be closer to Nina. He was not going to move to Daytona where she was currently living. He did love Daytona as he had spent many spring breaks vacationing there. For him, it was just not exactly the right move. If he was going back to Florida he wanted to move back to some familiarity. He was familiar with Daytona, but nothing is more familiar than home. Adding to that, he wanted to take this relationship with Nina with caution. If they lived in the same town that was her territory this would not benefit him if the relationship went sour. He wanted to take baby steps with this relationship. With him in the Peeking Islands and her only sixty miles away in Daytona they were close enough to see each other on the regular, but not in each other's back yards all the time.

The plan started with a phone call. It was a call he had made two weeks prior. Andy had called every radio and television station in the Peeking Islands. There were only three broadcasting companies, but each one had multiple stations they held. His first call of course was to his old employer, Q95. While they acted happy to hear from him, they, unfortunately, did not have space for him. Not only at just Q95, which he really had his heart set on, but none of the other stations in the conglomerate either. The second choice was a powerhouse of a national broadcasting company. It would have been great because the company was a powerhouse across the nation for radio and television and the paycheck would have been superb! They straight up told him they had no interest. They had put it simply. It was too long since his last stint in radio and they were only hiring seasoned people with a current resume. The last choice was a local broadcast company called Peeking Broadcasting. They were a small ma and pa business, but it was a job. Andy would have been happy with any job. He would have waited tables or worked on a boat as a mate. He would be closer to Nina and that is all that really mattered to him. Realistically though, it would be nice to know there is a job lined up and one with a steady paycheck so he could take care of Nina and her kids.

It had been roughly two weeks since he sent his media kit to Peeking Broadcasting. Since he was no longer in radio, he enlisted the help of some production friends in L.A. He had put together a faux demo reel. He did have shows from his previous radio days. Those were on cassette though and he had no way to transfer them over to a file or even CD. Plus, those were extremely cringing to him. He listened to them when he first hatched this plan of moving. He did not like what he heard. He wondered why people listened to him back then. It was so bad. He knew he was a young punk with zero tact back in that time, so he let it slide. He was not going to use those though. Instead, he came up with a mock demo that he felt showed who he was now.

Tino and Andy sat on the living room floor. They were playing with one of Tino's favorite toys. It was a feather on a string. Andy's favorite toy was a laser pointer. He liked it because it required much less effort on his part, and it was hilarious when he turned the light off and Tino would be left in total bewilderment as to where the little red light went. It made Andy laugh uncontrollably each time. Andy wanted the cat happy though, so for now they would play Tino's game. Andy would sit on the floor and wave the stick back and forth. The feather would follow the stick and Tino would follow the feather. If he got it he would put it in his mouth, then release for another go at it. Andy's cell phone rang from the table. It was the generalized ringtone, so it was not anyone important that he knew. It was probably just another scammer. They were relentless these days. Andy looked at Tino and asked, "You want to get that? Oh right. No opposable thumbs. Too bad for you." Andy stood up quickly and felt his head and legs go numb for a brief second as he temporarily saw stars. "Freebie", He thought to himself and smiled at his own joke. Looking at the caller ID it said, Peeking Broadcasting. His eyes lit up and he picked up the phone quickly.

He answered, "Hello, Andy Chelios speaking."
A voice on the other end asked, "Is this Andy Chelios?"
Andy reconfirmed with a yes.
The voice said, "This is Bob Overwrite. I am the general manager for 102.7 WVCX."

"Hi. How are you?" Andy said with a nervous excitement building up in his gut. He looked up to the ceiling, closed his eyes, and quietly mouthed, "Please, please, please."

"I am fine. You sent us a media kit of yourself a week or two ago. Is that right?"

Andy answered, "Yes sir."

"So, I take it you are looking for work here?"

Andy replied, "Yes, I want to come back home and thought it would be great to get back into broadcasting again."

Bob said, "Well, Jake, the program director you sent the package to, did get it. He and his music director, Rosie, brought it to me and we all sat down and listened to it together."

Andy just sat in tense anticipation. There was a short pause. Then Bob came back to say, "We all thought it sucked."

Andy's heart sank to the pit of his stomach. He suddenly had such an empty feeling. He could not form any words from his mouth. He had nothing to say.

Bob came back to loudly say, "I'm kidding! We liked it!"

There was silence. Andy just stared into the space directly in front of his face. He heard Bob's voice, "Andy? Are you there?"

"Ah, yeah Bob. Still here, just a little confused. So, you are saying I do have a job?"

Bob was laughing as he responded, "Of course! It was a joke. Laugh with me. They tell me you are a guy with a sense of humor!"

Andy feigned a chuckle and said, "Uh-huh."

Bob quickly responded, "Andy, we would love to have you back on the island working for us. Our program director, Jake, and Tim, the sales manager, remember you from your Q95 days and spoke of the fierce competition you gave us. Say, I didn't wake you up did I?"

"No. I'm just still a little in shock from your joke." Andy could hear the pride of the joke still in Bob's voice when he said, "Good. I wanted to make sure you are awake this time of day because it's the timeslot you will be working."

Andy asked, "So I'll have afternoon drive?"

Bob said, "No. It's 10:30 PM, Andy."

"Bob, it's 4:30 where I am at right now."

"Oh. So really you should have no problem adjusting. Your time awake there will be your time awake here." Bob said with enthusiasm.

Andy asked, "So the evening shift? Like eight to midnight?"

Bob said, "More like six to eleven. Now let's talk pay. We want to start you at thirty-seven a year. For remote talent fees, we pay all of our talent at the same rate of three hundred per remote. And to be clear, we are hiring you for the weekday evening shift six to eleven with one required weekend shift. I'd like to offer you more. But it's been a while since you have been out of radio. Does that all sound okay?"

Andy realized that was ten thousand more a year than he made in his Q95 days, it was a hell of a lot more than he made now. More than anything, it was his open door to be close to Nina. He calmly said, "I understand. That will work."

Bob said, "Great. I am very pleased you understand. Listen, how soon do you think you could make it here to start? We have our Arbitron ratings starting in about three weeks and it would be great to have you up and running before that."

Andy had no idea how long that would be. He knew that if he could, he would be on a plane tonight. In the reality of it all, he knew he had to close out a lease or find some way to sublet, figure out how to get his stuff from California to the islands, and he had to line up a place to live back home. That last thought hit him. He was going back home!

Andy said, "Well Bob, there are a few tight ends here I need to take care of. I am not really tied down by anything here. So, maybe by the end of next week?" All though, in reality, he knew it would be a month.

"Great!" Bob said, "I'll have Jake call you tomorrow and you can work through the details. I will see you next week! Are you excited?"

Trying to sound humble and calm Andy dryly replied, "Yes, Bob. I look forward to meeting with you."

Bob said, "All right. Goodbye Andy Chelios and welcome to the WVCX team."

Andy thought Bob had a cheesy get-up and go coach-like sound to his voice as he said that. He said, "Thanks, Bob. Good day."

Andy hit "End" and looked at the phone to make sure the call had ended. He then looked at Tino with excitement. "Did you hear that, Tino?

We are going home!" Tino looked up and Andy and gave him a meow. "Well, not your home, per se. But my home! Oh, you are going to love it so much on the island kitty cat! There are lizards there! Oh, so many lizards and birds and, well, so many other critters you can make friends with!" Tino grabbed the stick with the feather attached to it and dropped it at Andy's feet. Andy continued to speak with great excitement at Tino, "And you know what else, my little blue-eyed friend? We get to be close to Nina!" Andy was filled with excitement. He could not contain himself. Tino put his front paws on Andy's leg and then back onto the stick with a feather and gave him a meow. Andy picked up the stick with a feather and whisked it through the air as he continued to tell Tino how excited he was.

Tired from playing with the feather, Tino was taking a catnap on a windowsill as Andy was calling his friend Steve. Steve was a friend in the Peeking Islands that Andy had gone to the Rome Military Academy with. He was probably his closest friend. Steve was a little sadistic and narcissistic and perhaps borderline psychotic by most people's definition and treated women like dirt, but he was Andy's friend. He was one of his best friends from back in the day and they had been through a lot together. It had been a while since they had spoken but Steve had connections on the Peeking Islands and Andy needed a place to stay.

The voice on the other end answered, "Jell-Oh. This is Steve-Oh!"

Andy said, "Hey Steve."

Steve immediately said back, "I don't know who this is, but I had no idea she was married! I'm sorry man!"

"This is Andy."

"Yeah. Well, Andy, I had no idea she was your wife man. I'm sorry. But I probably just did you a favor."

Andy said, "Steve! This-is-Annndyyyyy."

There was a pause. "Andy! Andy Chelios?" He was laughing now. "Oh, bro. You had me fucked up dude. I thought you were someone else. How the fuck are ya, bro?"

"Good. Good. Listen. I'm moving back to the islands. I got a job with WVCX."

Steve answered back, "All shit music 102.7 WVCX? Really man. You can do better than that!

You're Andy fucking Chelios. KING of the island mountains!"

Andy said, "Uh-huh. It's a job and it will be better once I am there."

Steve asked, "Oh-yeah? Why is that?"

"You said it yourself, dude. I am Andy fucking Chelios." He responded with a laugh.

"So what brings you back man? And don't tell me a fucking girl."

With a slight pause, Andy replied, "Not a fucking girl, no."

Steve boasted out loud, "Good, cause I was going to have to get a fresh can of whoop ass on your whipped ass if you said a fucking girl."

Andy said, "You did not let me finish. Not a fucking girl, but an awesome woman! Dude, I know what you are thinking, but give her a chance. She really is the most awesome chick on the planet."

"Aren't they fucking all, man?" Steve said with a laugh, "So what's up? When are you coming out?

"That is what I am calling you for bro. I have a job, but I need a place to live. Do you have any ideas?"

Steve told Andy, "I know a dude who is looking for a tenant right now actually. It's on Isla Sirena.

So, you would be living and working on the same island. I can set that up for you right now if you want."

"Steve."

"Yeah man, what?"

"Bro, this is no bullshit. I need a place for sure right now. You're being for real right?"

Steve said, "Yeah man. I got you my cracka'. Are you gonna just fly out here, like tomorrow or what?"

"No, I have to figure out a few things here. Like how to get my shit from here to there."

"Aw man, just purge it all and come back here to start over."

Andy told him, "Dude, I've collected too much shit to start over the years."

Steve said, "Man, what happened to you out in Cal-i-forn-ni-eh? They make you all materialistic and shit out there? You all uppity in a playboy mansion out there, or what?"

Andy laughed, "Dude, I go to sleep to the sound of gunfire and helicopters every night. It's just I got some shit I'd rather not just up and leave behind."

Steve said, "All right dude. Whatever, but if it were me, you know what I would do."

"Thanks, man. What are you up to now anyway? Where are you working? You still selling watersports?"

He said back, "No sir! I'm a LEO!"

"A what? What is a LEO?" Andy asked.

"Law Enforcement Officer!"

Andy laughed hard. "A cop? Yeah. Okay. Seriously, what are you doing?"

"I told you, man, I'm a cop."

Andy asked, "How the fuck did that happen? Did you lie your ass off?"

"No man, you gotta take a lot of tests actually and one of those is a lie detector. Then you must go to an academy. This is no joke man."

Andy said, "But you, a cop? Really?"

Steve told Andy, "Listen, man, it is what it is. It's a job with a steady paycheck and good benefits. Granted it is a thankless job. Most people today hate me because of my uniform. But the ones that love me, they really love me. Dude, I had this traffic stop the other night, and let me tell you. This chick really did not want a ticket! I mean she really did not want a ticket. You follow me?"

Andy could hear Steve laughing, "Yeah I get it. You're a home-wrecking cop?"

Steve said, "Hey, don't hate the play'a. Hate the game. I'll see you out here next week, lil brother?"

With a sigh, Andy replied, "yeah, next week and you know I'm older right?"

Steve laughed, "Yeah, but I'm bigger and I get more pussy."

Andy asked, "How much do you think this dude with the place is going to want?"

"For the apartment? I don't know. I think the last guy in there charged like two thousand a month. But I'll talk to him and Jew him down for you. You have money to move in right? You can crash on my couch for a while if you don't till you get things going." Steve told him.

Andy ignored Steve's racist comment and cringed at the thought of living with him. He knew him as a close brother-like friend. But he would not want to live with him. Not the Steve he remembered anyway.

"No Dude. I'm good. I just want to make sure I am not jumping into someplace that is like forty-five hundred a month that's all. Because I'm not willing to do that."

"It's all good in the neighborhood lil' bro. I gotcha'."

"All right Stevo, I'll talk at you later. Thanks."
"All righty, Andy Chelios!" Steve said as he hung up.

Andy looked to Tino still sleeping on the windowsill. He walked over and lightly shook him. "Wake up pussy cat! Wake up! "
Tino opened his eyes and gave Andy an evil squint. "Oh, you don't like it when someone wakes you up do you? How does it feel? How does it feel?" The seal point Siamese made a long and low meow as it rolled back over into sleep. "Tinnno, did you hear all of that? We got a job and now a place to live! We be go'n to da islands mon! Now, what am I forgetting? Oh, I know! We should call Nina!"

Andy sent a text to Nina that said, "Baby! Good news. Got a job and a place to live. I'm coming home!" Andy got a reply almost immediately. It said, "I am glad you texted. I was just about to kill myself." His eyes bulged out of his head as he tightly rubbed both of his hands through his hair almost pulling it out of the scalp. "Oh my fucking God. Not again." He dreaded moments like this. She had such a hardcore thing with depression and was always threatening to kill herself. He knew that she had been dealt a bad hand in life, but he thought him being a part of her life had improved it. He called without hesitation.

He heard the phone pick up but no answer. He said, "Baby."

There was a silent and uneasy pause. Then it all came out. It was the same as it always was. In between the tears, he heard the same story he had heard a hundred times before. Her ex-husband had come over and beat down Nina's door. He beat the shit out of her. After he left in a rampage, she called the cops and as always, they said there was nothing they could do unless they saw it actually happen. They were just lazy and corrupt is what it came down to. One would think that a door beaten out of the hinges would be enough for proof. Or that she had video of his truck pealing out of the apartment parking lot after ramming one of her cars with it. One would think that would be sufficient evidence. Then she talked about being behind on bills and not having any money. It was exactly the same every time. It frustrated him that he was not there when this stuff happened. He wanted to be there to protect her. He was not though. All he could do was listen to her vent, then try to make her laugh and feel better. This was the cycle that had become his life. He loved her so much. He hated that she still had these depressive mood swings. He felt like he was failing her.

RAH!-RAH!-RAH!
(SPRING 2014)

A month had passed and Andy had somehow by the skin of his teeth made the move happen. He sat in the lobby of 102.7 WVCX waiting to meet the station manager, Bob Overwrite. Andy sat dressed in khaki shorts, a yellow T-shirt, and flip-flops. As Andy sat looking around the lobby of his new place of work, he could not believe he was getting back into this business. He could not believe that he was back home. He never in a million years would have bet he would be back on the island doing exactly what had caused him to leave. Even more startling to him was that he was now going to be competing against his old employer. Andy tried to remember what it was like in this business. He blocked out the bad thoughts that had made him leave and remembered the good times. Hearing a flashback song play in the lobby on the air currently made it easy to remember. Then he thought, "Wait, is this a flashback song now? Really? I remember playing this when it was new." His thoughts were interrupted as he heard a voice, "Andy Chelios?" Andy stood up and looked at the man, or boy rather before him. He stood about six feet tall with very short and carefully groomed blond hair. He looked to be very healthy but not overly concerned with hitting the gym. He did not look a day over thirty-four. His most striking feature was that he was dressed in what was probably an $800.00 suit. The man offered a handshake to Andy and said, "Hi. I am Bob Overwrite, station manager for Peeking Broadcasting. I run all four stations in the building. We spoke over the phone. I'm the one that hired you." Bob had a weird handshake. It was with both hands grabbing Andy's one and he had the smile of a used car salesman. The grip felt limp, and Bob's hands felt clammy.

Andy, a little taken back by the wardrobe shook Ben's hand and said, "Hi. I'm—"

Bob interrupted, "Andy Chelios." He said with a finger point. "Former Q95 superstar. Come with me to my office."

Andy stood in Bob's office and looked around. Everything was in pristine order. The whole office was minimalistic. The corners had a few fake plants. The wall was decorated with a business degree from Syracuse and a few pictures of Bob and perhaps his family. It was a beautiful woman with blond shoulder-length hair and three kids that were probably between eight and maybe fourteen. Based on the pictures of the kids, Bob was older than he appeared. Every picture appeared to be on ski slopes. There was a phone on the desk, a computer, and an exuberantly decorated box of tissue. Behind the desk was a window that overlooked the mountains.

Bob offered Andy a seat and said, "Andy Chelios." There was a laugh that came along with it. It was a weird laugh. It sounded forced but Andy assumed it was real. He smiled and said, "I am he." Unsure how else to respond. "Boy oh boy am I excited to see you here. I've spoken with some of the old school salespeople around the building and word around the campfire is you were a thorn in this station's ass back in the day! You offered up some good completion and cost this station a lot of ratings."

Andy shrugged his shoulders and smiled as he said, "And yet here I sit now. Ready to work for you, Bob"

Continuing with his weird laugh Bob said, "I remember I used to listen to you all the time. Well, not really me, my mother, Jodi, used to listen to you all the time. Which I guess means I used to listen to you all the time."

"I'm not that old Bob."

Andy was so confused. He felt as if he were in a job interview for a job he already had. Plus, who calls his own mother by her first name? He asked, "I'm sorry, Bob. Am I missing something here?"

"Oh no, Andy. I just want to get to know you. I want to know where you sit now."

"Right here before you, Bob."

Laughing again Bob said, "Right you are, Andy. But when I used to hear you on the radio, I pictured a superstar. Someone who was larger than life. A superhuman even. Like superman. But I look at you and I see a man who looks broken."

Andy tilted his head a little and asked, "I'm sorry? Come again?"

"Well in my head I hear the guy that was in my eyes, in Jodi's eyes, a superman of the radio waves. But I look at you and the way you are dressed, and I see superman in a poor suit. See Andy, around here we dress to win. Look at me. I am dressed to win. I believe that if you dress good, you feel good, and if you feel good, you play good. You dig?"

Andy was starting to feel a little defensive, "Well Bob, I dress for comfort so I do feel good, which means I will always play good. And if I heard you correctly you said I used to be a thorn in the ass of this station back in the day? Well, I was dressed then just as I am now. Plus, last time I checked I was hired to work in radio, not television, Bob."

"Right you are Andy. I just want to make sure you are comfortable around here. It has been a while for you and some things have changed in the business. Deejays are no longer just a hidden face. These days you are our number one selling commodity. We want to make sure you represent us well. You are not just the voice of the station; you are the face"

As he said that he laughed his fake-sounding laugh again and then waved toward the door with his hand. He yelled out, "Rosie! Rosie, come in here a second. I want you to meet Andy!"

Into the room walked a woman who looked to be in about her late forties. She had curly hair just past her shoulder and was dressed in business casual. She had tight-pressed jeans and a blouse with brand new-looking tennis shoes.

Bob said, "Rosie Rector, this is Andy Chelios. Andy Chelios, this is Rosie Rector." Andy offered a handshake to the woman and she said, "Hi. Good to meet you." Andy smiled and said, "Nice to meet you, Rosie. I've been listening to you all week. You have a fun show. Have you been filling in on nights?"

"Oh no Andy" Bob interjected, "Rosie has been doing the night show for five years by herself and will be joining you on the night show for what is hopefully a long time."

Andy questioned, "I thought I was hired to do the night show for you, not as co-host, but a host."

"Oh that you are, Andy. You are the host. We will have Rosie with you just to help rein you in a little bit. You have a reputation for pushing the envelope and while you were very successful at Q95 in the day, we cannot have the same type of humor now. Things have changed slightly. Rosie is just there to help even things out and keep it equal. Would you show Andy around the station, Rosie? The studio and maybe to his office?"

Rosie and Andy walked around the station; Andy asked, "So what's with the suit?"

"Oh, yeah. Well, Bob is just the new generation. He tries to have that let's go get em' boys rah-rah-rah attitude but it comes off as— "

"Phony?" Andy asked.

"I was going to say cringe, but phony works as well."

They walked into a studio and it was closet-like. It was small. Perhaps it was about ten square feet of space. It was dark as it was not currently in use. There was a small control board with a very large window behind it. The window had a curtain covering it. There were three microphones. Andy looked to Rosie, "So we work in this space? It looks like we are going to get to know one another really well."

Rosie replied, "No. This is the newsroom. This is where there the news people on the morning show broadcast from. We are in here." Rosie leaned over the control board and pulled on a string opening the curtains. Andy could now see through the window in a room that was larger than the average living room in a family home. There was an oval table with eight seats and a microphone for each. At two of the seats were control consoles. One of those was much larger than the others. Each seat had a laptop at its place at the table. The seat with the smaller control panel also had two computers. The room was decorated with banners that identified the station. At the seat with the larger control board sat a woman dressed in pressed khaki shorts and a buttoned-up bowling shirt. She had neatly combed mid-length blonde hair. At the seat with the computer, there was a man in jeans and a similar bowling shirt. His face was buried in the computer, as he seemed very engrossed in whatever he was doing. They both looked to the window and smiled as they waved at Rosie, and she waved back. Andy gave a half-wave and half-smile.

Andy asked, "So where does the music come from Rosie? I don't see any CD decks."
Rosie told him everything is all on a computer now. The woman is Stacy Davis. She is the midday host and the other man is her producer, Simon. Stacy runs the show controls and content from her control board and laptop. Simon readies all the music and stop sets. When we do

our show you'll be in Stacy's spot and I'll be in Simon's."

Andy looked to Rosie and said in a way trying to not sound condescending, "About that. I had no idea I was moving into this spot with you. I did not know. I thought I was filling a vacant spot. I don't want to come in as if I am stealing your thunder."

Rosie looked at Andy and said, "Don't worry about it. It's not as if I am losing any pay or sleep over it."

Andy said, "Cool. So, we are a team then? Because that's how I want to run this, or that is how I would like this to be run rather."

Rosie asked, "Have you been able to find a place to live yet"

"I found a place here, on the north tip of Isla Sirena. It's weird. I can see where I grew up on Vista Bahia from my humble little shack now. I wanted to be close to the station. What about you? Where do you live?"

Rosie told him she lived on Isla de Cabeza Martillo up by Aullando Cala Lobo with her boyfriend, Costello.

"Aullando Cala Lobo. You don't say? I went to military school there."

Switching topic back to the studio Andy said, "Looking at that studio. It's only computers and a table basically. A lot sure has changed. Is it okay if I get a closer look at what I'll be working with?" Rosie told him, "Actually, Bob has a very strict policy in place that only the air staff currently on the air is allowed in the studio. Don't worry, Andy, We'll get you up to speed. Plus you have me. I am the one running the music and flow. All you have to do is come up with content and talk." "Ah yes. I am the grinder monkey." Andy said as he chuckled. Rosie gave him a blank stare. He said, "Just wind me up and watch me go" Andy added. Rosie gave him another blank stare and continued to explain the hierarchy of the station. Andy drifted off into his thoughts as he wondered why his entire life, nobody ever got the reference to the grinder monkey. He thought back to his childhood.

THE GRINDER MONKEY
(SUMMER 1978)

Andy was about seven or eight when he met the grinder monkey. It was sometime in the late 1970s. Andy was on a summer break vacation with his parents in San Carlita Beach, California. The main strip on the beach was filled with all sorts of weirdness. It looked like a place that was frozen in time mixed with the ambiance of a carnival. Andy was in love with it. There were stores with funky souvenirs and even stranger smells. A few rides were available and games of chance were abundant. It was a forever carnival on the beach. Andy was awestruck. The one thing that caught the attention of Andy was all the street performers. One was a fellow dressed in old and patched-up pants that had wide orange and blue stripes. He wore a pullover sweatshirt type thing only it was not really a sweatshirt. It looked like the material was some sort of rope. The man had disheveled hair and an unkempt beard. He wore sunglasses so dark you could not see his eyes. He was a juggler, or was he a magician? Maybe was a stunt man on a unicycle. He seemed to do a lot. He appeared to talk more than anything else. He was constantly telling people to gather around for "the big show" and get ready for the big act. Although Andy never saw anything "big", he did see the man do a lot. Some of it would get applause from the crowd and some of it got nothing. Sometimes the man would say things and the crowd would laugh. Andy would look around confused, as he did not know why what the man said was funny. When the man did a stunt or told a joke that garnered no reaction from the crowd he would pause. He would hold up one finger in the air and briefly pause. Then the man would reach into a bag and take out a monkey. It was not a real monkey. It was a play monkey. It was dressed up like a circus monkey though and had a tall hat with a tassel on it. Similar to what his grandfather wore as a Shriner, only different colors. In its hands were two cymbals. It had one in each hand. When the man did a trick that did not get the desired attention, he would take the monkey out of the bag and wind it up. He would then place it on the ground. The monkey would move around in circles while banging on the symbols. The man in the striped pants would follow the monkey around in large and exaggerated steps while clapping his hands together and motioning for the crowd to clap with him. Then he would blow on a whistle, and as if under magic command the monkey would stop. The man would pick up the monkey and put him back in the bag. The man then stood up straight as he yelled out, "Okay, You folks are a much more developed crowd. Way too smart for the common tricks. Everyone gather around for the big act!" This would continue in a never-ending cycle. It never ended. The man spoke, did tricks, people clapped and then walked away. Some of them would drop money in a hat he had placed off to the side.

As the sun went down and the crowds had moved into some of the local tiki bars, Andy sat and watched as the man packed up his belongings. He appeared to be talking to someone. It would be easy to say he was talking to himself, as there was no one else around. But it looked as if he were having an actual conversation, as he would pause to listen as if another person were speaking. The man looked up and noticed Andy about twenty feet away staring at him. He looked to Andy and said with a smile and soothing deep voice and a very thick accent that almost had a snobbish sound to it. "Bonjour young man, come over here." Andy just stood in shock like a deer in headlights. He did not know what to do. The man spoke again and said, "I do not bite, young man, come here."

Andy shyly spoke as he said, "I'm not supposed to talk to strangers." The man got up from his knees and picked up a bag as he walked towards Andy. He was a very tall man. He must have been over six feet. He was a giant in Andy's eyes. He was larger than life. He had a funny smell to him. He smelled as if he had not showered. There was an oddly familiar scent to him though almost masking the foul body order. It smelled like the sticks his parents burned in their bedroom. The man took off his sunglasses and had dark soulless eyes. He smiled and said, "My name is Fiorello. But around here people just call me 'the mayor'. Tell me now, what is your name?"

"My name is Andy."

"Well, Andy, we are no longer strangers. So now we may converse. Oui?"

Andy just nodded his head up and down in an unsure manner. The man asked, "I have watched you watching me all day from this spot. You have not moved. You have not eaten; you have not drunk. Are you homeless?"

Andy said, "No sir. I live in a home with my mom and dad in Florida."

"Then what is your story? Why do you sit and watch me all day? Surely there are better things for a boy such as you to do?"

Andy said, "I like watching you do tricks for the crowd. I want to do that."

The man looked down at Andy and said, "Young man, trust me, this is not what you want to do."

Andy just looked up at the man with anticipation. The strange-smelling man sighed and said, "But I see that the more I tell you not to the more you will want to do it. Oui?"

Andy just nodded his head up and down. The man said, "I thought as much. I can see that sparkle in your eyes, the sparkle of a performer. It is a gift you know; entertaining the masses is not something that can be taught. You either have it or you do not. I can see that you have it. I tell you what—"The man got down on one knee so he was eye level with Andy. He reached into his bag and pulled out the wind-up monkey. The man continued with the monkey in his hand held out to Andy. "This is Marcellus. His sole purpose in life is to entertain the masses. He picks up where others fail. When people are down, he brings a smile to their faces by running in circles and banging on his cymbals. This is all that he does know. He does it without pay. His only reward is the applause of the crowd. One might say he is soulless as all he knows is the stage. It is easy for him as the only expectation people have of him is to bang on his cymbals. When they want to be entertained, he is simply wound up and he goes to work. He lives to serve. Young man, you can entertain if you want. If it is what makes you happy then chase it down and never reach any lower than the stars. The one thing, don't ever, ever become the grinder monkey" The man grabbed Andy's backpack and slid the monkey inside. Andy simply said, "Thank you, sir." He did not understand what the man was talking about. He may have only been enthralled that he just gained a new toy. Andy's mother had come up at that moment, calling him by his full name. She said, "Where have you been? We have been looking all over for you" She paused as his father walked up. She looked at the man and said, "I'm sorry if he bothered you. He can be so hard to control sometimes." The man smiled and said, "No bother at all Miss. He is a fine young man and very well-mannered. No doubt that he is the product of good parenting. He has sat here patiently all day watching me and has not caused any trouble whatsoever. He is a very upstanding young gentleman." His mother said, "Well yes" She cleared her throat and mumbled something to Andy's father. His father rolled his eyes as he reached into his wallet and handed the performer some bills. Andy's mother said thank you to the man as she grabbed Andy by the hand and scolded him as they walked away. "What were you thinking? You just walk away from your father and me and disappear without a trace! Do you know we are miles from home? Strangers surround us! Who was that man? Do you know him? No, you do not! For all you know he could have stuffed you in a van and nobody would ever see you again! What do you think of that? Andrew! Answer me! What do you think of that?"

"What do you think of that?" Rosie repeated. Andy shook his head to and fro back to reality. He said, "What? Oh, yes, I agree completely. I want to have a show that caters to the audience, not to the needs of the station. I want our show to be seen as a show for the people! I very much want you to not think of me as your replacement, but co-host. I want you to be just as much as this as me. We are a team and together we will win the ratings." Andy had no idea what he had just agreed to but hoped his political candidate like sidestepping would be a satisfactory reply to whatever she had just been saying.

BATS, GUNS, AND SMOKING TIRES
(SUMMER 2016)

Nina was delirious with excitement. In only a couple of days, she was going to drive and ferry to Isla Sirena and see Andy. She missed seeing him so much. They had talked every night using a video chat and that was good. It was better than nothing. But it was not the real thing. She enjoyed being around him as he uplifted her. He made her feel better about herself. She was so depressed with her life. She had four kids she was trying to raise on her own. There were so many bills that she could not keep up with. The way she saw it, her life was a mess and there was no hope. Andy did not see the same faults in her that she did. Nina knew that Andy was special and different from anyone else in her life. She was looking forward to this visit as they had discussed it for a long time. It was also going to be her birthday and she was happy that she would get to spend her birthday with him. Nina had her friend Natasha over at her apartment and they had been drinking fairly heavily. Perhaps it was Nina's constant talk of Andy that made Natasha want to go home for the night and see her boyfriend. As Natasha got up to leave Nina insisted that she not drive as she had been drinking. Natasha had questioned Nina on that as she had been drinking as well. Nina told her, "I am fine with it though. You look a little out of control. Let me drive you home and I will come back tomorrow so you can pick up your car." Natasha agreed as she knew there was no way to argue with her friend Nina. Once that girl had an idea in her head it had to be done her way.

They arrived at Natasha's apartment complex and pulled into the parking lot. Nina parked the car and as she got out, Natasha's boyfriend came out of the shadows. He was a big man. He was a big angry man. He was livid. He walked toward Natasha yelling as he carried a baseball bat. It was hard to make out what he was yelling about as he spoke so fast the words ran together. It did not help that he yelled a mix of Haitian and English rolled together. Nina could not just sit in her car and watch. She got out and tried to help Natasha. Natasha's boyfriend walked toward Nina and yelled at her in a language she did not understand. Her heart sank as the man three times her size and all muscle walked in her direction and then pushed right past her. With his baseball bat, he took swings at Nina's car. There was nothing either girl could do.

He was much too big for either of them to stop. Even if they had worked together, they were no threat to him. Nina's car took a beating for about a minute before she was able to muster up the courage to run to it and get inside. She put her keys in the ignition and started it up. The angry boyfriend continued to beat all sides of the car with his bat. Without taking time to think of a means of escape Nina threw the car in reverse and floored it. She hopped a curb and ran into a tree as her head jolted back. Her eyes were wide with fear as she shifted to first and hit the gas. She speed-shifted her way out of the parking lot with her tires smoking.

Andy was lying in bed when the phone rang. He was not sleeping. He was just relaxing with Tino purring at his side. He knew from the ringtone that it was Nina. His heart lit up as he picked up his phone and said with a smile, "Hello beautiful." He could not make out a word she was saying. She was crying and crying hard she was. She could not even get the words out of her mouth. She tried to explain why she was so upset. But she could not even take a breath properly let alone speak. She said she was going to call him back on video chat and told him to pick it up. Andy still mystified at this hung up his phone and waited for the call back on video. A minute later she called back and he answered. The sight he saw on his screen was horrifying for him to look at. Nina was visibly shaken. She could not control herself. She could not stop crying. Andy told her repeatedly to stop and breathe. He was really concerned. What could have happened to get her this upset? He figured that maybe her ex-husband had broken down her door again to beat her. He hated that man with all of his heart. He hated that situation, as it was one he was out of control of. He wished that he could be there to protect her from that cowardly troll. Andy was finally able to get Nina calm enough to speak. She was still crying and still very upset, but she could at least speak in a somewhat coherent manner. He found out that it was not the ex-husband that had her this upset for a change She explained the whole chain of events about taking Natasha home and what her boyfriend did to her car. She was upset about not being able to drive down to the Peeking Islands on her birthday and seeing Andy, but she was clearly more upset about her car. She asked him in a stressed-out voice, "What are we going to do baby? What are we going to do?"

After hearing the story Andy was upset inside. He was upset that she drove her car while intoxicated. It did not make sense to him. It made no sense for her to not let Natasha drive intoxicated but then get behind the wheel herself when she was just as drunk. But he knew that is just how Nina was. She had a huge heart for those she cared for and would do anything for anyone. He wanted to chew her out but knew this was not the time. Andy calmly said, "We will get your car fixed baby. We will get it fixed."

From behind tears, she asked back, "But how, baby? My cars are specialty cars. They are racecars! It is so expensive to get them fixed. Not just anybody can do it!"

Andy assured her not to worry about the cost. He would take care of it and wire any money she needed no matter what it was. She asked him, "But it could take a month to get fixed baby! What are we going to do about my car?"

Andy was doing his best to remain patient. He had learned that this is just the way she was. Her cars were her life. There was nothing that mattered to her more. He knew that she wanted a magical fix that would have the car ready to go tomorrow at six in the morning. Even though that was only six hours away. She somehow expected that to be the answer. If she did not get that as the answer, she would continue the tantrum that he had grown accustomed to when life did not go exactly her way. Especially when it came to her cars. He took a deep breath and said, "Listen, baby. I am just being real with you. The car is not going to be fixed tomorrow. We know this. We have been through this before. But please listen. Are you listening?"

He looked at the screen of his phone and saw Nina wipe her tears as she nodded her head up and down.

He continued, "The car will not be ready tomorrow. But it will get fixed. You will have the money to do so. I promise. Tomorrow take it to the shop, talk to your insurance adjuster and I will send you whatever you need."

"But will the insurance cover this? My car is so expensive to get fixed!"

Trying to make a joke Andy said, "Well I don't know baby. Do you have drunken, angry best friend's boyfriend, beating up your car listed on your coverage?"

She smiled and almost laughed as she wiped more tears from her eyes and shook her head back and forth. She said, "Probably not. I love you though. You can always make me laugh."

He smiled back and said, "I try baby. I do what I can. I live to serve."

The two had continued to converse and Andy did have Nina at least laughing now. It was going well until she brought up the car again. She stood up and said, "Come with me." He said, "As if I have a choice, you're holding on to me."

She put her hand over her mouth and ran to the bathroom. She got on her knees as she propped her phone upon the head of the toilet. Andy could only watch as she proceeded to hurl all of her stress into the toilet. He just shook his head as he said, "There you go, baby, let it all out." She peered up at him and wiped her mouth." She continued to throw up. Much of it was dry heaves. Occasionally she managed to work something solid up. Andy sat on his bed with his pillows propping him up. His phone held up in front of him all he could do was watch as Nina would hover her head over the bowl and spew the stress from her stomach. He spoke up, "Well I guess this means we are comfortable around each other."

She lifted her head up off of her arms that were supporting her and looked into the camera on the phone. She asked, "How so?"

"Well, most people would have told me they have to call me back. Most people would not want others to see them in this kind of situation. But you? Nope. You take me in your bathroom and let me watch you barf your brains out for twenty minutes. And me? What do I do? Do I say hey I will let you go and call me back when you feel better? Nope. I stick around and watch."

She wiped her mouth again and tried to hold back a smile. Andy continued, "I must really like you a lot. You know if I were there, I would be in that bathroom holding your hair back for you, right?" Nina looked at him through the camera and shook her head back and forth. She spewed out a mess. Andy yelled, "There you go, baby. Get it out. Demon be gone! " Again, she only glanced up at him without saying a word.

As she kept on trying to get more of that night's drinks out into the toilet Andy just kept on talking, "So I guess we must be comfortable around each other. I mean maybe not take a shit and shower at the same time comfortable, but at least you are comfortable enough to let me watch you puke and I am comfortable enough to stand by and not hang up." She lifted her head again and glared at him. She wiped her mouth as she said, "You have a funny way of putting things"

He said, "You have such beautiful eyes. Has anyone told you that today?"

She shook her head as she said, "No" and coughed a very wet cough. He told her, "Wow. I find that hard to believe. Well, in that case, let me be the first to tell you today that you have beautiful eyes. I could totally get lost in those."

She looked at him again through the screen as she stood and picked up the phone. She said, "Thank you, baby. You really know how to make me feel better. I'm always happy when I am talking to you."

He smiled with pride and said, "You're welcome."

She told him that she had to go and get cleaned up. He asked, "So wait, I can watch you throw up, but I cannot watch you clean your face?"

She looked at him with a smile and said, "I've got to get the kids to bed and get cleaned up. I will call you back in a bit." They ended their call and as Andy looked at his phone, he noticed they had been talking for an hour. It was the same every night. They would video chat and it would always last around two hours. They never ran out of anything to say. There was never a lull in the conversation. A smile hit Andy's face as Tino jumped up on the bed and cuddled into Andy and the purr machine started. Andy looked down at his feline friend and said, "I know buddy, and I think she is pretty cool too." He laid back and went to sleep with thoughts of his sweet Nina on his mind.

Andy was sound asleep when his phone rang. It was the video chat sound, so he knew it had been Nina. He reached over to his nightstand and answered. She was apparently outside in a breezeway of her apartment complex. He said, "Well, to what do I owe this surprise?"

She told him, "I told you I'd call back."

He said, "I thought you meant tomorrow." He could not help but notice she looked a lot more chipper than he had just seen her an hour ago. She seemed to have a lot more energy. She was very upbeat. She was walking around the breezeway briskly and she was holding her pistol. He asked, "Baby, why are you walking around outside with your gun?"

She told him with a crazy look in her eyes, "Oh, I'm waiting for that bitch to come over here."

"Who would that be?" He asked.

"Natasha! I called her and bitched her out for this whole thing. She got all ghetto on me and I yelled back. I am so nice to people and they take advantage of my generosity. I yelled at this stupid bitch and she yelled back. She said she was coming over so now I'm waiting for her and I am going to shoot her ass." Nina was very pumped up and full of adrenaline. Andy said, "Baby!

Please go back inside. Put the gun away. Do not shoot anybody. Please! We don't need this right now."

Nina just looked into the phone and said, "Oh, if this bitch comes over I am going to shoot her. Her boyfriend fucked up my car and she don't even care. She acted like it was my fault. Why? Why do people take advantage of me? I am so nice to people and I get fucked over every time. I could have let that drunk bitch drive home. But no, I drive her ratchet ass and the payment I get back is her angry drunk ass boyfriend destroys my car!"

Andy tried to plea with her and begged her to go back inside and put the gun away. She said, "Oh, it's okay. My son already got them back too."

Andy asked, "Oh? How is that?"

She said as she continued to walk around the breezeway waving the gun around, "He went over to his place and beat up his car with a baseball bat."

Andy shook his head as he could only watch helplessly as Nina continued her rampage with a gun out in the open at what must be at least 4:00 in the morning. He said, "Well, at least he loves and protects his mama. So, there you go. That piece of shit beat up your car. Your son beat up his. Tooth for a tooth. Could you please go put the gun away now?"

He watched as she waved the gun in view of the phone and continued to make her threats. Andy gave a half laugh and rolled his eyes. She asked what was so funny and he told her, "I feel like I'm watching a half-cocked reality show play out before my eyes."

"What show is that?" she asked still waving the gun around.

"Real Hoodrats of Daytona. I gotta tell you, baby, right now you are exemplifying why I would not live in your part of town."

"Why is that?" She asked.

"Because there are crazy-ass chonga's running around in the middle of the night with loaded guns ready to shoot the first person they run into."

She looked into the phone with a smile and said, "Oh, I am crazy now, right? Crazy enough to shoot this stupid ass bitch, who called herself my friend. Maybe I'll go shoot my ex after that. Or maybe I'll just shoot myself and I won't have to worry about any of this."

She walked into her apartment and sat down on the floor. She showed him the gun close up on the video chat. She took it apart and put it back together. Just to show she was very familiar with how it worked. Just as she had, time and time before. She said again, "So should I just shoot myself?" She put the loaded gun to her head and Andy yelled out to her to stop. He told her he loved her and her kids needed her. He begged and pleaded with her not to shoot herself. She was clearly upset. He hated it when she got like this. He knew she battled with depression. But he hated it when she took it to this level. There had been times when he would text her a simple hello and he would get a text back telling him it was weird that he had text at that moment. She was sitting there, with a gun to her head, ready to pull the trigger and his text had stopped her from doing so. It was such a stress factor for him he had a hard time dealing with it. He was pretty sure she would not do it as if she were real she would have done it already. It concerned him greatly, nonetheless. Andy was finally able to calm Nina down and get her thinking clearly again. Just as he had done in the past and just as he was sure he would have to do in the future.

He was just happy that she was smiling again. He was happy that she did not shoot anyone, especially herself. He was happy that regardless of how anything worked out that she was alive. They said their goodnights and hung up.

A song faded out on the radio as a familiar voice to the afternoon listening audience spoke, "102.7 WVCX. The station playing today's hits and yesterdays' favorites! It's the afternoon drive at five and coming up I have something for you that is completely unexpected. Stay tuned to find out more!" A jingle identifying the station played segueing into the next retro song.

MARRY ME (WINTER 2016)

Although this trip was some-time later than originally planned, Nina was coming to visit Andy on the islands. She was coming and they would be together. It would only be for a few days. Those would be three wonderful days though. One of the many things Andy truly enjoyed about Nina was that she was different from other girls. She was not the lovey type that always needed to talk about relationship stuff. She really did not like talking about it. She was not the type to show her affection openly. She was like a best friend that he got to sleep next to. They usually talked about everything and anything except the relationship. She was secure in knowing that he belonged to her and was loyal to her. That is why this night seemed off. She was not herself. She was affectionate toward him. More so than usual. She had been all over him the whole night with her hands in public. She had been very grabby. These public displays of affection were out of character for her. Especially considering how blatantly obvious she had been about it. She had no qualms on this night about grabbing his crotch in public. She was acting very strange.

They had just finished up a fun dinner at a tchotchke-filled restaurant and were in the parking lot next to her car. She stopped him and grabbed him as she pulled him in close against her body and gave him extremely deep and passionate kisses. Her hands were rubbing all over his body. He knew she could tell, that despite not being a fan of public displays of affection, he was very receptive to her physical attention. He knew that she had to have felt that with her hand through his jeans. There was no way she could not.

She leaned back a little and grabbed both his hands and put them on her breasts. As she held them there, she looked at him and said,
"I love you so much." He nervously looked back to her and said, "I love you." Not sure where this was going. She told him, "No, I mean I really love you. I want you" She rubbed his hands over her breasts then gave him more deep kisses and leaned back again still holding both his hands tightly and not letting go or not letting him step back. She said, "I want every girl on the planet to know you are mine. I want every person to know

we are together." She laughed. Her laugh had a hint of crazy to it.

Andy was taken back by her behavior. Nina had never acted like this before. Up till just now, they had always kept their relationship on the down-low. It was not something they advertised or talked about openly to the general public or social media. He was not even allowed to tag her in posts on social media as one time when he did, she was annoyed that her phone blew up with notifications. She was not used to that and did not like that type of attention. For Nina to be acting like this, something was up. Andy was unable to put a finger on to what it was.

She continued to kiss him and hold him tightly in the parking lot as she said, "I want to spend forever with you. You cannot say no. That is not an option. I will not be able to handle it. Tell me you will let the world know we are together and you are mine."
Andy was giddy with excitement. He was so turned on. The fact that Nina was taking this type of crazy possession of him was very arousing "Of course. I will let everyone know. I will do it

proudly. I love you." He told her dryly as he was still confused and shocked at her out-of-character behavior.

She grabbed him and put his hands on her breasts again as she said, "You have to accept. If you do not I will, well I will not be able to go on. I could not handle it. So, you have to say you will be mine forever and everyone will know. Please say yes. If you don't, oh, I don't think I will be...you just have to say yes."

Andy laughed, as he was confused. He thought he had already said yes. He wondered what she was going on about. He repeated, "Yes baby. I am yours and only yours. I will be with you forever." She smiled with glee and kissed him deeply again. Holding him tight up against her she made thrusting and gyrating motions. She leaned back again while holding her arms around his hips while laughing. It was not a, "I just heard a funny joke laugh". It was more of a borderline crazy person laugh. She said with a smile, "I love you. You make me so happy. I have to be with you. I cannot be without you and every person on the planet has to know this. They must know you are mine. I want to marry you."

Andy leaned back and looked at her as he asked, "Wait a minute. Was that a proposal? Did you just ask me to marry you?"

She smiled at him with a crazed look in her eyes as she grabbed his crotch again and said, "Yes, and you have to say yes. I will not take no for an answer. If you say no, I will not be able to take it. You will be mine forever. Don't say no." She grabbed her breasts and pushed them together and upward to make them pop out of the T-top she wore more than they already naturally did as she said, "These could be yours forever."

Andy thought before he spoke. He wondered why she would say something like that? Her breasts were not a reason he was with her. Actually, they were a little too big for his taste. He knew this was not the time to discuss that though. Gathering his composure, he smiled and told her with direct eye contact, "I love you, Nina. I want to spend forever with you as well. I am so happy you did this. I am just a little taken back. I mean, I guess I pictured me being the one popping the question. I am a little surprised and unprepared as well. Like, I don't even have a ring for you."

She continued to hold him tight, refusing to let him go she spoke with intensity, "I don't care about a ring. I just want you in my life. I want to be together with you. I want to move in with you now. Please don't say no. I will not be able to cope if you say no."

Andy assured her repeatedly that he accepted her offer and was overjoyed that she felt this strongly about him. She rubbed her hand on him again while kissing him all over his face. There was something really into her tonight. Granted, she had a few drinks. But even for drunk Nina, this was not normal. On a normal day, when she drank, she either became the life of the party and wanted to be everyone's friend or she became overwhelmingly depressed. It all factored on the situation or local. Tonight though, it was like she was a completely different person. The way she was acting physically was extremely aggressive. He looked at her and asked with a sheepish smile, "I take it my chances of getting laid tonight are pretty high?" She looked at him with a hunger in her eyes and nodded her head up and down. She told him one more time, "I love you and I need you in my life. I need to be with you. I want everyone to know. So, it's a yes. I will move in tomorrow." Andy's heart dropped a little bit at that statement. He knew that was not realistically possible. He also knew how her mind worked. Once she got an idea in her head it had to be worked out. Trying to explain the reality of a move to her at this moment would not work. She would just press on. Knowing her flair for emotionally dramatic situations and her inability to take no for an answer he knew this was one of those moments to just go with it. Besides, there was something sexually charging her tonight, and who was he to put a damper on that mood?

The two newly engaged couple hopped into Nina's car to head home after this dinner-turned proposal. Nina hit the ignition and put the car in reverse. She then backed right into a light pole in the parking lot. The jolt had thrown both of them back. It startled the hell out of Andy. He had no idea how that just happened. He was already aware of her driving skills. She was very good, as long as she was moving in a forward motion. It was going in reverse she had a problem with. This was not the first time she hit a light pole or some other inanimate object while moving in reverse. Nina was shaken. Andy told her to stay put and he would check it out. He walked to the back of the car fearing the worse as it was a sudden and hard impact. When he had walked to the back of the car, he felt a mixture of two emotions. One was relief that it was not as bad as it felt, or he feared it would be. Two was the fear that Nina was going to explode with anger when she saw this. To the normal person, this was only a small dent, and really it was. It was barely noticeable. It was only a flesh wound. The normal person would have been happy this was all it was. The normal person would let this go and would not stress about it. They may have even let it go a few weeks before getting it fixed. They might not even get it fixed at all. If they did, it would not cost terribly much. This would be how a normal person with a normal car would have handled it. Nina was not a normal person, and her Challenger was not a normal car. Somehow the dent was only the size of a fist and a quarter inch deep at most. Because this was a specialty car and based on experience with Nina's fender benders he knew would cost about a grand. He was thankful that is all it would cost as it sounded and felt a lot worse than it was. He knew Nina would not be happy though. As he got back into the car she asked how it was. He lied and said, "Oh, it's barely noticeable. We are really lucky. Now, how about we get moving before we attract any attention since you've had a few drinks." She did not move. He inquired what was wrong and why were they not moving. She told him that she was too flustered to drive. He suggested leaving the car in the parking lot since they were a short taxi ride away from home. He did not want to continue just sitting there and have a cop come up and start asking questions. He had only one month ago paid a DUI ticket for her. Not to mention she probably would have lost her license and gone to jail with another one. Andy felt uncomfortable just sitting there at the scene of an accident. He was not the type to commit a hit and run. With this accident though, nobody was hurt. There was no property damage, except to her car. So no harm, no foul. As long as a cop did not come into the parking lot they were now sitting in.

The idea of leaving the car sit in a parking lot overnight did not go over well with her at all. She explained to Andy, as she had a million times before, how much her cars meant to her. She loved those cars more than anything in life. It was a speech he could probably recite himself word for word. He asked, "So what do you suggest we do?" She looked him dead in the eye and said, "You drive." Andy felt like his world just dropped out from under him. Those were words he never expected her to say to him. These cars were Nina's lifeblood. She had never in a million years let someone else drive one of her cars. She was even particular as to who she let even ride in her car. The list of people who were allowed to ride in her car was much shorter than the list of people that could not. This was a once-in-a-lifetime opportunity. Andy was not going to turn this down at all. Why would he? This car was a dream machine when it came to barely street-legal racecars. He clasped his hands together and said, "okay!"

Andy sat in the driver seat of Nina's Dodge Challenger. The race bucket seat fit like a glove. The racing peddles at his feet were metal with holes. The all-digital dash illuminated his face with a glow. He could not believe this was about to happen. It was not just because he was about to drive the most powerful car he had ever driven. It was more than that. It was the fact that it was Nina's love. The one thing she held only to herself. She was about to trust him to handle her car. Her baby. The one thing she loved more than life itself. This was huge. "She must really, really love me. For real", he thought to himself. On the outside he was stoic but, on the inside, he was all smiles and cartwheels.

Andy parked the car in his driveway after an uneventful ride. One would think that being allowed to drive such a beast that they would take full advantage of the situation. He was happy though with the trust Nina had just put in him. He had worked so long and hard to get this feeling that she was the real thing and she really did love him. He was not about to screw that up over some tomfoolery on the road. A joy ride will only last a few minutes. The butterflies caused by the love of a girl like Nina could last an eternity.

Nina got out of the car and walked to the rear to inspect the damage for the first time herself. As was expected she freaked out. Andy tried to assure her it was not as bad as it appeared. Compared to other dents she has put in her car. He explained that it was nowhere near as bad dents on over half the cars currently on the road. She did not care about the other cars on the road though. She only cared about this one. The red Dodge Challenger parked in front of her. She went into her 'this needs to be fixed now' mode. Andy reminded her that it was two in the morning. She pleaded with him, "But baby! What are we going to do? This is my car. It cannot have a dent in it like this. My kids will be so mad at me for this! What are we going to do baby? What are we going to do?" Andy replied, "I don't think your kids are going to hate you for this and I told you. Tomorrow we will call the garage and have them fix it. We'll do this first thing tomorrow morning. But I will be honest with you. They are not going to have it done tomorrow. It is a garage. There are other people there with their own car problems. It might take a week."

By this time, they had made their way into the house and inside the bedroom. Nina just plopped down on the floor like a lifeless lump. She lay on the floor muttering repeatedly about her car. Andy tried to pick her up off the floor. She was convinced she wanted to be on the floor. Maybe that is where she felt she deserved to be. Andy had no idea. He hated it when she got like this. She always had to have her way, especially when it came to her cars. It was as if her whole world revolved around these cars. Andy had given up on getting her up off the floor. He sat down next to her. He put one hand on her leg and his other on her chin to lift her face so she was looking at him. She asked, "Baby, why didn't you tell me to turn when I backed out?" Andy was perplexed by this question. He almost laughed and probably would have if he did not already know better. He just squinted his eyes and said, "I'm sorry what? Why would I do that? I just assume since you are in the driver's seat you know what you are doing. Do I really have to tell you to turn when backing out of a parking lot? Or, no wait. You know what baby? You're right. I should have been watching out for you. I promise you first thing tomorrow morning we will get this taken care of." She responded by telling him, "But baby, it's going to cost so much. This is a specialty car. It's going to cost too much." He told her not to worry he would take care of it all for her. She looked down to the ground then back up to him and asked, "Promise?" He told her with a smile while touching her cheek that he promised. She smiled back and said, "I love you. I don't know what I'd do without you."

Andy got up and asked, "So we're all good now?" She nodded her head up and down from the floor. He offered her his hand and hoisted her up off the ground as he asked, "I can go take a shower? You're not going to do anything crazy?" She nodded her head back and forth. He said, "Good. I love you. I'm going to go shower.

Andy had finished his shower and came into the bedroom. She was on the phone. He asked who it was and she told him her ex-husband's girlfriend. She started to get mad and talk about how ratchet this girl was and that her ex-husband was not going to pay his child support. Which really, was no different from any other month so Andy did not understand the surprise.

He asked, "It's the middle of the night, what is she doing calling you?" Nina responded, "She's a ratchet whore, that is what she is doing and she said Leo is not going to be paying child support and he is not going to be giving me any money for the kid's Christmas. I won't be able to get any presents for my kids for Christmas!" She broke into tears.

Andy said, "Nina!" She looked at him with her big loving eyes. He continued, "He is an ass who never pays child support, you know this. It should not come as a shock to you. Don't worry about Christmas for your kids. I've got it covered. I'll take care of it." She tried to deny his offer, "No baby, you do too much for us already. You help pay my rent, my bills. I can't take anymore from you." He told her, "Listen, Nina. I am unable to go about life knowing your kids miss Christmas when I can fix that. They are kids Nina! They deserve to have Christmas. I'm not going to allow anyone to take that from them. So listen, this is the plan. Tomorrow when we wake up we call your garage over on the mainland and get an estimate on your car. Then we will go to the bank and take out money for that plus, a thousand for your kid's presents. Do you think that will be enough?" She nodded her head up and down and leaned in to hold him tight. She told him she loved him and he has had made her life so much better. She said she wished she had met him sooner in life. He kissed her on the temple and said, "Me too baby, me too. Now go take a shower."

Andy was lying in bed staring up at the ceiling fan. He was wondering where the hell did tonight go.? She was really happy. She had proposed to him. He said yes. She was very happy. She was happier than he had seen her in a long time. He was on a good track to finally have sex with the hottest woman on the planet who he loved and wanted to spend the rest of his life with. Then she reversed the car into a pole and it all went downhill from there. Andy congratulated himself on being the only guy he knows that could completely fuck up a perfect evening. He thought to himself, "Seriously dude, how the hell do you fuck this up? Why is this girl with you? You apparently cannot keep her happy. She was happy as a lark, then less than an hour later she is in tears on your bedroom floor!

His self-deprecating thoughts were interrupted by Nina walking into the room after her shower.

She was beautiful. Her long black hair flowed down her back. Her eyes filled with passion and love. A slight smile was on her normally solemn face. There was an air of serenity to her walk. It was as if she walked on air. She wore an elegantly dainty negligee that fit her body perfectly. It was crimson-like in color accented with black. The entire outfit was transparent and helped exaggerate every curve. Her complexion, although naturally dark, seemed luminescent in the dimly lit room. She had a glow about her. Andy looked Nina up and down with his eyes. He wondered why all girls wear such complicated shit to bed but all that came out of his mouth was, "Oh yeah. Now that is what I'm talking about." Nina only smiled as she thought, "he has a weird way of putting things." She continued to glide across the air to the foot of the bed. She looked at him coyly and asked, "Is this what you want?" She motioned with her hand over her body as if presenting a brand new car on a game show. Andy stared at her with his mouth ajar and said, "Oh yeah." While he slowly nodded his head up and down like a servant eager for payment. He was so nervous. He could feel his heart pounding out of his chest. He had been waiting for this moment since the day he laid eyes on her. He could not believe that someone so beautiful was willing to have sex with him. He could feel the temperature of his body rise drastically. As he fixated on her he could feel her passion as well. It was a solar flare reaching out from the sun.

She crawled onto the bed and next to Andy as she lightly ran her fingers across his chest and occasionally his inner thighs. She knew what she was doing was working by the look in his eyes. The way he gazed upon her was intense. At the same time, he had the look of a lost puppy dog unsure of where it was. She leaned in and gave him long slow kisses on his neck and ears as she continued to run her hand around his body. She could feel him tremble.

Andy quivered as he felt the love of his life rub her hand around various parts of his body. Her lips to his neck made him feel an unheard-of amount of warmth and craving. The warmth of her breath on him elevated the need he had for her body to an insatiable level. There were so many things he wanted to do. But where should he start? He was so confused. He was unquestionably nervous. He had never been to bed with someone this beautiful before. He was not sure what to do. That was okay for the time being as she seemed to be in control of the situation. The smell of her perfume went from her body, into his nose, and hit every sensory nerve inside his system. The aroma hit him like an aphrodisiac. She sent him to a level far above the Heavens. She was Aphrodite. He was Himeros. She was the tequila, and he was the key lime.

The two were exploring each other's bodies with their hands, lips, and minds. Nina was now on her back with Andy leaning over and on her between her thighs. He kissed her repeatedly all around her neck and face as his hands glided over her body. She felt excited as his hand made its way around her thighs. She started to breathe heavily. Andy slowly made his way from her lips to her neck. Then his face was between her breasts. She grabbed his head and pulled him in tight with a heavy sigh as he licked and nibbled. Nina had never felt so much passion from a man before. She took the moment in with every ounce of her being. The harder she rubbed her hands through his hair and the harder she held his head to her body, the harder his kisses became. He was breathing so hard and filled with excitement. She could feel his heartbeat through his chest.

Andy continued the exploration of her frontal body with his lips as he made his way to her belly. From her belly, he paused slightly to move down and breathe lightly on her thighs. He kissed her thighs and was staring directly into her vagina. With a strong desire, he went to kiss it and was stopped by Nina suddenly saying, "Awa hell no! I don't do that shit." Andy immediately felt failure. He felt lost. He felt as if he had once again screwed up the perfect moment in time. "What did I do wrong?" he thought to himself. "Fuck! How do I recover from this? Are we done? Did I just offend her enough to end this?" He continued to chastise his playbook in his head. He pictured a fighter jet going down in flames. He was about to quit when she simply grabbed his head and pulled him back to her level so they were face to face with Andy on top of her. He slightly hovered his waist above hers. She kissed his lips while grabbing his hand and holding it where his face was only seconds ago. He started to lightly caress her there. He was not quite sticking his finger inside, but he was only lightly caressing. He would occasionally rub her clitoris and maybe go a quarter way inside if only for a light tease. He was like a boy thinking about trespassing onto the farm but unsure if the fence was electrified.

Nina asked him if he had protection. She reminded him in a half joking way of how fertile she was. Andy affirmed a yes with a head nod and heavy breath as he continued to kiss and rub her body. He thought to himself that he was pretty sure he had protection anyway. He was almost positive there were condoms in his dresser. They were probably old and expired, but they were there. Why do condoms expire anyway? He questioned in his head. It is not like milk or bread that goes stale. He wondered why they expire. His current thoughts were interrupted by more thoughts, "Focus! Focus!"

he said to himself. As he continued to rub the very wet area between her thighs she said, "I am sorry. I did not come prepared for this." He stopped as he looked at her and asked what she meant. She pulled her lace panties down a little and said, "I am not shaven. I'm kind of a mess; I really was not expecting this. I do not normally do this." Andy gave a half laugh as he said, "Oh, that is more than okay. To be honest, I prefer it this way. I don't like shaven clean. That would be like having sex with a 12-year-old." She looked back at Andy and replied, "That is nice to hear." She thought a second and continued, "You have a weird way of putting things."

Still hovering between her thighs and fighting for breath he temporally got lost in his head again. He started to wonder if when she just said she did not normally do this, might be her subtle way of saying "no" in a nice way without hurting him. All of his life, Andy had been a strong proponent of no means no. Andy paused as he took a breath. He put his hand on her cheek and kissed her forehead before rolling off her and lay on his back staring at the ceiling. She lifted his arm as she rolled over so her head was using him as a pillow. Andy told himself in his mind that this was okay. It was probably the right thing to do. He made a promise to himself that he would wait till after they were married to have sex with this woman that was beautiful both inside and out. What was the rush after all he thought? This was true love. Unlike anything he had felt in his life. She was a remarkable person. The most awesome he had ever met in his life. Why simplify this with something like sex? She was a keeper and worth the wait. Besides, they were young and had all the time in the world. They both had a long life together ahead of them. There would be many times available after they were married to have sex. Andy whispered, "I love you." As he lightly caressed her back with the tips of his fingers and Nina smiled as they both drifted off into a sweaty sleep.

MERMAIDS AND MANATEES
(WINTER 2016)

Andy awoke and made a cat-like stretch in his bed. He came out of his sleepy somber quickly when he noticed Nina across the room packing her suitcase. He sat up with worry in his voice and asked, "Hey, are you okay?" All he could think of was that he had pissed her off or scared her away by trying to have sex with her. He felt an inner hatred for himself for trying that. He should have known better. Now the love of his life was walking out because he chose to take direction from his penis. She looked up and said, "I'm fine. I just have to get ready to go home." Still concerned that this was now all over he inquired, "But you were going to spend a few days here. Did I do wrong last night? I am so sorry if I seemed presumptuous. I was out of line and I promise I won't try that again till we are married." She looked at him and said calmly, "No baby. I need to get my car fixed, remember? I cannot get it done here so I have to get on the ferry and take it home. I have already made an appointment with the garage and they will get me in tomorrow." Andy searched his thoughts for the proper response. He felt he may have still been good with her but did not want to push her away with a feeling of neediness or lack of self-confidence. The best he could come up with was, "So we are good?" Nina looked to Andy and replied, "Of course. I feel safe around you. Nobody has ever made me feel safe before." Andy went back into his head and searched the available responses. He thought, "Okay, she feels safe. Is that because she thinks I am a pussy that won't follow through with having sex? Is it because I am a gentleman that respects her personal space? Or is it because I take care of her and her kids? Is it because I have talked her down from every suicide attempt since the day we met?" He was at a loss of what to say. Nothing was coming up for him. He smiled and said, "Thanks."

Tino jumped off his spot on the dresser and curled up onto Nina's clothes in her suitcase. She was not quite a cat person but she pet him anyway. She knew Andy loved that cat. He claimed not to. He claimed not to be a cat person at all. According to Andy, the story he told her was that Tino was a stray cat that just followed him home one day. Out of the goodness of his heart, he fed the cat, and set it on its way, but the cat was on his front porch the next morning.

He had said this went on for about a week and he finally gave in and 'adopted' the cat. The Siamese did not have a tag so he just randomly picked the name, Tino. She could tell there was a little more to it than that but had accepted the story he told her.

Andy said, "See, even Tino wants you to stay. Baby, it is four days before Christmas. How much work on your car do you think they will actually get done? I mean you can't expect them to work over Christmas, can you?" She responded, "Oh they will do it for me. Mike loves me. In fact, he keeps asking me to work for him selling Challengers. I know more about those cars than all his salespeople combined. He'll get it done."
Andy agreed, "I know, baby. So, about last night? Were you for real? Do you still want to get married or was that the drinks talking?"
She lifted her eyebrows and said, "Of course I want to marry you! I want everyone to know about it too!" Her face lit up with excitement as she continued, "Baby! This is going to be so great! I am so glad you agreed to let me move in! I can't wait to tell my kids we are moving here! They are going to be so excited. You have made

me so happy. You accept my awesomeness and you don't take advantage of it. I love you so much. This is the happiest I've felt in so long."

Andy was excited to know she was legit on the marriage part. He was still on the edge about the moving in so soon part. It was not because he did not want to rush a relationship. It was because he was unsure as to how they could afford a home big enough for all those kids. He could make it work on the mainland. That would be easy. But on this island, the rent was so high everywhere. He did not want to put all of them in a two-bedroom home. He wanted at the very least a three-bedroom home. One for them, one for the sisters, and one for the brothers. It was not ideal for him to force kids to be roommates. He thought that they should have their own rooms. But realistically a three-bedroom would be the best he could do and even that was grasping at straws. He knew this was a conversation they were going to have very soon. He knew that no matter how badly she pleaded with him that he was going to have to stand his ground on this one. He was all about taking this to the next level and living with her. Just in a place they could afford and still live a comfortable life. He was willing to give up his island life and move to the mainland for her. Right now, though it seemed as if her mind was set on moving here. He would talk about this with her later. Maybe after the holidays would be best. After all, he had all the time in the world. With Nina wanting to marry him, he had just been reborn. This was the first day of the rest of their wonderful lives together. This was a new fork in the road and the path they were choosing would be the right one. He would celebrate one victory at a time. Right now, he cherished being the luckiest man alive.

Nina was packed and it would still be a few hours till she could get her car on the ferry back to the mainland. He asked her what she wanted to do. They came up with the plan to go to Andy's bank and he would withdraw money from the bank for her to get the kids Christmas presents. They agreed on one thousand. As for the car repair money he promised once she found out the actual amount, he would wire the money immediately.

After leaving the bank, they walked around town. They did have plans on this trip of going parasailing and jet skiing. But Andy silently blew that off and avoided bringing up the topic. He had just dropped a lot of unexpected money on her and wanted to give his account a little room to breathe. He was a little stressed about it but kept his mouth shut. It was not something he would wave in her face ever. Taking care of her was just a fact of life he had, as of last night, accepted to be charged with. He asked if there was anything she wanted to do. She told him, "I am just happy being with you, baby. I love you so much." She grabbed his arm and interlaced it with hers as they walked the side streets of Isla Sirena. It was so out of character for her to show this type of affection, especially in public. She held his arm tightly with hers as they walked along the sidewalks adorned with palm trees and historic cozy homes. He stopped and looked at her as he asked, "How about a selfie?" He cringed in his mind as he said that. He hated seeing people take selfies with a passion. He hated the word even. He thought it was so self-centered. Besides, what had happened to human interaction? Why was it so hard to ask a stranger to take a photo? Nonetheless, he wanted a picture with his fiancée. They had not one picture together. They had plenty of pictures of each other. But none of each other together. They had not just been that type of couple that needed to take pictures together to show their love for one another. At this point though, Andy did want a picture of him with his love.

After the photo, Andy put his phone back in his pocket without looking at it and Nina mentioned she was hungry. They stopped at the first place they came to and it was a sub shop. Andy was not a fan of fast food-type places. He liked his food fresh. This sub shop claimed to have fresh food. It was their advertising motto even. But Andy was not sure about that. He let Nina order whatever she wanted, which was a steak sandwich. She asked if he was going to get anything and he nodded his head back and forth as he said, "I'm not too hungry" The two sat down and as Nina devoured her steak sandwich, Andy would pick off her plate. To his surprise, it tasted pretty good. He thought, "Okay, maybe I am a little bit hungry." But he did not want to be taking Nina's food. It was hers, he had his chance to order and he did not. He resisted as best as he could from taking her food.

They walked around the side streets and down to a small seaport. They sat in silence as they watched the schooners come in and out of the harbor. Nearby a fisherman was cleaning his catch as a small crowd of tourists had gathered to watch him. It was not only tourists that had gathered behind him on the wharf, but he had an even larger audience of pelican in front of him in the water anxiously awaiting any scraps. Below the surface tarpon circled waiting for their share. Andy grabbed Nina by the hand and said, "come on, I want to show you something." She walked beside him along the wharf to an area that was a little less congested. The two leaned against a wooden railing as they stared into the water. After a few minutes, Nina asked, "You wanted to show me something?" Andy asked back with a slight chuckle, "You don't see it? Look right there, down in the water." Nina's eyes widened as she finally noticed what Andy was talking about. She did not know how she could have missed what Andy was trying to show her, as right below her, under the surface of the water was a 1200 pound slightly grey mammal. It was a manatee and her calve. They sat under the surface for quite a while. Nina spoke up with excitement, "Oh a manatee! And look, she has a baby!" Nina paused and continued, "Oh, I miss my kids. Baby, they are so cute. Are they always here?" Andy replied to her, "Well, not always. But it is common to spot manatee here anywhere on the island. You know, when they named this island, Isla Sirena it was not random. I mean, of course, I guess that when drawn out on a map it kind of looks like a giant sea cow, but also we are the middle island in this chain so we have slightly warmer water and that is what manatee like." Nina said, "Baby, Sirena means mermaid." Andy said back, "Right. The sailors long ago told stories of seeing mermaids out in the sea and there were horrific stories of the mermaids luring the sailors to a watery grave. But theory shows that those 'mermaids' were most likely manatee." Nina looked back to Andy and asked, "So the manatee killed sailors? Why would they do that? How could they do that? They look so peaceful." Andy looked back at Nina slightly confused and then realized what she was talking about. Laughing he said, "What? No, the manatee did not kill sailors.

Nobody was dragging sailors to a watery grave, baby. That part was a fish tale." She asked, "Fish tale?"

"Yes. Fish tale. You know, an embellished story? A fabrication?"

She asked, "Why would they do that?"

"Because around the bar, it sounds more thrilling than saying" I went to sea and scared all the fish away when my drunk ass fell in.""

As Andy wrapped up explaining what a fish tale is the mother manatee and her calf came to the surface. Air came from a blowhole. As the top part of their bodies were breaking the surface of the water one could see the scars on the mother. Scars left by irresponsible boaters who refused to follow no wake rules in rivers and canals. She had been hit more than a few times as was the case with most adult manatee. Nina was giddy with excitement as they surfaced. Just as quickly as they had come up, they went back down. "Welp! That's it, folks. Next show in 20 minutes." Andy said as he laughed at his own joke. Nina asked, "That's it?"

"Well, yeah baby, what do you want? This is not some aquarium that holds sea critters captive and forces them to do tricks for meager food allowance. This is real nature! This is beautiful. I love manatee. They are so fun to watch."

Nina responded with, "Well, they don't do much."

Andy told her, "Exactly. They know how to...just be. They do not...do. They just...be, and they are content with that. Top that off with the fact that they don't pay rent and I'd say the manatee have got it figured out. You live in Florida! How do you not know much about manatee?"

She answered back, "I'm from the Bronx, and you know that."

"Yeah, but you've spent the past ten or so years living in Florida, haven't you? Oh well, I am happy to teach." Andy said with a smug but playful smile. Nina asked, "You'll be my teacher?" Andy looked at her and said in a playful sexy voice, "Oh yeah! I'll be your teacher baby and you will be my pet."

She shook her head and laughed as she said, "You have a weird way of saying things. "Seeing that he just made her laugh he continued with his impromptu act, "Oh yeah. And I will teach all the ways of nature in its rawest of forms." Still laughing Nina said, "Okay, you can stop."

"As your teacher, I will teach you all the ways of the wild. We will make unbridled, unpassionate, monkey love on the extra credit couch. Bow chica chica bow bow" Andy said as he made pornographic movie sounds. She looked at him and said, "Okay, you took it too far. It was funny, but you found the line and crossed it." Andy stopped there. This was one of the things he loved about her. While she did laugh at his corny jokes, she did keep him tactful. She would always let him know when he took it too far and whenever she did, he stopped. He loved her and respected her for that.

It was close to the time that Nina had to be leaving so the two walked back to his home and packed her car. Andy asked if she was sure she wanted to leave so soon. He did not want her to go. She told him she did have to get her car fixed and she missed her kids. Andy, on a technicality, could probably argue the car part. Nobody really needs to get a car that still drives fixed. He knew he could not argue the missing her kids' part. No man in his right mind would ask a mother to put him before her kids. With a sigh, he opened her door and she sat in her car as he lightly shut the door and stood beside the car looking down at her. She told him she loved him so much. He could see the look in her eyes that she actually did not want to go. She told him that she missed him already. He bit his lip and just looked back at her. She thanked him for their time together and a million other things. She was stalling and rambling. She did not want to leave. Nina told Andy she was so happy he accepted her proposal and she could not wait to tell her kids they were moving to Isla Sirena. They were going to be so happy she told him. Andy soaked in everything she was saying with the excitement she said it. He could tell she was very happy. With that, she said, "All right, I have to go if I want to catch the ferry home. Kiss me." Andy leaned in through the window and kissed the love of his life. Not a full-on tonsil hockey type of kiss. Just a simple lips to lips kiss. Not too long, and not too short. It was just right. To Andy, it was the essence of them able to just...be, and not do. It was perfect. Andy pulled away and stepped back from the car. They looked at each other. Nina said, "Thank you for making me happier than I have ever been. I look so forward to a life with you." Andy smiled and said, "Same. Now go get on that ferry. I love you."

With that, Nina drove away. Andy missed her already. He wished he had spoken up more to get her to stay. He figured it was okay. He had the rest of his life to spend with her. He had all the time in the world. As Nina's car hit the end of the block she turned and faded out of view like a manatee going back under the surface of the water. Andy knew, that much like the manatee, she would be back.

There was a sound effect of a radio dial switching stations along with a few bleeps and bops. A voice said, "If you're going to listen. Then listen responsibly! From the station giving away all the gifts, Merry Christmas!" A sound effect of a crowd yelling, "Happy New Year!" Overlapped that and was followed by the station voice identifying the station, "102.7 WVCX" The beat continued with retro hits.

CHRISTMAS IN PEEKING

The holidays around the Peeking Islands were something that was an astonishment to behold. If one had not experienced it, there was no way to prepare them for it. What the island lacked in snow it overcompensated for in festivities and lights. All of the islands celebrated heavily and welcomed the holidays with open arms. It was a time to reflect with friends that had become family. It was a time to share love and giving with everyone. It was a time to welcome in a new year to come!

The real celebrations happened on Water Street. Water Street was a two-mile stretch of road that ran parallel with the Peeking Highway. The street was filled with shops, restaurants, and bars. It had its own little side streets to find more off-the-beaten-path shops, restaurants, and bars. Most of the service industry workers would dress in red or green, along with Santa hats. One block had artificial snow blowing from a machine over the whole block. People would gather up what artificial snow they could and have snowball fights. Christmas music played publicly over speakers up and down the street. Every place was lit beyond belief. They all wanted to win the best light decoration contest. No prize came with that. It was the pride of holding that honor and having those bragging rights for a full year.

The whole week was filled with events. One bar had a shot-for-shot contest. This was an event that had each contestant going shot for shot and keep going till there was only one person left standing. Another bar might take the risqué route and have a sexy Santa contest. That was for both, men or women to strut their stuff on a makeshift catwalk dressed in a homemade sexy Christmas outfit, or lack thereof.

There were events for families as well. On one day a block of Water Street would be shut down to traffic so they could do the bobsled races. Which involved two people in a homemade bobsled on wheels being pushed by two other people. There were a variety of baking contests and on another day the street would be filled with people dressed as pirates and interacting with kids.

The big event was on Christmas Eve. It was the holiday parade. It started with the loud sirens of the Peeking police and fire. Followed by a plethora of floats, local charity groups, churches, and about eighty different Santa's. Everyone of course tossed out candy and stages were set up outside of the bars for live music.

It was the happiest time of the year, and it really was.

HIS STORY I (Decmeber 25, 2016)

Andy sat in the studio of WVCX with his producer/co-host, Rosie Rector, across from him. It was Christmas day. Together, they hosted the evening show from six to eleven. The show was best described as a variety show. Sometimes they would play music, sometimes they would talk, and other times they would take calls from listeners and discuss whatever topic came up. It was never serious topics. They always kept it fun and upbeat.

They sat at a table across from one another as a song faded out and the station's voice reverberated in their headphones, "Broadcasting live from high atop a mountain somewhere in the Peeking Islands. WVCX, serving Isla Sirena and all the Peeking Islands! It's the Andy and Rosie show! The sun goes down, but it gets hotter with your hosts, Andy Chelios and Rosie Rector!" That was followed by a jingle that sang, "Andy and Rosie, 102.7, WVCX!" Andy hit an orange button all the way to the left on the control board in front of him as he said, "102.7, WVCX Good evening everyone, and good evening to you, Rosie!" Rosie returned the greeting as he continued, "Merry Christmas Rosie! First things first. Thank you so much for coming in to do this show live with me tonight. You know, radio stations all across the country right now and all day have been running pre-recorded shows so that their on-air talent can have the day off and spend time with their loved ones. I am sure many people are wondering why we are here live on Christmas night when we have the capabilities to also take the night off" Rosie responded, "Merry Christmas, Andy, I was wondering the same thing myself."

"Well, I tell you why my sweet, hardworking co-host. It is because there are plenty of other people also working tonight. People cooking food and serving tables, working retail stores for the tourist who don't want to spend the day in their hotel, and the hotel workers! In fact, everyone in the service industry is working right now. These people are our listeners, and they deserve a live show from us! Plus, I have some really important news to share"

Rosie asked, "What is this news, Andy?"

He quickly responded, "I am engaged, Rosie!"

Rosie said, "Congratulations! When and where did this happen? How did you propose? Please tell me you kept it simple and did not make a scene and embarrass the poor girl."

Andy quickly responded, "Actually, it was she that proposed to me!" Andy continued to tell Rosie and their listeners the tale of how Nina proposed to him in the parking lot of a restaurant. Rosie asked, "So did she get down on one knee and give you a ring?"

"No Rosie, she grabbed my tallywhacker and put my hands on her breasts!"

Rosie interjected, "Okay, that's probably enough. Should we be talking about this on the air? Isn't this getting a little personal?"

"Absolutely we should be talking about this! That was Nina's whole point! She wanted the whole world to know that we are in love and that I belong to her! So I am here now saying to the whole world, I love and belong to Nina!"

"I see. That is a little better. I don't think our listeners want to hear about your sex life."

"Well see, Rosie, that is the thing. It would be about my lack of sex life. We did not have sex! We mutually agreed that we could wait till after we are married. You know, to make it special."

Rosie responded, "Well that is very special Andy. I am very happy for you! On behalf of all of our listeners let me say, congratulations!"

A song started to play as Andy spoke, "Thanks, Rosie. Hey gang! We have a fun show planned tonight! We have music, we have contests, and tonight I want to hear about your strangest Christmas ever! All that and more coming up on 102.7 WVCX!" The second he stopped talking a vocalist started singing the song. Andy turned the microphones off and looked at Rosie and with his hands up in the air said, "Well, how about that?"

Rosie looked to Andy and while off the air asked, "So was that all for real? Are you really engaged?"

"Yes," Andy laughed and shouted back at her, "Can you believe it? Some chick wants to actually spend the rest of her life with me!"

"That's great. I am so happy for you. Don't you think that was a bit much sharing some of those details? I know the show we do is risqué but come on, it's Christmas night." Rosie was often Andy's good angel on his shoulder. She was the part of his brain that contained a moral compass and also kept him grounded spiritually. Without her, the show would have gone in one direction and be lost at sea.

The show did have a reputation for pushing the envelope of what should be discussed on the airwaves. It was never serious or political. It was just a little over the top. Rosie was Andy's pull back though. She was the one that would reel him back in if they were wandering into the territory of getting fined by the FCC. It was not only because she was that type of person it was also her job. The two continued to talk to each other in the studio off the air as the song ended, a jingle played identifying the station and another song started.

A song had ended, a music bed started, and Andy spoke, "102.7! It's the Andy and Rosie show on your radio. Coming up after the break we have a special prize for you! We have…" Andy paused and made a sound of shuffling paper, "What do we have for them, Rosie?"

"Andy, we are giving away two movie passes to the Star Movie complex on Isla de Cabeza Martillo. We also have food and drink vouchers to enjoy with your movie. Complements of our friends at the Star movie complex where everyone gets the red-carpet treatment."

Andy responded, "That's awesome! Your chance at movie passes and more of today's hit music or Christmas music rather, are next on 102.7 WVCX!"

As the commercial break started Andy's cell phone lit up indicating a text. It was from Nina. His heart skipped a beat of delight. He picked up his phone and held it to his face as it unlocked. Then as he read the text he felt as if all of the blood had left his face. It said, "I am going to kill myself. Please forgive me."

Andy responded quickly, "Please don't do that." He wanted to say more. But he was at work. He had a contest coming up in three minutes and twenty-three seconds. The phones would be slammed. This was the worst moment in the world to be doing this. His phone lit up with another text from Nina,

"Please tell my kids I love them. Promise me you will take care of them."

Andy could not believe she was doing this now. She had to know that he was working at the radio station right now. She was out of the listening area, but she knew his schedule. What was she thinking? Her suicide threats were frequent in the past but only three days ago he saw her and she was the happiest he had ever seen her. She had sent him a text only yesterday explaining how she was the happiest she had been and she could not wait to start a life together. She had sent him many selfies of her smiling. It was Christmas night. Why was she doing this now? Who kills themselves on Christmas? One minute and fourteen seconds till Andy and Rosie went live with the on-air contest. He texted her as quickly as he could, "Please don't do this now. We will talk when I get out of work. I love you. Your kids love you. Neither of us could survive without. Pls don't."

They were halfway through the commercial break Rosie noticed something was up with Andy. He was responding furiously via text on his phone. This was not normal. He was always focused on the show. It was not normal at all for him to be texting like this, especially minutes away from a peak busy part of the night. He looked grossly concerned and in-depth with whatever he was texting. All color had left his face. She tapped her hand on the table to get his attention. He looked up and with her arms in the air she gave up a look asking if everything was okay. He nodded up and down and held his forefinger up in the air.

The station came back from break, a music bed had started and Andy's voice could be heard over the airwaves, "102.7 WVCX! It's the Andy and Rosie show and it is time to give away some cool crap. Caller number 102 we are looking for you." He paused briefly as he looked over at his cell phone on the table. It was lighting up indicating a call. Andy took a deep breath and continued "Caller number 102 on the hitlines right now, this is your chance for two free movie passes! "He pointed over at Rosie who spoke, "From the Star Movie complex on Isla de Cabeza Martillo, where everyone gets the red-carpet treatment"

Andy's cell phone lit up indicating a call again as Rosie pointed back to him. He ignored the cell phone and picked up where she left off, "This is for two free movie passes from the Star Movie complex and food and drink vouchers. Caller number 102 we are looking for you. Good luck! It's 102.7 WVCX!" A song started and every light on the station's phone bank was lit up like a Christmas tree. Andy indicated to Rosie to start going through the calls and find a winner. He picked up his cell phone and texted Nina back, "At wrk in mddle of contest. Call u aftr wrk. Please don't do it! Lov u!"

Rosie had found caller number 102. Andy took the caller and spoke with her off the air while the rest of the audience was either listening to the song currently playing or trying to be caller number 102. He started to set up the DAT to prerecord the call. When they did contests, they always prerecorded the calls. They never went live with contests because there were too many variables that all led to an air catastrophe. This time, however, the DAT machine was not allowing them to record. There was only a minute left in the song. Even if the DAT worked this second there was no time to record the call and have it ready for playback. Feeling copious amounts of stress, Andy looked at Rosie and coldly said, "Fuck it, we'll go live" Realizing what

he just said, he bit his lip and was relieved when he looked down at the control board and saw that his microphone was not all ready accidentally not on.
Fifty seconds.

He spoke to caller number 102 off-air very quickly. He said, "Hey what's your name?"
The voice said back, "Shelly. Hey, Am I the winner?"
 Andy said back, "Yes, Shelly you are but—"
She shrieked loudly over the phone.
 Forty seconds.

Andy's cell phone lit up with a text notification.
Thirty seconds.

Andy spoke back, "Shelly, Shelly, Shelly! Hold on. We are not on air yet but will be soon. That is great excitement though. I appreciate it and I need to you hold on to it to it for me, okay, sweetie?" She said, "Uh-huh"
Twenty-five seconds.

323

Andy continued, "Shelly, in about 20 seconds we are going live. I need you to be loud, okay? Shelly, do you know what station you are listening to?" She responded with an uh-huh.
He asked, "Okay, what station, sweetie?" She asked, "What?"
Fifteen seconds.

"Oh dear God," Andy thought, maybe out loud, who knew. He asked, "Shelly, what station is this?" She screamed out, "102.7!"
Andy shook his head back and forth. What an imbecile he thought. Clearly, she thinks we are on the air. But she's excited and she knows what station she is listening to.
Ten seconds.

Just before the text notification had dimmed on Andy's phone, he picked it up and read, "G'bye".
Five seconds.

The world around Andy started to move in slow motion as his cell phone fell out of his hand. The lights on the phone bank that normally flashed quickly seemed to fade on and off at the rate of one beat per minute.
Four seconds.

The music playing seemed to play as if it were a tape player running out of battery and slowing down to a deep voice.
Three seconds.

Every minute he had ever spent with Nina flashed through his head. He saw every smile. He saw her laughing with him on a dock. He saw her excitement as she described how amazing her cars are. He watched her face fill with joy when she opened presents from him on her birthday. The face of his phone shattered as it hit the floor at his feet. Andy looked at Rosie, who was holding a number two with her fingers in the air in the same slow motion that a referee counts out a boxer in the movies.
Two seconds.

A modulated deep voice filled his ears as it said, "102.7 WVCX, It's time for some freebies from the station that keeps on giving." It was followed by a rushing sound of touchtone sound effects. The meters in front of Andy pulsated in a way that they were listening to a sloth play classical music, despite it being a very upbeat dance track of a Christmas song playing. Andy pictured Nina in her car, alone and afraid. Rosie now made a number one with her forefinger. Andy wondered, "Why do we even use that stupid touchtone sound effect anymore? Over half these fucks listening don't even know what that is. Rosie held a fist up in the air. A vision of Nina with a gun to her head flashed in front of his eyes.

one second.

A strong music bed filled Andy's ears as Rosie pointed sharply at him. He saw Nina's face. It was lonely. There was a flash of orange light as a sign that said, "ON AIR" lit up as Andy hit a bright button all the way to the left of the control board.

Zero seconds.

He spoke with excitement, "102.7 WVCX! The station giving gifts live on Christmas! Who is this?" The voice on the other end said, "This is Shelly!" Andy said back, "Shelly, where are you calling from tonight?"

"Um. I'm on my liveaboard on Vista Bahia"

"Shelly, did you have a good Christmas?"

She answered with an, "Uh-huh"

"Did you get everything you wanted?"

"Yeah, I'm on my liveaboard drinking with some co-workers right now. We are the trailer park of the ocean! We're getting drunk and mooning all the richies in the mountains above us! Whoooo!"

Andy looked to Rosie and shrugged his shoulders with his arms out to his side and palms up. She just shook her head back and forth while laughing.

"That's great, baby! Love to hear you are spending time with the people you love but we want to make today a little sweeter, is that okay?"

She asked with excitement, "Am I caller 102?"

Andy said, "Shelly....You -are –caller- one!-oh-two!"

He reached his hands up to remove his headphones off his ears slightly as the screaming coming through was loud. The meters in front of him tapped the far-right side of the window they sat in. Putting his headphones back on Andy said, "Shelly, you and a friend are going to see the movie of your choice at the Star Movie complex where you always get the red-carpet treatment! We are also giving you vouchers for all the treats, soda, and fixins that your heart desires! Shelly, tell me what station is the station that keeps on giving all year long?"

There was a small pause as all that could be heard was laughing and screaming from other people in the background and then a voice came back and said, "Huh? What? Oh, 102.7! Whoooooo!" Then there was the sound of a phone call ending. An upbeat jingle with a choir played that identified the station and a Christmas pop remake played.

Andy turned off his microphone and looked across the table at Rosie and asked, "Did that just happen? Did she seriously just hang up without sticking around so we could get her information?"

Rosie said, "It sure did. It's okay, I'm sure that tomorrow if she remembers winning, she will call the station. She was excited though. She did not swear and she knew what station she was listening to. Not bad for a live call I'd say."

Andy looked to Rosie and said, "I think she just killed herself." Rosie replied, "Oh I don't think it was that bad. She was drunk with her friends and having a good time."
"Not her, I mean Nina. I think Nina just took her own life."
Rosie questioned him, "What makes you say that?"
Andy explained all the texts and the two missed calls and then said, "I mean, she has threatened this before many times over and I have talked her out of it every time. But this time something feels off." Andy put his head down in front of his control counsel and his hands over his head. He sat up and back while running his hands over his face. "I don't know dude. Something about this is not right. I need to try and call her. We are not due to talk for another seven minutes. Do you mind?" Rosie told him, "I'm surprised you're still here.

Andy stepped out of the studio and tried calling Nina. There was no answer. He tried five more times. Then he sent a text. Nothing. He tried calling one more time. Still nothing. He looked up her social media. There was nothing posted recently. He then clicked on one of her friends and sent a message, "Hi Natasha, I just received some very cryptic and suicidal messages from Nina. I am very worried she may try to hurt herself. Would you please go to her place and check on her? I live in the Peeking Islands and have no way of doing so. Thank you very much~ Andy" He was not sure if she would get the message or not. But he did not know what to do.

Andy walked back into the studio and Rosie asked if there was any luck. He explained what he did. Rosie asked, "Do you want to cookie cut the rest of the show?" Andy looked to her and said, "No, of course not. She is there and I am here. No plane or ferry can get me there from here till morning. So, what is the difference?" With thirty seconds left in a song, Andy and Rosie sat down at their separate control consoles facing one another and finished out their show. The rest of the night was spent playing upbeat Christmas remakes by pop artists, discussing listener's most bizarre Christmas' ever, and another contest. The last song of the night played out and Andy came on one last time for their shift, "102.7 WVCX, That's it for me and the wonderfully talented Rosie! We will see you when?" Rosie interjected, "Same great station, same great time."

"That's right! J.J. Reinhold is up next, taking you in the overnight with LoveLight at night!" He then said in a dark and muffled voice, "The love light...is lit...Good night! Talk at ya tomorrow!!!" There were some heavy staging sound effects, a montage of people screaming the station name, a deep over modulated voice identifying the show, and the station. It was about thirty seconds of airtime pumping up the show now leaving the airwaves. The only true purpose it served was satisfying the ego of the Deejays it was pushing.

J.J. walked into the studio. Rosie was cleaning up her workstation, as Andy seemed to make a mess of his. Rosie and J.J. exchanged hellos and wished each other Merry Christmas. J.J. handed Rosie a small present that was all wrapped up and said, "I got this for you." Andy said out loud without even bothering to look over his shoulder, "She has a boyfriend, asshole!" "Don't mind him" Rosie said softly, "He has had a rough night. But thank you. That is very sweet."

J.J. looked over to Andy and asked if he was all right. Andy turned and paced quickly to J.J.

"Am I all right? Oh, I'm way better than all right. It is midnight on Christmas night. Do you know what that means? Do –you- have- any- fucking – idea-what –that-means?" He punctuated each word in the question by throwing a show note out of the playbook and tossed them around the room. J.J. just looked back at Andy with wide eyes as he silently shook his head back and forth. "It means, What, it means my follicle challenged night owl is that I don't have to hear another fucking Christmas song for a whole mother-fucking year!" He grabbed J.J. by the shirt, pulled him forward, and kissed him on the cheek. Then he threw the rest of his notes in the air and ran down the hall as if in the excitement of someone who hated Christmas music and did not have to hear it anymore.

Rosie had gathered up Andy's personal effects that he had left behind as well as her own and walked down the hall to the lobby. It was half-past midnight and nobody was in the lobby except for Andy who was sitting on a couch, leaning over with his elbows on his legs and his hands supporting his face. As Rosie walked into the room, he looked up at her and his face was red, his eyes were swollen and bloodshot. He wiped his face with his hands and feigned half-smile. She could tell he had been crying. He showed her a message he received from Nina's friend, Natasha, that had verified she had gone through with taking her own life. His phone rang. The caller ID indicated it was the station general manager, Bob Overwrite. Andy showed her the incoming call and said, "Yeah, I don't know what this dipshit wants now. I can't right now. I just can't."

Rosie took Andy's phone in her hand and answered, "Merry Christmas from Andy Chelios's phone, this is Rosie speaking, how may I help you?"

The voice on the other end yelled so loud it felt like the phone shook. "Rosie! Don't give me shit! Where is Andy? I want to talk to Andy!"

Rosie said in a super soft but direct and cheery voice, "I am so sorry sir. Mr. Chelios is not available right now. May I take a message?"

"Rosie. This is Ben. I am not even playing right now. I am on vacation in Aspen with my family it is the middle of the fucking night on Christmas and I have one deejay calling me freaking out that another deejay is going to kill him in the studio! Get me Andy!"

Rosie got serious and said to her general manager, "Now is not a good time Ben. I assure you that whatever you have been told is an exaggeration of the truth and I promise you that there will be no murders in the studio tonight. Andy has had some personal issues come up and I have taken his phone from him. I have this under control. Sorry, your vacation has been interrupted. You may go back to sleep. I got this. Merry Christmas" She hung up. Andy waited for a good minute while starring at Rosie holding his phone. He looked at her and asked, "What? That's it?" she asked what he meant. "Well, the phone has not rung back. Anytime I sass off to that asshat and hang up, he calls me back in seconds. You'll have to show me that trick." Rosie asked Andy if he wanted to talk. He told her not right now. He just wanted to go home and try and figure this out. They made plans to meet up the next day.

Andy sat on his bed scrolling his phone. He was looking at pictures of Nina. Mainly he was reading through past text threads between the two of them. He read every single one. Both in text form and social media message form. He felt an overwhelming amount of sadness. Occasionally he would crack a small smile as some messages brought back fun memories. Then he would seep back into darkness as he realized all those memories are all he would ever have of his sweet, dear, amazingly awesome Nina. There was one photo he looked at for a long time. It was a moving picture photo. Kind of like a short two-second video. He put it on loop and would stare at it retentively. It was a photo that Nina had sent him on the day before Christmas. The look in her eyes and the curve of her smile showed a picture of someone in love. Because the picture moved it was as if she were there in the room looking at him in admiration. This was the last picture she had sent to him. It would have been about twenty-four hours before she, well, before she left. She looked so content in this picture. How did she go from the way she felt in this photo to feeling so sad? Another photo he went back to frequently was one of them together after lunch at the sub shop. They both looked so happy holding each other in their arms. She was leaning on his shoulder. Why did they not take more pictures together? Andy took a deep breath as he continued his trip down memory lane. He closed his eyes and tried to picture what it would have been like as she sat in her car. What was she thinking? What was going on in her head? How did she feel? A million questions ran through his head along with images of her sitting in the car feeling lost and alone. Tears continued to roll down his face onto his neck as his body shut itself down into the abyss of forced sleep as if it were a laptop that had run out of juice.

Andy woke to a loud bang. He shot up and looked around what was going on. He was having a dream, or no, a nightmare that his sweet Nina was about to shoot herself while sitting in her car. As she was about to pull the trigger there was a loud bang. The bang though was not in the dream. It was in real life. Andy scanned the room quickly and then heard the pitter-patter of a cat's paws on a wood floor as Tino quickly vacated the area. Andy rubbed his eyes and noticed a speaker had been knocked to the floor most likely from the cat. He rubbed his hands as he thought to himself, "What a fucking way to wake up." As his mind made its way to the land of the awake and aware, it hit him that the dream was not a dream. His head was foggy. He looked at his phone text history and saw that was no dream. His Nina really did leave him in the world of the awake. He saw a message from her friend Natasha that verified that. Nina was gone. This was real. She was not going to come walking through the door. Yet for some reason, he could not accept it as real. He got up out of his bed and showered, cooked some breakfast for Tino and himself. He was not sure why he was making himself breakfast as he was meeting Rosie soon at the café. Perhaps it was an involuntary force of habit. As he poked his food around his plate, memories of his sweet love now gone entered his head

From a radio perched up on the counter of Sal's Street Meat a song faded out and a voice said, "102.7 WVCX! I am Jake Robison and that is it for the all cool, all request, retro power hour. Andy Chelios and Rosie Rector are up next and getting you back to speed with today's current hits on 102.7 WVCX!"

ACT III

MIRRORED IMAGE (WINTER 2016)

Elsewhere on the island at the same time, Ariel Villarreal was working dispatch when the call came through. She answered, "Peeking 911. This call is being recorded. What is your emergency?

The voice on the other end said in a hushed and scared voice. "She is going to kill me. She is in the house with me."

Following the protocol, Ariel asked, "What is your current location, ma'am?"

The scared-sounding voice said. 345 Dey Street on Martillo. You've got to send someone. Please help. She is going to kill me."

"Okay ma'am, help is on the way. What is your name?"

There was panicked breathing coming from the other end with a small sob.

"Ma'am, can you tell me your name please?"

The breathing continued and a whisper came back to say, "She is outside the door right now. Help."

"Okay, ma'am. An officer is on the way now. Is this person outside of your home now?"

The frightened voice responded, "She is outside my bedroom door. I am in my closet. Help me, please. She hates me. She is going to kill me."

Ariel asked, "Who is trying to kill you?"

The caller said, "She is. She hates me"

Ariel responded, "Ma'am, police are on the way. Please stay on the line with me."

There was a loud noise that came from the other side of the phone. Ariel could hear rustling from the other end of the phone. She heard a scream and another voice. It was another female voice that had a husky grovel to it.

"Who is that you talking to?" The voice could be heard asking out loud. "Quit your crying. You're always crying. Who is that on the phone? Give me that!"

Ariel heard the other voice loud and clear now as it asked, "Who is this?"

"This is Peeking 911. Who am I speaking with?

The angry-sounding voice yelled back, "This is the police?" She could be heard now yelling at the original caller, "You done called the damn police? Oh, girl, you are good as dead now!" Arial heard the original caller screaming for help and what sounded like a struggle.

The husky voice came back to the phone. "Hello! You still there?"

"Yes ma'am. Could you tell me the nature of this dispute? We can work through this."

The husky voice said, "Aw, you done got me fucked up. There ain't nobody working through nothn'. We are all going to die tonight and that includes any pigs that come bustn' through that damn door."

Corporal Steve Steube and his partner Sergeant Amy McGuire arrived on the scene and notified dispatch. The response on the radio said, "10-4. Contact has been made with the suspect. Female, with a husky voice. Assumed to be dangerous. The victim, also female. Names are unknown. Proceed with caution."

As the officers approached the door of the home, they could hear two voices coming from within the home. One was yelling and the other was screaming for help. Corporal Steve knocked loudly on the door. "Peeking police. Open up."
They heard a voice yell back, "Ya'll get or the bitch is dead and so are you!" The two cops heard a blood-curdling scream for help as they battered through the door.

Once inside they were in a kitchen, which appeared empty. They heard the commotion coming from another room on the other side of the house. They quickly made their way to that room while carefully clearing any room or area they went through.

They made their way to a closed door. It was obvious that the victim and her assailant were in the room on the other side of that door.

Sergeant McGuire yelled, "Peeking police, ma'am. We want to speak with you. Please come out slowly and with your hands up. We can get through this." Both officers had their weapons drawn and pointed at the door. There was another loud scream for help and the sound of flesh hitting flesh, followed by a loud thud.

A voice cried out in pain as it begged, "Get off of me. Get off of me. Help!"
The husky voice could be heard yelling, "Shut your bitch ass up. I am sick of you always crying. I am here to help you. That is all I ever want to do. But all you do is cry. Shut the hell up!" There was another sound of flesh hitting flesh and more cries of pain. The husky voice could be heard, "All right. I warned you. I am going to end

this now!" At no point to Corporal Steube, did it seem off that two people in a domestic dispute were not yelling over each other. It as if they took turns respectfully in their shouting.

There was the unmistakable sound of a gun being fired. Sergeant McGuire made some quick hand motions to Corporal Steube. Without hesitation he put his shoulder hard into the door, breaking it open on the second lunge. Sergeant McGuire rushed into the room. The corporal noticed his partner fall forward as if she had tripped over something. There was a flash of light and a loud boom. The sergeant went to the ground face first as Corporal Steube rushed in behind her with his pistol thrust firmly into the air. He yelled, "Peeking police! Get down on the ground! Get down on the ground!" He realized there was nobody in the room. Nobody he could see anyway. Except for his partner on the floor and a small, bloodied female sitting in a chair with a shotgun at her side. Kneeling to his partner he had one hand holding his pistol out and with the other held his hand on his partner's neck. She was still alive. He could feel a pulse. With his free hand, he keyed his radio, "Officer down at 345 Dey Street. Request immediate back up and paramedics! Suspect still at large! The victim is dead with a shotgun wound to the head." He repeated the call and nervously scanned the room. With both hands on his pistol scanned left and right and saw no one in the room. He rushed over to a window. It was shut and locked from the inside. He turned around quickly and walked to the open closet. Gripping his pistol tightly with both hands he yelled, "Come out of there now! This does not have to end like this." There was no response. His heart throbbed so hard he could feel it in his head. The corporal thrust into the closet and found no one in there. He quickly turned around still scanning the room. The only noise he could hear was his partner groaning, his breathing, and his heartbeat. He could not figure out where the suspect could have gone? There was only the door, that he had come through and the closed window. There was no place else to hide. He pointed the gun at the bed. He said out loud, "Come out from underneath the bed!" He approached the bed and kicked it. Nothing happened. He grabbed the bed and shoved it to the side. Still, nothing happened. In a brave, yet maybe stupid move he quickly threw himself into a prone position facing the bed, and pistol held out in front of him. Looking under the bed, there was nobody there.

He heard a commotion from the front of the house as he heard familiar voices yell out, "Peeking police!" Corporal Steube yelled out to identify himself and give his location.

Paramedics walked in and attended to Sergeant McGuire and the victim. They came to the corporal, and he brushed them off, telling them he was fine. While other officers continued to clear the house, corporal Steube felt a wave of adrenaline rush off of him. Still breathing quickly he looked around the room. He saw his partner starting to stand up with the assistance of the paramedics. She had a confused and lost look on her face as she held a hand to her ear. On the ground where she had fallen, he saw a long and thick thread. Still lumped over in a chair, with detectives now looking at her he saw the victim. Her face was gone. Her body was covered in blood. It was hard to determine anything about her at that glance. He tried to reenact the scene in his head as a detective approached him.

"Corporal Steube?"

"Yes?" He answered back.

"We need to ask you some questions. Would you step outside with me please?" Before following the detective out of the room corporal Steve Steube, looked at the shooting victim and then over to a full-size mirror. He looked at himself in the mirror as he readjusted his uniform and utility belt as he winked and said, "You're beautiful." He looked back to the slumped-over body in the chair one more time and walked out of the room.

HIS STORY II (WINTER 2016)

Rosie walked into the café where she and Andy usually met before going to the station for work. It was a good place for them to meet, as it was not at the station so they would not get interrupted. They could discuss what they wanted to do on the show that day and go over any issues before they happened.

As it was every day, Andy was already there. On the small two-person table he had both of their drinks and food. She approached the table as he took a sip of his double espresso and said, "Your double bullshit mocha latte awaits." He motioned to her drink and a blueberry muffin at the empty seat. She sat down and thanked him as she took a sip. Rosie asked, "So what's up?"
"Well, I was able to line up a great live interview tonight. We are going to be talking to Tina Romeo live minutes before she takes the stage for her first of three sold-out shows in New York! This will be great as we get to catch the excitement of a popular performer just before they start her concert. I see on social media there is a new 'challenge' the kids are doing. It involves dipping candle wax on each other. I want to get into that with some calls, and I have a great idea

for a new contest that is going to be pushing it to the edge just a little bit-"Rosie interrupted, "That is not what I meant. What's up with you? What's up with Nina?"

"Nina? She is dead. You know that. Nothing has changed. She is still dead. If there is any change in her condition you will be the first to know."

Andy could be ugly with his sarcasm at times. Rosie took a breath of diplomacy and replied, " I know. But how are you handling this?"

"How am I handling this? Well, Rosie, the girl I loved with all my heart is dead and it is all my fault."

"It's not your fault Andy, there is nothing you could have done."

Andy replied, "There is plenty I could have done. I could have canned the contest. I could have taken her call when she called. After multiple texts and two phone calls, I should have known this was serious. I should have taken those calls. I should have called her back to help her out. She always depended on me to get her out of the dumps when she was feeling down. I should have been there for her. Rosie, Nina's blood is all over my hands!"

Andy paused as he looked around him. Other people in the café were looking in their direction. He did not think he was speaking loudly. He thought he was keeping it quiet and private. But he must have been a little louder than he thought because people were taking glances at the two talking over coffee and muffins.

Andy continued in a quiet tone, "I should not have even been on the air, Rosie. Every other deejay in the country was doing a pre-recorded show. Why did I feel we had to do our broadcast live?" Rosie answered, "Because it's who you are Andy. You believe in the show so much and caring about our listeners so much is part of who you are. It is part of what makes our show popular. We are seen as one of the people."
"Fuck that one of the people shit. We could have pre-recorded, and no one would have known any different. I took you away from Costello, on Christmas. That is not fair to you or him. I...I was not available to the woman who depended on me when she needed me most. On Christmas of all days! I should have been there for her. I should have sent her more text after she left. I

should have pressed harder so she would not have gone home in the first place!"

Rosie tried to assure him that it was not his fault, but Andy was determined to put the weight of the whole situation on his shoulders.

Andy continued, "She told me to take care of her kids, Rosie. How am I supposed to do that? They barely even know me. I have no legal rights over them. We are not married so I have no legal right to them. Her ex-husband, their father has every legal right to them. He is going to get them and this is so unfair. He does not give a shit about them. He does not send one penny of child support. He never buys them anything and he beats the shit out of their mother. I am the one who should be rewarded with the kids. He did not give Nina any money for their Christmas. Do you know who did? Me. I gave her one thousand dollars to spend on her kids. So who cares about those kids? Me. But because we live in a fucked-up country with fucked up child laws there is no way I would get custody of her kids."

Andy paused as he looked down at his moist and fresh blueberry muffin. Eating this was usually one of the highlights of his day. It sat there in front of him untouched. He took a sip of espresso and swallowed hard as it went down with pain.

He looked up at Rosie. His eyes were swollen. They were bloodshot. The skin on his face looked as if it had been rubbed raw. He said, "The real kicker? Those kids will not see that thousand dollars. All the inventory in her car that she shot herself in goes directly to Leo, that fucktard ex-husband of hers. Do you know what he's going to spend it on? Not those kids I can assure you of that. Probably drugs. It's so unfair. This is my fault. I should have been better for her. I should have been there when she needed me. She needed me many times before when she was on the brink of suicide and each time, I was there to stop her. Except for this time. You know, we all have friends who talk about killing themselves and we all listen and talk to them. But you wonder if they would really do it or is it just a cry for attention. Well, apparently this was no cry for attention. She meant it and she fucking did it."

Rosie tried again to remind him that it was not his fault.

"The worst part about this, Rosie, is her soul. According to the Bible, she is now going to burn in Hell."

Rosie's heart sank as he said that. She could not believe he had those thoughts. She told him, "Well, actually the church has changed its beliefs on that. She was a good person. I am sure she is not in Hell."

Andy asked, "Well where is she then? She sure is not here anymore. We have been taught since we were kids that all sins are forgivable. All but one, that one is taking the gift of one's own life. God gave us this gift out of the goodness of His heart. For us to take our own lives is saying fuck you to God and that shit He does not forgive. That is what we are taught. For as long as I can remember."

Rosie answered back, "Well, as I said, the church has changed its beliefs on that and it is now said that as long as you are close to God you may enter Heaven. I am sure she is in Heaven now."

Andy thought for a minute. He desperately wanted to believe Rosie. He wanted to know that Nina was not spending eternity in a damnation of flames. He wanted more than anything for her soul to be at rest and at peace. He wanted to believe Rosie. Everything he had been taught by his parents and schools though said otherwise. He was trying his best to block those lessons out and sway toward Rosie's words. He spoke with a glimmer of hope, "Well, she was found with a Bible on the passenger seat next to her. So there is that. Perhaps she prayed to God and Jesus before she did what she did. Perhaps she made peace with the Lord before taking her own life. I don't know. I was not there. GOD! I should have been there for her! This is not how it is supposed to be! This sucks! I hate this." He closed his eyes and took a deep breath.

Rosie asked, "Do you think we should be doing a show? Don't you think you should take some time off?"

"No, the show must go on. I am a professional and beat must continue so to speak."

"Well, the beat can continue without you for a little bit, you know. Not sure if you remember but

I ran that show by myself for five years before you came along."

"Rosie, I don't mean it that way. I know you ran a very successful show before I joined. Very successful. I know you have the capabilities. I have full trust in you. It is not that. That show is the one thing that keeps my mind occupied. So for those five hours on the air are the five hours of the day I am not thinking about anything else. It is like free therapy. I need that show."

She asked, "Are you at least taking time for her funeral?"

"Oh God, I don't even want to think about that right now. Do you know the last funeral I was at I was only about six years old? I had no idea what I was doing or what was going on. I was in an uncomfortable corduroy suit. It was a weird experience. I don't even remember who it was for. It was for someone my parents knew, that is all I remember."

Andy and Rosie continued their conversation. It would weigh mostly on Andy blaming himself and Rosie trying to convince him otherwise. The entire time visions of Nina's smiling face were seen in his head. He just could not fully shake the feeling that she was gone, and this was real.

After spending an hour in the café, the two deejays picked up their trash and tossed it in a can. Andy picked up his uneaten blueberry muffin and handed it to a homeless man on the walk to the radio station. Somewhere in the world, a new baby was born, a little girl's cat died, a young man was the first in his family to graduate from college, while another man lost his job of twenty-five years. All of this happened and the beat continued on today's best hits, 102.7 WVCX.

Andy sat out on the lanai of his humble home on the north tip of Isla Sirena, taking in a cool night breeze. From where he was, he could see Vista Bahia and all the lights that came off the liveaboards. He could also partially see lights coming from the oversize homes that sat nestled into the mountains overlooking the bay. That is where he grew up. His home now was much more humbling than what he grew up in. He enjoyed his smaller home and where it was. It was his and had his personality to it. It was home. It was welcoming. He remembered what it was like to grow up in one of those large houses up in the mountains. It was nothing like what others perceived it as. They were big. So big that one could feel lost and alone in one. Everything was pristine. There were even one or two rooms that he was not allowed in for the most part. There was a living room in the middle of the house that no one used. It was only there for looks. Since it was in the middle of the house he would have to walk through it of course, but he had to walk around the outer edges. Nobody was allowed to walk through the center. It had furniture that nobody was allowed to sit on or even touch for that matter. Every Christmas there was a fake blue tree by the bay window. That tree was only for looks. There would be an actual Christmas tree in another living room where the presents would be. It was absurd. Also in this living room was a piano that no one was allowed to play. It was the type of house that was quiet. He grew up in that house knowing he was only to speak when spoken to. He could go days without seeing anyone in the home except for a servant or nanny. "Yeah". He thought out loud. "Those homes are not what people think they are." He enjoyed his home now. It was small. He knew where everything was. He was close to work. He had this awesome lanai where he spent most of his time. He loved sitting out there early in the morning or late at night, smelling the sea and watching boats pass by. It was very comforting and took him away. Most importantly he did not feel alone. It was too small to be alone in! It was a simple one-bedroom, one-bath apartment. He had a very humbling kitchen with only a four-top stove, oven, and fridge. There was a total of five cupboards. One below the sink and four above the oven. He had a living room, which he never really used for anything other than a place to store his boxes of books. In the living room, he had a pastel couch that he never sat on, and two large screen TV's that he never watched. There were two tall shelving displays that had several knick-knacks on them. Mostly they were filled with pewter pelicans or manatee. In front of the couch, there was a glass table that had nothing on it but drink coasters and dust. There was also a small and depressing looking faux wood dining table that he never once ate at. He normally ate on his lanai. The lanai was a screened-in area. Around the edges were some plants in pots. In one corner sat a few wicker chairs with a small glass table in front of them. Going all around the top he had strung up party lights in the shape of palm trees that he would on rare occasions, plug in and light up. This was his home. He did not feel alone in it. Until now.

To Andy, Nina had become everything. She was such an amazing woman who had it going on a lot more than she thought. She just did not give herself enough credit. But she was always there to support others. She was that friend who would drop everything to help someone else. She always put her needs after everyone else. Many people took advantage of that generosity.

Before Nina, Andy was not really alone. He was living his best life in California away from this island chain he had tried so hard to escape. He may have not been doing exactly what he wanted, but he was working on it and he was living life by his own rules. Nothing was holding him back and he had a great circle of close friends in California with which he created some fun memories. There was the kind of wild nights that only happen in a movie. Yet, they happened to him for real. Life definitely was not lonely for him there. It was because of Nina though, that Andy gave up that life he had made out west and move back to the island chain that taught him everything he knew.

Nina added to his fulfillment. What started as a friendship and a cool chick to talk to, turned into something far more than he would ever have of dreamed. He did not plan this. It just happened. One day he woke up, opened his eyes, and thought, "I am in love with Nina." He could not explain it to even himself. Sure, he knew what he enjoyed about Nina. She supported his aspirations. When he had an idea he wanted to do she was all in and told him to go for it. She appreciated his writing. He used to wait up late at night just so he could write her a short story or poem. He would then send it to her email while she was asleep so it was the first thing she would see when she woke up in the morning. She would call him every morning at 7:15 to wake him up and get him motivated to write his books. She would call him again at 7:30 to make sure he had actually gotten up. When they spoke, she listened to him. It always seemed as if it were in baited anticipation. As in she was interested in what he had to say. To Andy, she was way out of his league. On the outside, she was a total bombshell. She was the most beautiful girl in the world type. On the inside, she was so caring and compassionate. He never understood what she saw in him. The way she treated him was unlike any other. It was as if she were his biggest fan. She loved listening to him on the radio and she loved his books he would write. She would consume them usually a day or two after they had been finished. Then she would text him questions non-stop about the book. That part was kind of weird to him, but it was a small part of what made Nina, Nina. Even though there were boxes filled with his books in his house, she always wanted her own copy and she wanted it autographed. That, however, would sometimes make him apprehensive. He would start to think she was playing him. He would always question her on that. He would say, "Seriously? You sleep next to the author, and you want this autographed." She would get so giddy with excitement over it when she yelled with a resounding yes. There were also times that she would seem overly excited about the simplest of gifts. He would get her flip-flops or maybe a Mopar T-shirt and she would act out of her mind happy. As if it was the best gift in the world. The situations like that at times made Andy feel as if he were being played. In his mind, it was not normal for a girl like Nina to be in love with a guy like him. She did complete him in many ways. He thought she was as awesome and with her, in his life he would never be lonely. Except now, she was no longer in his life. She was really no longer in his life. It was not as if they had a bad break up and maybe there was a chance of them getting back together someday. She was gone. As in gone, gone. Forever. There was no second chance. It was sudden and without warning gone. His heart had just been ripped out of his stomach and there was nothing he could do to bring her back. This was one hundred percent for real. Andy was alone. Except for Tino. He would always have Tino.

As if on cue the seal point Siamese walked from inside the house to the screened-in lanai. He gave his greeting to Andy and Andy asked, "What's up buddy?" Tino just looked at him and answered with a meow. Tino walked around the lanai as if he were looking for something and just could not find it. He looked back to Andy with another meow. Andy said, "I don't know what you want, buddy. I wish I could understand you. I feel that you need a bigger vocabulary." Tino walked over to an aloe plant in a pot and sniffed it. Andy said out loud, "Tino! Don't even think about it." The cat licked the plant, then started to eat it. Andy clapped and yelled out, "Tino No!" The Siamese then walked to the screen, jumped and in a second was hanging from the screen. Andy reacted immediately. "Tino! Bad kitty! Get down!" The cat just hung there. He tilted his head back so he could say one thing to Andy, "Meow". Andy grabbed a squirt gun off a table next to him and gave Tino a couple of quick squirts. The cat continued to hang there in defiance and once again tilted his head back to look at Andy and give him a single meow. Andy shook his head back and forth as he got up out of his comfortable wicker chair and said, "I don't know what has gotten into you tonight" He grabbed Tino off the screen and held him up in the air so that they were face to face. He asked, "What is wrong with you? You got da debil in you tonight?" He spoke in a deep and slightly dramatic voice as he said, "Do I need to exorcise these demons that have taken over your blissful soul?" Tino squinted his eyes then looked around the room as if he had not a care in the world. Andy put the cat on the ground and engulfed Tino's entire face with one hand. He said in his overdramatic voice, "Demon, I command thee. Begone! Leave the soul of this otherwise peaceful kittah alone!"

There was only the sound of a purr. Andy said, "Now that's more like it." He sat down in his wicker chair again and Tino went back to the screen. This time he did not jump. He was watching an anole climb on the screen. He then started to do what Andy referred to as 'lizard speak'. It was weird to him. He had never heard a cat make that kind of sound before. It was kind of like a broken meow mixed with a deep chirp. Tino only did it when he had his eyes on anoles. Andy asked, "What is the lizard saying, Tino? Are his people coming to take over the world?"

Tino slowly walked over to where Andy was sitting and jumped on his lap. Andy, in an almost automated response pet and rubbed Tino. The Siamese responded with his loud, deep, and vibrating purr. Andy said, "Now this is how a cat is supposed to act." The two sat in silence. On occasion, Tino's ears would perk as they could hear bottle rockets being launched. It was most likely from the service workers living on their boats in the bay below Vista Bahia.

"Now there are people who know how to live their best life," Andy said to Tino. He continued to speak out loud, "They have whatever job they can get. Server, bartender, boat mate. Does not matter. It is a paycheck and that is all they care about. They go to work. They come home and party. They don't save a dime. They live paycheck to paycheck and live each day as if it may be the last. Fucks given? Zero. That is the life, Tino, my friend." Without warning, Tino tensed up. He jumped off Andy's lap and ran like a bat out of Hell into the house. Andy put his hands in the air palms up and said, "I guess it's time for bed".

SMALL CRAFT ADVISORY
(SEPTEMBER 2017)

It was mid-September and the smell from the barbeque pit was amazing. Three campers had spent the past two hours doing their own thing and now they were about to enjoy hot dogs, beans, and s'mores. That was till Ranger Will came along.

Shelly, Alan, and Carissa had plans to spend a few days off from work camping at Isla Fantasma. They all worked together at a bar in the historic seaport on Manta Ray. They lived in Vista Bahia Bay on small sailboats. Since they lived on sailboats they were already roughing it by most landlubbers' definition. For these three, this was a good escape from the tourists. Camping out on this island was not a huge tourist activity. If a tourist had been out there, they would have known what they were getting into before they even signed up. Therefore, been like-minded people. In Shelly, Alan, and Carissa's book, they would be cool.

Compared to the other four islands in the Peeking Chain it was the smallest. Isla Fantasma was only two miles by half a mile. It was a national park. Except for a ranger station, there were no buildings.

There was not even a commode. For anyone camping on the island, aqua dumps were probably the choice way to use the bathroom. That meant sitting in the ocean and letting it all come out. While a little repulsive to some, for the experienced, it beat hovering over a bush and using a leaf. It was primitive camping. Anyone that was going to camp there knew that ahead of time. Campers had to bring all of their gear. This would include obvious tents and sleeping bags. They also had to bring their own food and water. A gallon of water per camper per scheduled day is what was required. If they needed sunblock or bug repellent they would have to bring that as well. Of course, it had to be environmentally safe. Because it was a state park, they were not allowed to build fire pits. At the campsites, however, were a couple of archaic standing grills leftover from the 1970s. Campers had to bring in their own charcoal. The main thing for a camper to remember was that whatever came to the island with them, had to leave with them. For anyone that loves to camp, this was a great way to do it. For a person that thinks the more modern glamping is roughing it, this would not be a trip for them.

The island was in the northwest quadrant of the island chain. It was two and a half miles west of Bear Island and two miles north of Manta Ray. It was the only island that did not have a bridge connecting it to the rest of the chain. There was a small dock slightly below the northeast part of the island. It was partially tucked away in what could almost be called a cove. The dock had enough room for the daily small ferry that brought the day-trippers or overnight campers out and three more boats. The only way to get there was by the small ferry that could fit twenty people at a time or a private boat. The island would never allow more than twelve campers at any given time. For anyone with the desire to camp there, did have to plan ahead and make reservations.

Shelly, Alan, and Carissa had tied off their johnboat at the dock and started unloading their gear. A park ranger was waiting to greet them on the dock. He introduced himself as Ranger Will.

Ranger Will stood at about six foot four. He had a good amount of weight to him, but it was all muscle. His biceps fit very snug into the rolled-up sleeves of his park uniform. His dark green uniform shirt looked to be made of the same thick and uncomfortable material that cop uniforms were made of. It was neatly starched, as were his dark green shorts that went to his knees. He wore thick black socks that went up to his shins and tan hiking boots. His hair was short and jet black, and he was clean-shaven. His shirt had three strips on the sleeves. He wore a utility belt that carried a flashlight, knife, small first aid kit, handheld radio, pepper spray, handcuffs, and what appeared to be a stun gun. Upon first glance, this guy was no joke. Like all the rangers who worked Isla Fantasma, they worked in teams of four and would be on the island for thirteen weeks, and off thirteen weeks then back on again. If one enjoyed nature, people, and long hours it was an amazing job to have.

The three were unloading their gear from the boat to the dock and the park ranger spoke. "Howdy. Looks like y'all are fixin' to camp. May I have your name?'

Carissa spoke up. "Hi, sir. It will be under Martin. We come out here all the time."

As the ranger looked through and made notes in a small notebook he had taken from his pocket slowly said, "Yes ma'am. I got you for three people and it looks like three nights."

"Yes sir," Carissa said with a grunt as she lugged a cooler onto the dock.

Alan asked, "Howdy? You're not from around here, are you?"

The ranger said, "No sir, I have recently transferred here from San Antonio." The way he said it though it sounded like San Ann-tone. My name is Will."

The three campers offered a handshake and introduced themselves. Shelly said, "Good to meet you, Ranger Will. As Alan said, we come out here a lot. We live over in Vista Bahia Bay and camp here a few times a year."

Ranger Will said, "That's fine, ma'am. You'll understand then that I still have to go through the routine as if it's your first time."

Alan tossed the last of the gear onto the dock and while brushing off his hands said, "Have at it."

The ranger said, "Okay then. There are no drugs,

guns, or any products that are unfit for the environment. This includes any sunscreens, soaps, shampoos, or any other kind of liquid or ointment. Do you have any of those?" The three all said, "No sir."

"Good. Snorkeling may only be done in three designated areas. You've been here before, so you know where those are?"

They all affirmatively nodded their heads.

"I don't see any kayaks, so don't suppose all y'all plan on doing that. Moving on then. Be sure to protect the vegetation here. Do not attach anything to the trees. All your camping gear must be free-standing. Your campsite does have wooden posts that you may tie one clothesline to. We do not allow wood fires. Use the barbeque pits and use only match-lit charcoal briquettes that I assume you brought. I see it looks like you brought your food. You know to keep it in hard-sided containers at all times?"

Shelly said, "We will keep the food in the coolers, Ranger Will. We know about the rats."

Alan said, "Oh, we know about the rats."

The three chuckled at some inside joke.

The ranger said, "Okay then. Be respectful of any other campers here and keep quiet time from 10

PM to 6 AM. I'll have no late-night ragers' in my park."

"We got you, Ranger Will," Carissa said with an enthusiastic smile.

The ranger continued, "Stay out of any roped-off areas. Right now I only have one area roped off and that is by the lakes. On that note, you know that if you see any eggs to leave them be. They are not free souvenirs. Do y'all plan on doing any fishing?"

They answered yes and produced all of their fishing gear and licenses for the ranger to look at. The ranger said, "Looks like y'all are about ready to go. You live here so you know what's in season. You also know that I am a park ranger. I am not your front desk clerk, concierge, massage therapist, room attendant, or tour guide. If everything goes well and all y'all behave then this will probably be the last time you'll see me." Pointing to a couple of wheelbarrows at the end of the dock the range said, "I'm also not your valet. Since you have done this before you know where the wheelbarrows are to get your gear to the camp and you know to return them."

A call came across on the rangers VHF radio. "Ghostrider One to Fantasma ranger station."

The ranger said, "Go for ranger station."

The voice on the radio said, "Ghostrider One inbound with sixteen-day tripping and two overnight souls. We will be 10-56 at your twenty in ten minutes."

The ranger said into his radio, "10-4 Ghostrider one. Ranger copies. See you soon. Fantasma ranger out."

The ranger said goodbye to the three and walked away from the dock. Shelly, Alan, and Carissa loaded their gear into a wheelbarrow and followed a small trail to the campsite area of the island.

The campsite was on the Midwestern coast of the island. It was an area that was tucked into an area surrounded by trees and about twenty paces from a beach. It looked out over the water and provided a great view of the sunset. There were eight campsites to set up a tent. In the camping area, there were three barbeque pits and six picnic tables. Each campsite had two wooden poles to put up a clothesline to hang wet clothing. All of the campsites were empty so it appeared that other than the two they had heard about on Ranger Will's radio, they would be alone.

The tents had been set up and it was time to cook. Alan had brought some burger patties along with some other food he had prepared for the trip and cooked up a delicious meal for the three of them. They did notice the other two campers come in while they were eating. Shelly had invited them over for a friendly lunch. It was a couple and they appeared as if they wanted to be left alone. They were really into each other. They may have been newlyweds from the mainland on a honeymoon.

After lunch, they cleaned up their area and put any of their trash into a zip lock bag and into an empty cooler. They had done this enough times to know that rats did infest the island and they are not the type of guests one would want around the campsite.

Carissa retrieved a book from her tent and sat down at a picnic table. Alan was down on the beach flying a kite that he had attached a go-pro to. Catching aerial footage of naturalistic areas and posting it online was a hobby he had created for himself. He did not own a drone or did not feel the personal need for one. He was content doing this the way he had been doing it. Many friends had suggested he invest in a drone. Perhaps he was stubborn in his ways. He had his kite and go-pro. This was the way he was happy doing it.

The day-trippers had gone back to Manta Ray on the small ferry and the campers had the island to themselves. As a camper, this was the time that one appreciated being there. It gave one the feeling of isolation. A few hours later the sun was about to set and Alan was just taking some freshly caught fish off the grill as he put it on paper plates. Shelly had come back from her tent carrying two large bottles. She said with a little bit of singsong to her voice, "Guess what I've got?"

Alan looked up with anticipation, "Is it something that will get me drunk?"

Shelly answered, "Oh, it will get you drunk all right."

Carissa grabbed one of the bottles. The bottle itself was unmarked. It had no label or markings on it of any sort. The bottle was a clear glass bottle that was the typical size for maybe a bottle of wine. The liquid had a light tan color to it. Holding the bottle up in the air, as she appeared to investigate it Carissa asked, "What is this?"

Shelly answered, "You remember my cousin Sandy that was just visiting from St. Croix? Well, this is a little somethn' – somethn' that they make there."

Alan looked to Shelly and asked, "As in homemade? Like moonshine?"

Carissa asked, "This ain't moonshine, is it? I don't do that shit."

Shelly laughed and told them, "No it's not moonshine. It's more of" She paused to think for a second. "Think of it more like a rum. It is homemade by my cousin's friend. It is some sort of family recipe from a family that is generations deep into St. Croix. This stuff is amazing. Try it."

Alan grabbed the bottle and smelled it. It had a sweet smell to it, like caramel. He put the bottle to his lips and took a large swig. The flavor was one of the most amazing flavors he had ever tasted in a drink. It did not have the slightest hint of any alcohol to it at all. It was like drinking liquid candy. A very, sweet candy. It was not hard or biting like whiskey. It went down very smooth like an espresso with cream."

He looked to Shelly confused and asked, "There is alcohol in this? I don't smell or taste anything."

"Oh, there is alcohol in it, you just wait."

Carissa grabbed the other bottle and took a swig. She responded as she wiped her mouth, "Holy shit, that is amazing. It tastes like candy! I love it." She tipped the bottle back again.

Looking at the clear bottle with no labels asked, "So what is it?"

Shelly said, "They call it Mamajuana."

"Mamajuana." Carissa and Alan both responded in unison.

"Yep. Not sure what it is exactly. Other than pure awesomeness."

Alan asked, "How did she get here? Don't TSA frown upon unmarked bottles of liquid in bags?"

"Too many questions! Drink up! I have plenty more!" Shelly shouted.

The sun had just completely set and the three campers were enjoying their fresh fish dinner along with what was left of the two bottles of Mamajuana that they had passed around. The maybe newlywed couple walked past the picnic table from the shore to the campsites. Shelly made an offer to sit down for some food. The man politely declined and the couple went to their tent to retrieve their dinner to cook up. Although it seemed as if they knew what they were doing around a campsite, they did not act like regular campers.

Alan rolled his eyes. Shelly asked what that was about. He said, "Just don't seem like normal campers."
Carissa agreed, "Yeah, it's not like they are not nice. They just don't seem neighborly."
Shelly teased as she asked, "Would it make you happy if they came over to sing Kumbaya with us?"
"No," Alan said. "But I guess I'm just used to campers hanging out with other campers. But to each their own I guess."
Shelly asked, "You know what you need? More mamajuana." She handed him one of the nearly empty bottles.
Shelly looked at Alan and said, "They are probably newlyweds. They are in love. This is their time alone together."

Carissa said, "Speaking of being in love. Let's talk about Ranger Will! Hubba, hubba. She giggled hard.

"Oh my God!" Shelly added, "Did you see those pythons for arms? And that slow southern accent? And his voice? That man makes me want to do illegal things just so he can cuff me!"
The two girls giggled as the mamajuana was starting to take its effect.

All three felt a wave of warmth hit their bodies. It was not just one wave. It was multiple waves. Calming waves, slowly going over their body. Each one would be followed by another. It was a warm and tranquilizing tide coming into the shore. It was not mind-numbing though. It did not make them tired. On the contrary, they felt quite energized. They felt aroused. It was not sexual arousal. It was more of an arousal to awareness and life. Their senses had been amplified to everything around them. Suddenly there were more stars in the night sky than ever before. The Milky Way above was a rush to look at.
The crickets seemed to chirp louder. The rustling of the breeze through the surrounding trees

seems to sing its own song. The breeze itself felt like a hug of warm island air. They were very much awake and aware. They were happy. They could feel the smiles on their faces as each corner of their mouths felt as if it were being stretched beyond its limits. Even if they wanted to, they could not lower the smiles in the least bit.

"Hold on. B-R-B." Shelly said as she got up from the picnic table and stumbled face-first into the sand. Carissa and Alan laughed hard enough to feel their guts. Shelly stood up, wiped sand from her face, and giggled, and said, "As I was saying, Be right back."

When she returned she had another bottle of mamajuana and a small duffle bag. Alan grabbed the bottle and opened it up. He took a deep swig and asked, "What's in the bag?"

"Glow-sticks. Come on, follow me." She walked to the shoreline, further down the beach and away from the campsite.

Carissa and Alan sat down in the sand and facing the water. Shelly took two glow sticks out of her bag and dropped them to the sand at her feet. With the glow-sticks held together in both of her hands, she gave them a quick and slight bend. There was a snapping sound as they came to life with color. One was a hot pink color and the other was yellow. They stood out brightly on the dark beach. She took one glowstick in each hand and wrapped her fingers around them. It was in a way a glow-stick would go over her two middle fingers and under her forefinger and pinky. She approached Carissa and put the glow-sticks by her temples. Carissa giggled. Shelly then started to move them slowly to and fro in front of Carissa, only a few inches in front of her face. As the glow-sticks moved elegantly through the air a long streak of light would follow them. Alan used his hands to create a tribal breakbeat on his legs. For Carissa, it was like a private light show. The bright colors surrounded her everywhere she looked. It started slow and as the speed would progress so would the tribal breakbeat being produced right next to her. It got to the point where all she saw was a world of blended color. It was a truly euphoric experience. The three would switch off roles as the night went on. One creating a beat, another would wave the glow-sticks, and one receiving an amazing experience. They cycled through this experience of visual pleasure a few different times. Then Shelly decided to change it up.

She grabbed the small duffle bag and dumped what must have been fifty glow-sticks on the beach. She grabbed two and activated them with a slight twist and snap. She looked to Alan and Carissa and laughed a sinister laugh. They giggled back unsure what she was doing. It did not matter. They were all in a blissfully cheerful state of mind.

With a glow stick held tightly in her hand, she bent it hard and the glowing bright blue liquid spilled out onto her hands. She laughed again as she made a large motion from left to right with her hand. The liquid from the glowstick sprayed all over Alan who was directly in front of Shelly. He looked down and was covered in a spatter of glowing dots. Shelly put her hand over her open mouth and laughed again. Alan reached down to grab a glowstick and broke it apart. He then did the same thing that Shelly did to him and now she was covered in bright yellow dots. Carissa followed suit with two glow-sticks and had nailed them both. They would continue to have this makeshift glow-stick war, as they would chase each other up and down the beach. Time did not matter so neither of them knew how long this had been going on when they unleashed the last of the glow-sticks on one another. They paused. Took deep breaths in between their laughter and could not help but notice the beach now.

For what must have been the space of half a football field, the beach was lit up. The beach looked like a luminescent abstract work of art in the night. It was a neon rainbow that shined brightly into the night. The three stared in silence at it for a moment. Then at each other. Then back at the beach and broke out in laughter. In each of their minds, they were probably wondering how the noise they had made did not attract the attention of any park rangers. They kept expecting to hear a loud voice come out of the shadows yelling at them and then be hauled off in shackles. Thankfully, that did not happen. They admired their work of art as they caught their composure. Carissa looked to the two of them and said, "Well. That was fun." The trance-like emotion of the mamajuana was starting to come off as they began to feel a little more like themselves. They retired to their separate tents and had dreams of rainbows as they slept through the night.

When Alan stepped out of his tent, Shelly and Carissa were already up. He could smell the unmistakable smell of fresh eggs and bacon being cooked on a pan over a small fire in the barbecue pit. They sat down to their island made breakfast that included orange juice, diced pineapple, and plantains. After breakfast, they cleaned up the area and went about their midday separately. Alan had gone on a hike around the island that would lead him to the north part of the island where there was a small mountain. He would sit at the top and overlook the island. He would stare out over the small lakes below and all the foliage beyond that. In the distance he could see Manta Ray Island. Shelly had gone to the beach and get deeply lost in a book while listening to the waves come in on the sand. Carissa walked to the south end of the island on a very small section beach and recharged her chakras with yoga. They would all meet up for lunch later in the day. For lunch, they snuck onto the ferry that had brought a new batch of day-trippers in. One of the amenities of that excursion was food and drink. The three would walk onto the boat as if they were passengers that day and snipe some food. It was not really sneaking or stealing since they knew the people that worked the ferry and those people did not care if these three were taking food. It was only some bread and deli meat along with some fruit they took. It was not really a big deal.

It was late in the afternoon and time for the ferry to leave. The three campers noticed the two newlyweds pack up their camp and get back on the ferry. One night of camping just did not seem worth the trip to the three. But it was no skin off of their back.

At sunset, they sat at the beach with their feet buried in the sand. They passed the last bottle of mamajuana around for a few swigs each. They had no intention of doing a repeat of the night before, as fun as that may have been. This was just enough to get a slight warm buzz. The bright orange ball of light was dipping close to the water. It painted a pretty picture on the clouds above. The three sat in complete silence as they watched the last minutes of the day lower into the ocean. Just as the sun tucked itself in there was a flash of green light that lasted about a millisecond. Shelly laughed out loud as she clasped her hands together, "Whoa! Did you see that?" she asked. Alan said back. "The green flash," Carissa added. "A sailor lost at sea has gotten his soul back."

Except for a camping lantern on the picnic table and the briquettes glowing on the barbeque pit, it was dark around the campsite. Tonight they were going to have hot dogs, baked beans, and s'mores. The baked beans smelled so good as they heated up in a pan on the grill. This was going to be so good. It was just the three of them and other than their light conversation it was pretty quiet. That calm was interrupted by a voice out of the shadows. It was Ranger Will. He appeared out of the shadows like a ghost. They did not even hear him walking through the woods. They did not know he was there till he was in the dimly lit camp area and said, "Hey guys."

All of their hearts dropped into their stomachs. Not only because of the sudden startle they just had, but also because they feared they were about to be in trouble from last night's activity on the beach. Ranger Will's warning about not having ragers on the beach echoed in their heads. Not to mention they had spilled glow-stick fluid all over the beach. They did not know what or if there was a fine for that. If there were, however, none of them could afford it.

Ranger Will said, "I've got some bad news. I'm afraid you are going to have to wrap up your weekend a little early. A storm has started to form without warning in the Atlantic. It has already grown to a cat three, and all the models are bringing it straight to the Peeking Islands. We are going to have to batten down the island which means tomorrow morning we're going to need to you leave."

They all felt a small bit of relief knowing that they were not about to go to jail for poisoning the environment of a national park with glow-stick fluid. They thanked Ranger Will, he disappeared into the darkness of the trees and they finished their dinner as they talked about hurricanes of the past.

The automatic printer in the newsroom of 102.7 WVCX spat out a message from the weather service.

"Storms are forming in the east and heading in a westerly direction. Expect rain with gusty winds. Small craft advisory. Dark days are ahead."

EYE OF THE STORM
(SEPTEMBER 2017)

All Andy could do was imagine. Imagine. Imagine one has only two hours to decide what is important to them that will fit into one rolling carry-on suitcase. Could they do it? What would they pack? Pictures? Perhaps they would pack a small family heirloom? Maybe they would find a way to pack a favorite plush teddy bear that has been with them all of their life. Think about it. What would they pack? Those were the thoughts living in Andy's head as if he were writing a blog.

Andy looked at his open suitcase at three in the morning. Hurricane Tonya appeared as though she had a chance to sneak through a small corridor and hit the island paradise of the Peeking Islands head-on. He had been watching this storm intently and thinking of all the probabilities. Andy flip-flopped between leaving and staying. He had never in his life evacuated from a hurricane. He had never even given it a second thought. He had always believed God would protect him. He thought of Psalm 23:4. Andy had always told himself that unless the Peeking Islands were under direct threat of a Cat 5, he never would evacuate. Perhaps he said this, as he knew that a Cat 5 would never hit. Or, as it may turn out, his father was correct when he taught Andy to never-say-never.

The signs all pointed toward the Peeking Islands taking a hard punch from Tonya. How many times can one person flip-flop between one of only two options? Common sense said to leave. He feared the airport being destroyed along with the entire wharf. If this happened, it would be weeks before he would be able to return home. He would be stuck, on the mainland, with no way of knowing what had happened to his friends or home. He would be stuck, on the mainland, with no way to help. He would be totally out of control of the situation. Andy would be stuck, on the mainland, a refugee displaced with no place to go and spending a lot of money on a hotel and fast food. These were, are, and always will be contributing factors to anyone put in this situation. Particularly anyone that lived on an island that was far from the mainland.

The decision was made. Andy was staying. He had discussed this with his friends. The people close enough to be considered his island family. Some of them were staying and a couple would be leaving. It would not be long before he started to question the dilemma. He was confident in his home. It sat on a lower part of the island, but it was at least eighteen feet above sea level. He lived on the second story away from Cat 3 and 4 surge levels. To the south, there was a large cement structure. Facing west was an open yard covered in a canopy of palm trees blocked in by another large and secure structure and to the east was the street. To the north was an open channel that led to the mountainous Bear Island. To the east of his little island was Isla de la Cabeza Martillo. That would hopefully work as a good barrier island. Andy felt safe where he was. He may have had one of the safest homes on the island. If worse came to worse he could always hunker down in the radio station, only two miles away and in the mountains. There would be nobody else in the building as the plan for a natural emergency was to simulcast with the national broadcasting company on the island. So he was staying.

Andy was starting to receive text messages of concern regarding being in the cone of concern from his friend, Judy. Judy and her husband, Chris were a couple he had met many years ago. They were kind of like older siblings to Andy. These messages had made him once again change his mind. It was around 4:00 Tuesday morning when he started to look at flights off of the island. He looked at Wednesday's flights. This was way too soon to leave. What if he booked this flight and the hurricane turned? As they almost always do. He looked at Thursday flights. They were disappearing fast. Apparently, Andy was not the only one up at this hour that had changed his mind. He found one flight that looked okay. He wanted better. He looked at some other flights and it appeared that the first flight he looked at was the best option. Andy went back to that one and it was gone. Having learned that lesson quickly he booked the next best option without hesitation. Which had him leaving on Thursday. It was a good thing he did. Five minutes later, no flights were left.

At this point he had insurance and peace of mind that he had a way off the island should he decide to take it. Judy called Andy to run her plan of action by him. At the time, she was in Tennessee with her husband on vacation. She was thinking about flying back to the Peeking Islands to make sure her island house was secure and flying out on Thursday. Andy told her that sounded like a good plan. Hurricane Tonya was not scheduled to hit till Sunday night. What were the chances of flights being canceled as early as Thursday? Judy decided to fly from Tennessee to her home in the islands and fly out the same day that he was. As luck would have it, they were even on the same flight.

As for his plan of action, it was still up in the air. He was staying at this point, but at least he had the option to leave the island with the airfare he had purchased. On the chance that he would be flying off the island, Andy needed to pack a bag. This is when it hit him. What mattered to him the most? What could he not live without? What was so important to him that it had to be saved from the hurricane? He starred at the empty suitcase for a good twenty minutes. Andy walked around his home looking at items that held some factor of importance to him. After the bag was packed, he knew the answer to the question of what meant the most to him. The answer was clothing, basic toiletries, and his recently expired passport also mattered. This was a hell of a time for a passport to expire.

Since he was still planning on staying regardless of having a ticket off the island Andy had to re-up on his hurricane kit. His kit was already well supplied. He was a Floridian after all. He knew how to do this properly. A few cases of bottled water, canned foods, candles, batteries, flashlights, a battery-operated clock, and most important after the water, a battery-operated fan. These are items that were in his kit on day one of the hurricane seasons. Taking into consideration the size of this storm he had to make his kit stronger. After a long day at work, he got out just before midnight on Tuesday. Andy went to the local convenience store in hopes that they would have something, anything. To his surprise, they had full shelves. He purchased two more cases of water, five boxes of breakfast bars and as luck would it, they had beef jerky. Andy bought sixty-dollars' worth of beef jerky. He got home and he was ready. He had a meeting on his porch with his neighbor, Joseph, who was a very good, trusted friend. Joseph and Andy were going to be staying. The two discussed the plan to get through this together. Andy was glad to know that he would not be alone going through this. The noise a hurricane produces is scary, loud, and relentless. In the moment it seems to be never-ending. Sometimes just having another person nearby that one is close to is something that can give an unprecedented amount of inner strength. Sometimes that inner strength is all that is needed. Andy was ready for this. He was nervous. He was apprehensive. He was as ready as he could be for impact.

Wednesday was a beautiful day on his island paradise home. It is always picture-perfect weather before a hurricane hit. This is how to predict if it is going to happen. There is no need to watch an overly sensationalized fake newscaster delivering doom and gloom on the TV. If the weather is perfect for three days straight, one could expect a massive storm on the way.

Andy was happily enjoying the day. Then it happened. The residents of the Peeking Islands got the official announcement from the governor. They were under mandatory evacuation. Something to understand about mandatory evacuations is that does not mean people have to leave. It is still a free county after all. It only means that should the choice be made to stay. A person is on his or her own. There will be no 911.

An hour later Andy received a notification on his phone that his flight had been canceled. The great day had suddenly turned sour. His safety net of having a flight off the island had just disappeared. He received another notification that the Peeking Islands was going to take a direct hit. Or at least it was extremely likely. Knowing what a Cat 5 is like and what it can do put things in perspective for Andy on where he lived exactly. It was an island in the middle of the ocean that was only four miles long and two miles wide, surrounded by four other small islands.

It was now that he wanted to leave. But he could not. For some reason, after the governor had told the island they had to evacuate, the head of TSA at the airport decided to get those officers out of harm's way on Wednesday night rather than wait until after Thursday. This decision affected approximately sixteen hundred people that had plans of evacuating on Thursday. In a time of imminent threat and when the people needed a plane the most, TSA had abandoned their post. Despite the massive storm being still four days out.

On Thursday morning around 3:00. Andy had gotten a text from Judy. She had said, "We are leaving the island, I hope you can come with us. If you come with us, bring a pillow, blanket, your laptop, and a small bag. I want to leave by ten." Judy had secured a boat with a friend. It was big enough to fit a few people. It was not quite a yacht, but it would make the trip to the mainland ahead of the storm.

At this point, Andy knew this would probably be his last chance to leave the island. He suddenly had an important decision to make. His gut was telling him that he needed to stay. He could not explain it to himself. There was something inside of him telling him so. Perhaps he was meant to stay and help those who could not help themselves and were left behind. Maybe his plan of flying off the island being canceled was God's way of telling him this. The Lord does work in mysterious ways after all. Common sense was telling him that he needed to jump on this last opportunity of evacuation.

Andy contemplated both sides of his dilemma. One thing that was holding him back was that Judy said, "small bag". He knew that she was the champion of purging. If anyone could pack a bug-out bag in a small backpack it would be her. He tried. Four separate times he took what was in his previously packed suitcase and narrow it down to a backpack. He could not, not even close. He was beginning to think that maybe this was the final sign that he should stay. Again, his gut was talking to him. He had text Judy and asked what she meant by a "small bag". She had said a small carry-on suitcase was fine. At that point, against his gut but going with common sense Andy told her he would go with her. Andy repacked his original roll-on suitcase with a sigh of relief and suddenly realized that he had no idea where she was going. He was not sure that Judy even knew. The plan as far as he knew was, to take the boat west to the mainland, get a rental car, and continue north.

Andy arrived at the wharf where the boat Judy had secured was parked. He walked up to the boat on the dock and was greeted by Judy, who smiled at him and said, "Hey buddy, glad you could make it. Good to see ya!"

"Yeah, I wish my day on a boat with you could be under better conditions. But I have always wanted to spend a day on the water with you, so I'll take my opportunities as I get them", Andy replied.

She said back, "A true opportunist that you are, my friend."

He said back with a smile, "I learn from the best."

Andy then found out there would be some traveling companions. Of course, Judy's dog, Clyde and then there was her best friend, Sonya. Sonya was Russian and her version of English, while very broken, was understandable as long as one would listen carefully. Andy and Sonya knew each other mutually through Judy but were not that close so Andy was thinking this was going to be an interesting trip.

They arrived on the mainland and picked up a car rental that Judy had previously reserved. They hit the highway and started their trek north. Judy was driving with Clyde in her lap, Sonya was in the back, and Andy was in the front passenger seat navigating. He pulled up a traffic app on his phone. The original plan Judy had was to drive up to Tennessee. After looking at the app though it may have been time to change the plan. The highway traffic on the east side of Florida had become a parking lot. It also looked like the storm was leaning a little to the right, which would take it up the east coast. A new plan came into action, which was to head to the west side of the state and try to make it to Tampa. Judy had some friends there and that would give them a night's rest and a clear mind to figure out what to do next. Plus, it would get them out of the current, herd of evacuees.

They did arrive in Tampa and at that point, Judy had driven as far as she could go for the day. As luck would have it, Judy had really good friends in Tampa that were willing to put them up for the night and they would wake up the following day to continue the trip north to Tennessee.

The following day they woke up to an update on hurricane Tonya. It was taking more of a trip to the east and up the east coast. Judy's friends, Thomas and Carrie, convinced them that it would be best if they stayed in Tampa with them rather than get in the messy traffic and continue north. The media was building this up as a storm of the century and mass hysteria would of course be the result. Looking at the helicopter views of the highways on television, it was made to look as if the entire state was evacuating. Andy saw that and wanted no part of it. This is the reason he never evacuated before. Judy's pride was not allowing herself to accept the offer from her friends. Andy wanted to speak up but knew he would be out of place. Thankfully, Thomas was finally able to convince Judy to stay with them in Tampa.

Andy was relieved. He felt much relief. Looking around the house, he felt safer here than he would anywhere else. Thomas was a superstar record producer that traded rock careers for souls. Since of course, he delivered well on that trade, he owned one very pleasing mansion. Just the pool house was more gracious than his apartment back on the island. They had an endless supply of food; a comfortable home with exquisite amenities like a very large pool and it seemed like a strong structure. Even if the storm shifted back west, Andy would feel safe here. He was in a good state of mind.

While it was very good to have the opportunity to bug out to this place, he did feel bad. There were people stuck on the island still, there were his fellow islanders paying money to stay in a hotel, or some that were probably sleeping four in a car. He had been blessed at this point. It was a good blessing, but at the same time, it was not. He was safe, he was housed and fed in the absolute best of conditions. But he did not feel good about it knowing people he cared about were in much worse conditions. Then there was the fact that these are friends of his friend, Judy. He was a stranger and they were taking care of him. For free out of the goodness of their heart. Andy felt guilty on so many different levels.

To say this home they were staying in was a mansion, really would do it no justice. The three evacuees were given a tour of the house and options of where to sleep. There were, at least five bedrooms shown. For some reason, Judy and Sonya chose to sleep in the same room. Andy chose the pool house. Which really, was more like a very nice efficiency apartment. He chose this, as he was a smoker. Knowing a home like this is going to have an alarm that chimes every time a door opens, he wanted to be in the pool house, a building separate from the main house so he would not chime the doors every time he woke up in the middle of the night to smoke.

The next couple of days were spent sitting around the house. Once a day Andy, Judy, and Sonya would go out for food. It was not really because they were hungry. There was already plenty of food in the house. They did a lot of cooking. Sonya made the most amazing salsa Andy had ever had in his life. She made many other great meals over that small period of time. They were all so amazing. She nailed his love of spicy food. One day some time was spent in the pool. Most nights were spent sitting around drinking wine and sharing conversation.

It was around ten o'clock on Saturday night. Andy was texting with friends that were left behind on Peeking Islands. The moment of truth had arrived. The outer bands of a Category 4 hurricane were about to touch his island paradise home. The latest updates of the storm had it wobbling back to the west. This meant the island was going to take a direct hit. Andy sat on a bed in an amazing pool house that he would be willing to pay a high monthly rent to live in. To the people who owned this palace, it may only be seen as a pool house or guesthouse. To Andy, it was a super nice efficacy apartment. He was sitting in his super nice efficiency apartment watching the live radar on his phone. Since he had been through hurricanes before he knew what they were going through on the island. He knew the fear that would be in their hearts. This is the moment one would have prepared themselves mentally, with false self-confidence. Those that had decided to stay or were forced to stay would have spent the past couple of days building each other up with confidence to override the deeply hidden fear. This is the moment when those friends would not be around. They would be in the same place mentally, but a different place physically: Lying in a bathtub with a backpack filled with some food and water, a flashlight, and covered in a mattress.

Knowing what they would be going through, Andy texted a few people on their phones while they still had power and phone service. Even though it was only text messaging, he could hear the tone of fear behind the words. Some of them even admitted to being scared. He gave them whatever strength and power he could through text messages. This might be the last moment he had with them. One would never say that though. One would never say final good-byes at a moment like this. Andy knew it and they very clearly knew it. This was the moment when one starts to doubt his or her personal decisions.

This was when a person becomes very close to the Lord.

He was so scared for his friends and loved ones left behind. As the hurricane approached and the island lost power, he knew that they were all on their own. He was sure they knew it as well. It was at this moment he felt so powerless, so helpless. There was nothing he could do for his friends except pray. He stayed up all night watching the radar on his phone as the hurricane ravished the island.

PENELOPE (SEPTEMBER 2017)

She sat in her historic home on Isla de Cabeza Martillo. She was Penelope. A five foot six, half Samoan half Korean girl. She was slightly overweight. It was not for lack of trying. She worked out often, or at least she was always dressed to work out. When at home on the island, Penelope, would always be seen in brightly colored spandex yoga pants and shirt. She blamed her weight on her dad. She would often joke that it is the only DNA he passed on to her. Penelope was addicted to tech. She always had the latest phones. She was constantly looking at and interacting with her smartwatch. She had an unhealthy amount of friends that she only knew through social media. As for those who only knew her through social media, they would think she led a first-class, world traveling, jet-setting lifestyle. In reality, she was merely a simply complicated small-town island girl. She was a beautiful disaster. Despite her shortcomings, Penelope was a true gem of the ocean. The infectious smile on her face was always alert. She had a heart the size of Jupiter and was the type to put everyone else's needs before her own. She always had a boyfriend but not able to keep boyfriends as she was too good of a girlfriend. That is to say, she gave too much attention and may have come off to some men as clingy.

Only six hours ago she was at a friend's house sitting by a swimming pool playing cards with the neighbors. In the background, they could hear the weather updates from the news. A neighbor down the street blasted rock music from the 1970s, someone else nearby cut plywood to put the finishing touches on their homemade home protection. Scooters could be heard buzzing up and down the streets as people made their final preparations and last-minute adjustments. A police car patrolled the streets playing an announcement on a loop that in one hour the island would be on curfew. It was a moment of clarity for them. The playing of cards and talking shit was only a distraction of the inevitable. The smiles were sincere as they enjoyed this moment in time together.

That was six hours ago. Those friends were no longer there to make her laugh. It was just she and the thoughts in her head. All day, rain bands had hit the island on and off. Some were mild and others were quite strong. None were close to what was about to come. The storm of the century was about to make its headlines.

Penelope sat on her couch listening to the howling of the winds as they started to pick up around her old island home. She had her phone in one hand as she texted back and forth with her friend, Andy, who had evacuated to the mainland. She had plans of evacuating but those plans were changed when TSA had abandoned their posts about four days earlier than they should have. Penelope was one of a few thousand left behind and stranded because of their actions. In her other hand, she held a whistle that was hanging on a string from around her neck. She was a fourth-generation native to the island. There were many tips and tricks she had learned from her family about surviving a storm. One of those was to wear a whistle around the neck. This was so that if the house collapsed on top of a person it would be easier for rescue teams to find them or at least know they were there. It was a grim thought but that was the reality of anyone that sat waiting to go through the storm of the century. She rubbed the whistle lightly between her finger and thumb as if it were a Rosary. It may as well have been, it was going to have much more practical use than God if the worst were to happen. Penelope closed her eyes tightly and shook her head back and forth for a few seconds, as she knew she could not be thinking like that. She needed to remain positive for the next few hours. With a noticeable increase in the wind, the lights flickered. Brownouts had been happening all day. It was only a matter of time before the power went out for good. She sent her final text to Andy saying the power was about to go out and she had to conserve energy. They wished each other well and she powered down her phone.

Penelope plugged in her phone and got up to take one final shower. She tilted her head up toward the showerhead and let the water pound her face in massage mode. She took in this moment of peace and tranquility, as she knew it might be the last shower she took for a while. Once the island lost power the water would no longer be good either. So it could be four days, it could be four weeks. There was no certainty. It was always better to hope for the best but plan for the worst.

After the shower, she sat on her bed listening to the wind outside. She could not see what was happening as all of her shutters had been latched shut. Even if they had not been she could not have seen anything, as it was the middle of the night. "Why do these things always attack in the middle of the night", she wondered to herself. The lights flickered one more time and then went out without coming back on. There was no longer cool air blowing from the air conditioning window unit or any of the floor fans. This was it. Hurricane Tonya had arrived.

She could feel the house sway back and forth in the thunderous wind. Penelope's house was an old house. It was over 150 years old. Many years ago the homes were put together without nails. The builders would interlace the wood, which would help the house survive a storm because it had flexibility. It was like a giant tall wooden puzzle that did not fall over. It was a trick that had been mostly successful with many of the old homes on the island.

She could hear the destruction going on all around her home. The wind was relentless. It sounded as if a Harrier jet were hovering directly over her home and did not let up. Not for a second. For as many storms that she had survived, this was one part she could never get accustomed to. It was the worst. It was a sound that no matter how hard she shut her eyes or covered her ears she could not escape. Then there was the sound of coconuts hitting her home like cannonballs. The sound of a tree collapsing on a neighbor's home or the sound of a car hitting another as they were tossed about. There was the sound of her house flexing in the wind. She could feel the house lean back and forth as it fought to survive and stay in one piece. None of those sounds around her, as bad as they were, even came close to the sound of the wind. It was inexorable, unforgiving, and persistent.

As she sat in the dark with her hand holding a Crucifix tightly, she prayed. Then she heard a noise she did not want to hear. It was the sound of a window shutter becoming loose. It banged up against the house furiously. As it swung back to the window the unmistakable sound of glass breaking was there. The shutter continued to beat against the house. Then she heard another shutter come loose. This one sounded as if it were in the bathroom. With now, two open windows, a wind was bellowing through her home with a fierce updraft. Collectables and keepsakes were flying off of the shelves. The updraft had entered the bathroom and pushed the hatch to her attic open and actually up into the attic. Her shower frame around her claw-foot style bathtub had become twisted in a way that now resembled abstract art. Penelope knew she had to do something. She had to get up from the security of her bed and blankets to defend her home against this bitch known as Tonya.

As Penelope fought the windblown shutter trying to grab it and somehow reattach it to the house, she realized this was a pointless task. She had no chance. She was about to give up and then she noticed something in the street. She saw a bunch of shadows scattered and running in the street in front of her house. Some were small and some were larger. In the matter of one second, she realized what they were. It was a heard of cats and dogs. She knew immediately that they must be all the furry family members left behind at the shelter. Cats and dogs teaming together in harmony to outlast this terror-causing event. As an animal lover, she knew what she must do. It went against every grain of common sense in her being. It went against everything she had been taught by her family. She must go out into the storm. She must get these loving creatures and try to get them into her home for surely the shelter had failed these helpless bundles of joy.

Penelope was now in the street striving for any sense of balance in the fierce wind. She held on to whatever she could to keep from being blown over. She yelled at the pets of the island but they did not respond. She screamed with all of her might to get them to come to her and the safety of her home. They did not listen or maybe they just could not hear her. They did not respond. She was so focused on these poor animals and keeping herself grounded to a palm tree that she did not even notice the sudden rush of a five-foot-high wall of water rushing her direction. It hit her with the force of defensemen blitzing a quarterback. It was like being hit by a train. Resistance against this force of nature was futile. The water swept Penelope straight off of her feet. She was carried in one direction and without warning, carried in another. Within what was probably only a few seconds but seemed like an eternity Penelope was swept out to sea with the island pets. She had no idea how far out she was, but she knew she was land out of sight far. Even in the darkness, she knew she should be able to see some shadows of the buildings or mountains on the island. The towering waves crashed over her repeatedly with no mercy. In between gasping for air and trying to stay above water she would get a brief moment of somewhat calm. Occasionally, she would hear the whimpers of the animals she had failed to save. In between the crashing waves she could feel herself being carried by the strong tidal forces. It was at this moment she looked to the sky trying to catch a glimpse of stars through the thick clouds. She was striving to see one more nighttime sky, as she knew this would be the last chance to see the stars before being among them. As she churned water from her throat she choked out a few Hail Mary's and for one brief second caught a view of the stars. Hurricane Tonya continued to thrash the island and its homes with a vengeance.

AFTERMATH

(LATE OCTOBER 2017)

Andy had not slept a wink all night. He got up to watch the news in hopes of hearing what happened. All of his thoughts were to the Lord and Jesus in Heaven and were for his island paradise home. "Please God, let the island still be there. Please God, let my friends be alive." He said aloud. The island did survive. It got quite lucky actually. The eye of the storm missed its target by about twenty miles. Make no mistake; the island did take a beating. But it was still there. Most of his friends, as he would find out in time, were still there.

Upon finding out the island chain had survived he had new feelings seeping into his head. They were feelings of guilt. He felt guilty for leaving his friends, his island family as it were, behind to fend for themselves. He felt guilty, as he had turned his back on his faith. God would always watch over him and he should have known that. He lost faith in his island. The island had survived many storms in the past and would survive many more in the future.

The storm had passed through. The stress of worrying about that was now over. Now there was new stress to deal with that would be delivered to Andy. While hurricane Tonya did spare the

Peeking Island chain, she still left her mark. The ferry terminal had been destroyed. It was not completely destroyed but it was going to be a few weeks minimal before it was operational again. The airport was ready for immediate operation but the island itself was not. There still was no power and the islands were still on a boil water alert. All forms of communication were intermittent. Supplies were very low even as the national guard via helicopter was delivering them. The island was not a good place to be right now. The governor had issued a state of emergency and banned all traffic into the island chain. Which meant unless a person was part of a rescue and recovery team or with the military. They were not going to be let in. In Andy's mind, he just went from being an evacuee to a refugee. They had spent the past week waiting out the storm at a friend's house on the central part of the Gulf. Though the friends had wanted them to stay, the refugees felt they must move on. Granted the place they were currently in was a very comfortable mansion with every amenity known to man. It was not right though for the three refuges cursed with a moral compass to stay.

Where to head from there was pretty much left to a dart. They remained hopeful that the day would come when they return home would come soon. If not tomorrow, then maybe the day after. Till then they would make the most of it and travel to parts of the county they normally would not get to see. The plan was to leave the rental car in Tampa at their friend's house. They would purchase a map of the United States and a dart set. Wherever the dart landed is where they would fly. This random jet setting would keep them occupied until the time came to come home. At which point they would either fly back to Tampa, pick up the rental and drive to the ferry terminal in South Florida, and ferry to the island or they would fly directly in. The ferry terminal in Daytona had taken a hit almost as bad as the one in the Peeking Islands. That is why they would most likely have to fly from Miami to the Peeking Islands. It all depended on the situation at the moment. They did not know. The goal was to not stress about the unknown. For now, they would travel. With some slightly skilled throws perhaps the dart had kept them mainly on the east coast. It never landed anywhere out west. In their travels, the three refuges had ended up in Tennessee, Ohio, Michigan, and North Carolina.

About halfway through their travels, Andy, Judy, and Sonya met up with Judy's husband, Chris. Judy and Chris were an odd couple whose relationship would be hard to describe any other way than perfection sprinkled with a few punishments along the way. This was a second marriage for both of them. They had been married to each other for twenty-some years. From the beginning, the two had started a variety of businesses together. Which is to say they always worked with each other and were always at home with each other. Sometimes that wear and tear of constantly being around the same person with no alone time would come through. When they bickered or fought it would get ugly. It was very awkward to be a witness to, as they would take it to very personal levels. It was like watching two young siblings fight. There were moments in their lives when they would be separated for a long stretch. It was moments like these that both Judy and Chris truly realized their love for each other. They understood that one could not survive without the other. These were the moments when being around them was a truly remarkable experience. Upon seeing each other for the first time in a couple of weeks, they looked at each other as if it was the first time they met. The look of love, admiration, and respect were alive in their eyes. They did not do a slow-motion movie like run towards each other. They did not even hug, kiss, or hold hands. They were never intimate in public settings. Perhaps they saved that for the privacy of things that go on behind closed doors. That would be something that would remain a secret to the world. What they did show publicly was much better than a hug or kiss. It was the knowledge that they had indeed found each other. There was no other couple on the planet that was stronger than them and they had found their match made in heaven.

After maybe five weeks of traveling the day had arrived. The announcement had been made that the people of the Peeking Islands could return home. It was at their own choice though as they were warned the island chain was still not back up to full sustainability. The power and communications were still intermittent at best. While the boil water alert had been officially lifted, it was still advisable to boil the water. People were warned that while the island chain did not take a direct hit, it still took a hit. It would not be the home they left that they were returning to. There was noticeable damage but people could return home now if they wanted to. That was the story from the news. The story on the local social media was slightly different. Those who had stayed behind were making pleas to those who left not to return yet. They urged that the island was not strong enough to take care of its full population. Water was unusable. The power was not reliable. Communications such as the internet did not work so well either. Despite the fact there seemed to be a lot of them making updated posts on the internet they claiming to be down.

There almost seemed to be an unspoken war going on. It was a divide between those who stayed and those who left. Those that left wanted to return home and get back to normal. Those who stayed almost seemed to take ownership of the island and built an imaginary wall to keep all outsiders out. The commentary between the two sides would get very nasty in the online forums. This broke Andy's heart, as he knew this was not how the people of his island home were. They were supposed to be one big happy family that would support each other through thick and thin. Now they seemed to be a mere reflection of a country divided over for whom to vote. This was not a political vote divide though. This was a divide over who belonged on the island and who did not.

Nevertheless, decisions were made. Andy was no doubt returning to the island, as were Chris and Sonya. Judy was going to stay on the mainland until the island was fully functional. She did not want to deal with the random loss of power and water. She did not want to deal with that when she had access to those simple pleasures on the mainland. To her, it made no sense to go back now. She may have also taken to heart that she was not welcome there by those who stayed and claimed the island as their own. Those people had just been through the most traumatic experience in their lives and were probably suffering from some PTSD. She wanted to give the people of the Peeking Islands a chance to simmer down.

As for Andy, Chris, and Sonya. The time had come. They were returning home. The plan was to fly into Tampa, pick up the rental truck, and drop it off in Miami where they had picked it up. They would stay one night in Miami and start fresh with a flight to the islands.

It was Andy's final night of being an evacuee. He was sitting in a hotel room somewhere on the outskirts of Miami. He did not know where exactly, he did not even know the name of the hotel. FEMA booked the room for him. This was the eve of the day he was to return to his home. He had been away for a total of five or six weeks, or at least what seemed like six weeks. He was not sure. He did not even know what day it was. He just had his first shower in that time that was not in someone else's home. He would be sleeping in a bed for the first time in six weeks that was not somebody else's bed in somebody else's home. Neither of them was his either. It was a hotel. But he was not couch surfing at the mercy of really good and thoughtful friends. He was not splitting a hotel room with others and getting stuck with the roll away because he was the shortest of the group. More importantly than anything else, tomorrow is the day he would get to return home! By all means, he should have felt as if he were marked with good fortune. The reality is that he was quite depressed.

The room he occupied was not exactly ghetto and not exactly a resort. It did have a big television, coffee machine, and even an alarm clock. Something about it seemed off, however.

The curtains were a lace-like material that could be seen through. That is to say that really, there were no curtains. He was on the ground level with a giant sliding glass door. He could see everyone walk by and was pretty sure they could therefore see him. Andy had the feeling that this was the type of room that someone either gets murdered in or purchases a five-dollar bottle of wine, swigs it down, and puts a gun to their head. That is exactly the type of depression he felt at this point. He tried calling several people in his contacts but it was late so understandably they did not pick up. He felt that he needed someone to talk to. He felt alone. He reached one friend, Marisa. But she sounded like she was out with friends and in really high spirits. Andy did not want to be a buzzkill so he cut that short. Though he knew Marisa could tell by the tone of his voice something was not right. She kept asking Andy repeatedly if everything was all right. He kept trying to change the subject to anything but the truth. It was hard to find someone to talk to that late at night. Now Andy knew how his loving fiancé must have felt that Christmas when he was at work and could not pick up when she needed him the most.

Thankfully there were no liquor stores nearby and he did not have a gun. Andy knew that he would be able to make it through the night. Provided he did not get murdered anyway.

The rooms Sonya and Chris occupied were far nicer. They had to pay for their rooms since for whatever reason their FEMA aid did not go through. Since they paid for the rooms they got second-story balcony rooms on the nicer side of the property. As Chris put it, "the FEMA trash gets the trashy rooms." Both Sonya and Chris got a hysterical laugh out of that one. Andy sat alone in his room. He was common FEMA trash, in his trashy FEMA room by himself. He was happy with sarcasm that a good laugh was provided to both of them at his expense. He knew it was a joke and he should not take it personally. But for some reason he did. For some reason being referred to as FEMA trash and being laughed at kind of hurt. Even though he knew it was meant as a joke.

Andy was not sure if it was really depression he was experiencing. He had spent the past six weeks on edge. Stressed about what has happened to his island paradise home. He was relieved that so far he had heard from many people that stayed who had made it through the storm. There was one he had heard rumors that did not. He was going to try and not think about that right now and focus on going home instead. He had been living from place to place off of other people's generosity for the past six weeks. He was going to owe some big favors. Having the feeling of being an imposing nuisance was a huge stress factor. Staying in somebody else's home, infringing on their space, was a massive stress factor. His hours had been all bent out of shape. Waking up every day at 7:30 in the morning and not getting to sleep until an hour or two after midnight. He had no daily naps that he was accustomed to. Not working, not making money. These were all things that weighed on his mind.

Now, as he sat in a true moment of solitude for the very first time in six weeks, the reality of it all came crashing down. It had the same feeling as being on a massive adrenaline rush and then, without warning, it was gone. There was nothing left. He was so tired. Andy was mentally and physically spent. He was on fumes and had nothing left inside of him. Yet he knew that when he got home the next day he was going to have to turn it up and get to work on rebuilding. For the first time in six weeks, he heard quiet. He was on the home stretch and rather than relief he felt a deep sadness. He thought about all the eighties' hair bands and their one required ballad song that had a video showing their tough life on the road. Always on a bus and missing home. He wondered if this was how they felt at the time.

Maybe he was not depressed. Maybe he was sad. Sad at how privileged he was yet at the same time he felt disadvantaged. After hurricane Tonya hit everyone was in a rush to get home. Yet, the powers that be would not let them get home. They were not allowed in. Everyone had gone from being evacuees to refugees. They were people without a home. They were people with no glimpse of the future. Everyone had been terribly upset that they would not be allowed to return right away. This was not fair. Many felt slighted at this. It was an outrage even!

If one took the time to think about it, how bad did they really have it? A large percentage of the Peeking residents still had a home to get to. They just could not get to it this second. But they knew they would eventually. It is not like everyone would be forever without a home or even a month. They would all eventually be allowed back home. That is a given.

Which lead to the thoughts that made Andy sad. How could he honestly call himself a refugee? He thought to himself as he sat staring at an open suitcase that had in it what he had imagined to be the essentials to take on a trip. He asked out loud to himself, "How bad do I really have it?"

It is not like his hometown was bombed and he lost everything he had. His home and everything in it was still there waiting for him to return. It is not like he was forced out of his home by some religious nut jobs and sent searching for any cave he could call home. Nor had he been exiled from his country with no way to enter another. He was definitely not starving. He had not once wondered where and when his next meal would be. In fact, he figured he might have gained weight in the past six weeks. He did not have a wife and kids; He had not stayed up late at night wondering what will happen to his family tomorrow. He did not have to fight for food and water. He had showered at least once every day. As he sat there truly alone for the first time in six weeks, he thought about the people in the world who do have to go through those types of daily routines. They don't go through it for only six weeks as he did. They go through it for much longer. Sometimes, perhaps even a lifetime. To Andy, those were the true refugees. There were nine-year-olds on the other side of the planet who were far more mentally tough and hardened than he could ever know. They did not know depression. They knew survival. They did not take happy pills. They created solutions. Those are the ones on the run that do not know if where they sleep tonight will be where they sleep tomorrow. Those are the people he was sad about tonight. Those were the people that will be in his prayers tonight for a better tomorrow. For he remained to be a very lucky individual with a soft bed to sleep in. He would have a shower tomorrow morning with a cup of coffee and a home to drive to. Then again, he may have only been tired.

The flight back to the Peeking islands was surreal. The surface of the water they flew over was not water. It was all floating seagrass. As they circled the islands they could see that the trees had been stripped bare. They were naked. They looked, as trees must in the north during winter, minus the snow. One could see a whole lot more than before without the trees. There was no green. The islands were all brown and wind-burned. Boats that had been tossed across the road were still on the side of the road. Small homes had been moved. Trailers overturned or demolished. Parts of the Peeking islands no longer existed. Where once a small community stood, was now only barren land. Businesses had been destroyed. During the flight over everyone on the plane had taken it in with his or her own coping mechanisms. There were people like Chris, who was unable to shut up. He was commentating constantly on his memories of what used to be and what is now. Others like Sonya could only say, "wow" and "Oh my" repeatedly. There were a few like Andy. He was silent. He could not think of any vocal response. He was stunned and perhaps in shock. It was surreal.

Chris, Andy, and Sonya had landed and picked up Chris's car that had been left at the airport. Thankfully that parking structure and everything in it was spared. Sonya was first to be dropped off. As they drove around the island chain the mood was somber. Not one word was spoken. It may have been because they were in awe of what they were seeing. Perhaps it was they were travel weary and they knew the end was near. They were all on the home stretch. The great thing about experiencing a traumatic event like this with friends nearby is that they were always nearby. The bad thing was, they were always nearby. Everyone was on his or her last string. As they surveyed the damage they knew peace and tranquility were only moments away in the middle of this disaster.

After they dropped Sonya off, Chris and Andy headed to the animal shelter to pick up Andy's cat, Tino. As they crossed the bridge to Isla de Cabeza Martillo they could tell this was a part of the chain that got hit the worst. This is what took the brunt force. As would be expected. The island was nine by three miles. Its length covered all of the island chain. It was fairly mountainous and served as a barrier island for the rest of the island chain. Now it was mostly barren in some areas.

Homes had been completely flattened. All that was left of many of the homes was a foundation and cement steps. Beach sand still covered some of the side streets. One could see clearly through the areas normally hidden in foliage as all the trees had been stripped bare. Andy wondered about his home and what it would look like, as he was only one island over. Chris felt optimistic because he lived in Vista Bahia. He had good feelings his home would still be there. Andy was not thinking about his home at this second. He was thinking about Tino. He felt so bad about leaving the cat behind but he had no choice. He did not know where he was traveling to or how he would be getting there. Having Tino would have been a huge hindrance. He knew that was a horrible way to think of the companion that had provided him with so much love. He had just hoped that Tino would forgive him and be as happy to see Andy, as he would be to see Tino.

That answer came soon enough as Chris and Andy approached the animal shelter and parked the car. Or at least, what should have been the animal shelter. Chris parked the car and they got out and stared at an area where there should have been a building. There was nothing left of a structure. It had been leveled. There were cages, tables, toys, and equipment scattered over the entire area. Both men stood in silence. Chris was the first to speak. He said, "Well, the cages are open. Maybe he got out and found a place to hide."Andy only looked at Chris. There was no vocal response. Chris added, "If he did, he will find his way home. He is a cat. It's what cats do." With his hands on his hips and still surveying the land, Andy said in a distant tone, "Yeah." Chris said, "Well, not much we can do here, you ready to go home?"

Andy stood at his doorway after being dropped off by Chris. He was relieved to see his home still standing from the front. He put his key in the door, closed his eyes, and took a deep breath. When he opened the door he was thankful to see the ceiling fans on. It meant he had power.

It was a disaster inside, but not from anything hurricane Tonya had done. It was just as he had left it. Hurricane kits were open and ready to be used. Cases of water ready to be drunk and about sixty dollars worth of beef jerky and energy bars ready to be eaten. It served as a reminder that his original plan was to stay. The rest of the house was the same mess he left it. Andy was not messy in a disgusting way. He was just a man that lived on his own and was comfortable with everything around him. The living room was more of storage space or a room he threw stuff on days that he did clean. He rarely threw away stuff as he was a bit of a hoarder. The living room had stacks of empty cardboard boxes because one never knew when it would be time to move and those boxes would come in handy. That and many other useless items covered the floors and corners of Andy's home. It may have been filthy to some but Andy knew where everything was at all times.

He had stepped out on the porch and viewed his street. It still had a light dusting of beach sand covering it. Relief workers mostly cleaned the street but there was still sand there. Large piles of debris and foliage were stacked up on the side of the street. The trees were naked. Normally he could not see halfway down the block with the trees blocking the view and making him feel secluded. Now he could see all to the end of the street. He was out in the open. The smell was the worst part. It was a mixture of he did not know what. It smelled putrid for starters. Perhaps it was a mix of dead trees and plants and some of the island critters that did not fare so well. It was bad. Andy knew that much. The hot midday sun baking it all did not help. Andy stood on his porch surveying the damage of his neighborhood. It was not as bad as he had thought it would be, but it was not great. There was some rebuilding that would have to be done. Some fresh re-starts had to be ignited. It was not just the island he was thinking of.

One of the things that Andy had noticed while he was away was the war that seemed to be taking place on social media. There seemed to be a divide starting between those who stayed and those who left. Thankfully one of the first things he noticed was that this drama existed on social media only. Once back home he noticed the Peeking Islands were a community again. Everyone would bust ass working and helping each other out all day. Then when the sun went down they would go to a bar and drink. It was like the old days that he had missed so much. The love between everyone was something that could be found nowhere else on the planet. This island chain was something special that way.

Andy walked the beach on Isla de Cabeza Martillo. It was a beach where if one looked on a map of the island it was shaped like the silhouette of a man's face. The old-time locals called it 'First Sunrise Beach'. The name of the town it was located in was Looking Man. It was like if this were a man, he would be facing east and he would be the first person in the U.S. to see the sunrise. Andy sat on the beach looking to the ocean taking in the past three years of his life and the storm. The past three or four years have been nothing but a storm. In the aftermath of it all, he realized a few things. First and foremost, this little slice of paradise was strong. Big things come in small packages. He always knew it was a tightly- knit community. The way this chain of islands came together to start to clean and continue to rebuild went way beyond explanation. He loved his island paradise home and all of the people here that made it unique. He promised himself that he would never leave this place as it would always be home. He also learned to not take the little things for granted. Every day he could walk out and see that he was surrounded by natural beauty. At times he had forgotten to take notice of it. Perhaps he started to take it for granted. He did not realize how lucky he was to have his commute to work be a five-minute walk through the streets surrounded by tropical trees. The old saying, "You don't know what you've got till it's gone" rang very true in his head right now. Once this all grew back he would never take it for granted again. The thing that mattered the most though was the people. The people that made this place what it was to him. Everyone may not all get along or run in the same circles. But they all share a common bond. They all love this place, even if for different reasons. When it came down to it, they would do anything for one another. They may be different from one another in their special ways. They may have differing opinions and some of those opinions ran strong. One fact remained. Everyone there, was now a family. As Andy sat and looked out into the ocean, he heard some old school breakdance music play from behind him. He looked over his shoulder and saw a jeep filled with younger people. It took off with its music blasting. Andy noticed he was looking in the direction of where the animal shelter used to be. It was now an empty lot with a for-sale sign on it. As the jeep drove away the music faded. That was the music he remembered from his younger years. The world was a different place then. He looked at the empty lot where the animal shelter used to be. He heard the music. A smile hit his face as Andy had an idea. A seed had been planted.

ROSIES DAY OFF

(FALL 2017)

Rosie walked into her house after a blissful Sunday morning service at Our Lady of the Lake, located in the middle of Isla de Cabeza Martillo. It was in a small hollow in the middle of the Centro de la Isla mountain range and almost right on Round Lake. She wanted to change before going out for the rest of her day. Sunday was Rosie's special day. It was Rosie's time. She had dedicated what seemed to her, most of her waking hours to other people. She had her boyfriend that she devoted much of her time, as that was what she wanted. He was her knight in shining armor. He was her world away from the world. He put her up on the highest pedestal and worshipped the ground she walked on without smothering her. He treated her like a queen while keeping himself equal. Although he was the type that could get a different woman of his choice every night of the week, he was fiercely loyal to her and would always be there for her through thick and thin. She had found him at a rather low point in her own life and he was the one that brought her out of despair, other than God, of course.

Rosie was the music director for 102.7 WVCX. Which meant that before or sometimes after her daily air shift she would spend a couple of hours on a computer designing the music playlist a couple of days ahead for the radio station. It was a job that was neverending and had to be done by someone. She was that someone. Then she co-hosted the night show with Andy. Which led to Andy. He was a special case just in himself. Whether on the air or in his own life, he needed guidance and it appeared she had been the one charged with providing such guidance. She did not mind doing this. She enjoyed working with Andy. At times he could be a handful of never-ending drama, but he was a good soul with his heart in the right place. Occasionally he needed to be nudged onto the right track from time to time. After all of that, but not any less important was her time given to the church and a variety of charities she worked with. None of this was a hindrance to her life. These were all things she sincerely loved to put her heart into. They were her life.

Sunday, after church service, was Rosie's day of Rosie. The plan was usually the same. She would gather a basket of fresh bread, deli meat, fruit, and some juice and head to Los Pradas de Olas. It was a large wooded area that, because of its shape, would look like a forest area waving from the view of a plane flying over it. It was a mixture of wooded areas and meadows that took up roughly 800 acres of space on Manta Ray Island.

From her home in Aullando Cala Lobo, she hopped into her jeep and took a right onto the Peeking Highway. The Peeking Highway was the main road that went around the outer edge of four of the five islands. It hit all of the islands except for Isla Fantasma, which was a national park and had no roads on it or no bridges to it. If one were planning on island hopping, it was the road to take.

Rosie could have taken a left and been to her destination a lot sooner. She did enjoy the drive through and it gave her a chance to take in some of the island's natural beauty that had attracted so many people there. The first part of the journey would be about an eight-mile stretch to the southern tip of Isla de la Martillo. Almost as soon as she had started the journey she had to pull over to make way for a platoon of cadets jogging from the opposite direction. They were from the Rome Military Academy that she shared the town with. As they went by she could hear their adult cadre sing something about going to wake his leader from his bed and rolling him over to find out he was dead. Then the cadets would take over the cadence by chanting they were men at war or something like that. It broke her heart to wonder what they were teaching those poor boys locked away in there and she said a small prayer for them. As they passed she pulled back onto the highway. It would take her past Our Lady of the Lake on her right and First Sunrise beach to her left. Then down to the southeast edge of Martillo where she would pass Shady'tn. That was where those who chose to live a life away from others lived in tents. As she passed by, she said a prayer for them.

Rounding off to the right she drove across the bottom of Martillo, which took her through a marshy area and another right turn took her six miles up the west side of Martillo, passing by some small seaports and towns along the way. Rosie would then take a left onto a one-mile bridge that would put her on the southeast corner of Bear Island. From here she could take the short and easy route to the left or the longer and scenic route to the north. She took a right and went for the scenery. This would take her up towards the north part of the island where she would be on the backside of the Vista Bahia Mountains and three small fishing seaports. At the second seaport was a sign that said, "Charleston, SC. 260 miles." It had an arrow pointing north into the sea. The highway would continue to wrap around Bear Island and take her past the bottom of the island. To her left, she would see the Vista Bahia mountains tower above her. To her right, she would see Isla Sirena across the water. This drive around Bear Island would be a seven-mile trip around the whole island that took her almost to where she got on it.

Next, she took a right onto the half-mile bridge to Isla Sirena. Once again, instead of taking the short route, she took a left for the long route. This would be about a six-mile trip. Heading from the north tip of the island to the south tip she would have the water on her left and the Sirena Mountains on her right. Her place of work was at the top of those mountains. She would breeze by two small fishing seaports. Small enough that if one blinked, they would be missed. She would then cross the Little Daku river. It was a river that cut directly through the middle of the island from east to west. She would then be taken to the southern tip of the island for a quick turn back to the north. On her right were the mountains and on her left, she could see Manta Ray island. She would cross the Little Daku river again and at the northern tip of the island take a left onto a bridge that may have been a quarter-mile long onto Manta Ray. She was almost there. One left hand turn off of the highway and onto Los Pradas de Olas road, where she would drive one mile, and then she would be at Los Pradas de Olas. She could have continued on the trend of taking the scenic route. That would have added another fourteen or sixteen miles to her trip. She would have crossed the Big Daku river twice, gone through more mountains, and beyond the main seaport. The seaport was two miles long and traffic was always packed and dangerous as it was filled with tourists' blind to everything around them. She also would have driven through a couple of small towns along the way. She was satisfied with her journey today, she pulled into her final destination.

She parked her jeep and grabbed her picnic basket and blanket. She saw a sign that said, "Future sight of Blue Sea Condos." It had a number to call Swarnson Reality. They were the big realtors on the island chain. It broke her heart to know that someone was willing to tear all this down in the name of money. It did not stress her out too much though. She knew that sign had been up for quite some time. There was a legal battle over who owned the property and who could do what with it. So, it would most likely never happen.

She stepped into a shady part of the meadows. She had trees all around her as well as palm fronds. Beautiful trees that only seem to be found on islands that surrounded her. Rosie took out her lunch. She had some fresh deli ham that she had topped off with pineapple and cilantro. She spread some mustard on the ham to add a little more flavor. She ate some star fruit as a side and an all-organic juice to wash it all down. Rosie sat on her blanket in her private little world and said a prayer thanking God for the meal she was about to eat. She prayed for those less fortunate and then enjoyed her lunch one bite at a time. Slowly taking it in, as she had nowhere to be today. Enjoying the moment that was hers. When she was done, she neatly packed everything back into the basket and put any scraps into a zip lock bag.

Now it was her time to speak to God one on one. She took in the nature around her. The grass beneath her bare feet was soft. It was not the thick hard feeling grass found in most of Florida. It was short, thin, and soft. Almost like cemetery grass soft. Even the ground seemed to have cushion to it. The breeze lightly blew through the leaves and fronds around her. They made a comforting sound as it let her know God was listening. The air around her had an almost perfect feel to it. It was warm, but not muggy hot. The smell of the flowers around her was an intoxicating pleasure for her to take in with her nose. Rosie took a lung-filling deep breath. She would hold it for ten seconds. Then she would let it out through her nose. She would do this for a couple of minutes. Almost going further into a deep trance with every breath. She reached into her pocket on her loose-fitting yoga-style pants to retrieve her Rosary. It was not there. She checked the other pocket. It was not there either. She must have left it in her jeep. This was okay. She was not going to leave the place she was at now. That meant either physically or mentally. For every problem, there was always a solution. To keep track of where she was on the Rosary she would touch the thumb of her left hand to her forefinger in place of a bead. With each Hail Mary, she would move her thumb to the next finger. On the fifth, she would close her fist. Then she would do the same on her right hand. When she closed her right hand into a fist she would know she had gone through ten beads. As for keeping track of the decades, well she was just going to have to remember that. When she finished her Rosary she clasped her hands together as she looked to the sky and said out loud, "Thank you, Lord, for this beautiful day."

Next on her agenda Rosie would head back to her home on Martillo and enjoy an evening off with her boyfriend watching movies and sipping on wine. But these past few hours belonged to her. She did not feel guilty about turning her phone to do not disturb. For all of her hard work and devotion, this was her time. Rosie did not have the self-righteous belief that she was a Saint. She just did the job of one…three miracles at a time. This was okay. As even Saint Monica, occasionally needed a break.

ANDY'S DAY OFF

(FALL 2017)

It was Sunday and Andy did not have to work. He had been out all day at the beach on the main island with his friends Steve, Mick, and Tony. They had spent the day playing volleyball. None of them were great at it. They had fun playing the game with each other though and it was just a good excuse to go to the beach. After a few drinks at a tiki bar overlooking the beach, Mick and Tony had left. They had families to get home to. Steve and Andy sat while watching the sun dip down into the water. Steve had a beer and Andy had tea. Andy asked Steve, "You remember the music we listened to in the late eighties? The dance music?"

Laughing, Steve said, "I remember the clothes you wore! You looked like a total dork dude!" Keeping a straight face Andy said, "You wore the same clothes, dude." Steve told him, "Yeah, but the difference was that I made them look cool." Andy shook his head, "Always be the same Steve, won't you? Anyway, I want you to remember back to those days and hear me out on an idea I had the other day." Andy spoke of his idea and Steve appeared to listen. When he was done Andy asked, "So, what do you think?" Steve said, "I don't know man, sounds a little old school. You think there is a need for that? Plus running a business like that is a very hands-on business and doing so would be a nighttime gig. You already have a nighttime gig." Andy asked, "What? The radio station? I'll quit." Steve perked up, "You can't quit that! You are Andy Fucking Chelios, king of the island mountains, a man of the people."

Andy did not know if Steve was playing with him or not. He was probably playing with him. Andy just said, "Dude, you are supposed to be my friend. How about some positive support here."

"Okay, okay. You want to do that? Go ahead. Hell, I'll even help you when and if I can. I mean what was it that old carney bum in California you told me about said? Grab the stars?" Steve made air quotes as he said that in a mocking tone. "Never reach lower than the stars and he was not a bum. He was a very smart man that gave me the most profound advice anyone ever gave me."

He also gave you that stupid monkey thing you still keep on your dresser, right?" Steve said still laughing. "The grinder monkey. Yeah"

"Dude, you realize it's not a real grinder monkey right? A grinder monkey grinds an organ. Hence the name GRINDER monkey. All that thing does is dance around banging symbols."

Andy said back, "You missed the point. He is not called a grinder monkey because he grinds an organ. He is called a grinder monkey because he works the grind. He is a never-ending street hustler who works the daily grind entertaining the masses. It's the basic story of my whole fucking life, Steve."

Steve put his hands up in the air, "whoa, okay. Hands up, don't shoot. Hey man, I am your friend, so whatever you want to do I am one hundred and fifty thousand percent behind you." Andy thanked him and Steve's eyes lit up as he said, "Oh, there is the chick I totally want you to meet". Andy replied, "Dude, I hate being set up. And I don't need a woman, I am already in a relationship remember? Nina?"

"Bro, Nina's dead."

"Okay, so it's a long-distance relationship."

"Between here and Heaven? Yeah, I'd say that's some distance bro. Anyway, this chick, her name is Marie. She is super hot but"

"But what? See, this is bullshit, dude." Andy interrupted.

"Well, she's a little crazy. Okay, okay. She is a lot crazy. Like to the point it can be almost embarrassing speaking to her. But she is totally hot. You dig? So I guess she is like a Vespa."

"Vespa?" Andy asked.

Steve said with a dirty smile, "Yeah you know. The scooter. Everyone wants to ride one, but nobody wants to be seen riding one."

"You know I own a Vespa right?"

"Huh? Yeah man, so she is perfect for you! Plus…"

Andy put his face in his hands and said, "Oh fuck, here we go."

"Well, she has this friend that I really want to hook up with but she will only go out with me if there are other people there."

"Smart girl. I see, so this is not really you trying to better my life. This is so you can get laid! You know there is something seriously wrong with your head right?"

"Yeah man, but it's not that head that I'm looking to use with her. You get me, bro?"

"You're a fucking asshole man. But you're my fucking asshole. So, sure, what the fuck."

"Oh, I'll be fucking her asshole all right. I'll set it up and let you know when."

"Cool, In the meantime, bro, get some help and take whatever meds they give you. And you best wrap that stick boy when your finger banging Mary Jane Rottencrotch!"

Steve responded, "I left that bitch behind at the academy twenty years ago bro. Who's the best?"

"Bravo Company!"

"Who's got it better than us?"

Andy yelled back, "Nobody!"

Steve asked, "What's wrong with your arm son? Is your arm broken? Get that salute in the air. "

They stood at attention, saluted each other, did a chest bump, and barked at each other like vicious dogs ready to fight for money. Laughing, they paid their tabs, left the tiki bar, and headed to their homes.

REBOUND (FALL 2017)

Andy and Marie sat at the Wharfside Bar overlooking the historic seaport on their second date. The historic seaport was on the main island and was the largest on the island. It was two miles long. It hosted a variety of watersport companies for the tourists, the ferry terminal, and of course an endless supply of shops, eateries, and bars. As it was on the west side of the island it faced west and was an excellent place to view a sunset while people watching. The Wharfside bar was fitting to its name. It had a rustic look to it. It looked old. It was mostly a place for locals to go as it looked too run down for the typical tourists. The house musician had been there for ages. Andy could not remember anyone else filling the daytime slot. His shift would start very music intensive. Then as the day wore on to late afternoon the setlist became a little more talkative. It may have been the beer. Andy and Marie were on their second date. The first was with her friend Stephanie, and Andy's friend, Steve. Stephanie and Steve did not hit it off so well. On the other hand, Andy and Marie made a slight connection. It was good enough to call for a second date anyway. They sat over appetizers and drinks and watched as the ferry left the dock for the mainland.

"I'm so sorry about my friend Steve. He may seem like an asshole, but when it comes down to it, he's someone you want on your side"

Marie smiled politely and said, "Well, I'm sorry it did not work out for him. Stephanie was more than a little put off and I am glad that you were my date and not him."

Andy said, "Yeah, well. Deep down." He paused and took a deep breath, "Deep down, he is a good guy."

Marie asked, "Deep down? Just how deep do you think?"

Laughing Andy said while motioning down to the ground with his hands, "Maybe like the abyss level deep."

Andy continued to speak as he changed the subject, "So you were saying you lost everything during Tonya?"

"Yeah, everything. My house was flattened. There was nothing left. Not even what was in the house out by First Sunrise. I'm so devastated by it."

Andy asked with sincere interest, "So what did you do? I mean where are you now?"

"I found a place with roommates here on the main island. It's not my house, but it is what it is."

"And you said you had a boyfriend at the time? What happened to him?" Realizing what he had just asked, Andy quickly prayed that the answer was not that he died in the storm.

She answered, "I don't know. He was an asshole and I just got sick of it. When we got back home after Tonya I told him I wanted him out of my life."

Andy, trying to sound sincere, said, "Oh. I am sorry."

Marie said, "It's okay. It was all for the better. Now I'm just going to keep on keeping on."

They finished up lunch and walked along the seaport. As much as it was overrun by tourists Andy loved the seaport. It was a fun place to be and do. Which made it a great place to take a date. There were enough distractions around that would remove any of the shyness, getting to know you, awkwardness of a second date.

They passed an area that was filled with carnival-type games for cheap prizes and Marie asked, "Oh hey! You want to play some games?" Appearing to have a reflective moment Andy said, "I'm not so sure. I have had some bad experiences with those in the past."

Marie asked, "Oh really? Do tell. What happened?"

Andy said, "Ah, a bad experience. But hey, look, there is an arcade, you up for some foosball?"

She agreed and they went into the arcade. In addition to foosball, they played pinball and some other games. Andy was intrigued. Here stood a girl that enjoyed geeking out on old school arcade games as much as he did. There might be something here he thought. But was he ready for this?

The two were leaning on a railing looking out to all the boats coming in and out of the seaport. Some were filled with tourists returning from snorkeling excursions fishing charters earlier in the day. Some were old wooden schooners that were just a cruise on the sea. They were enjoying milkshakes. Andy had chocolate and Marie had strawberry. Andy had a giant pretzel. He was not really eating it, as he was still rather full from lunch. He was feeding it bit by bit to the pelicans in the water below the old wooden dock that had been recently repaired from the hurricane.

Andy nervously spoke. "So, Marie." She answered, "Yes?"

"I've had a great time today. I'd like to see you again. I know you just got out of a relationship, but would you want to see each other again?" To his surprise, a big smile lit her face and she said, without hesitation, "Yes!"

"Cool, cool" Andy said. He was surprised as she was a hot girl. She was nighttime soap opera hot. Why would a girl like that be interested in him? Plus, if he were honest with himself, why would he date someone now? He was nowhere near over Nina. That situation was still fresh in his mind. Perhaps he asked because he was not expecting her to say yes. He said, "I mean, I'm not talking about dating exclusively right now. You still have your ex thing I'm sure you are getting over and need some space from men. But, maybe in a while, given some time, we could give it a try and see where it goes?"

Marie smiled big and said yes.

"Cool, cool," Andy said. So we can hang out like this for now and I won't bring it up again till you are ready and you let me know. Cool?"

Marie told him, "Absolutely."

Andy said, "Awesome. Because a long time ago there was this chick I knew that I wanted to date. She had broken up with her boyfriend and I wanted to make a move but did not want to swoop right in. I wanted to keep silent, give it some time, and make a move when she seemed ready to move on. Meanwhile, while I was waiting, some other dude moved in and I lost my chance."

Marie said, "I get it. I understand."

Andy told her, "Cool, because like, I want to be respectful and give you your space but, learning from my mistakes in the past, I don't want to lose my chance."

Marie laughed and said, "okay."

Andy smiled and put out his hand for a handshake and asked, "So, we good?"

Marie laughed again and shook his hand as she said, "We're good. Thank you."

For the next two months, Andy and Marie saw a lot of each other. They did not go on any dates or even hang out for lunch. They would see each other in passing. She would always smile when she saw him because he always had something positive to say. He always seemed to have something great to say about his day and seemed like an upbeat kind of guy.

She appreciated those small moments of her day when they would see each other in passing. Whether it be, in a grocery store or walking around downtown. Even if it was something as small as a wave and smile as he walked by the restaurant that she was a server at. She would look up from the table she was serving and see him walking by on the street as he gave her a smile and wave. His positive attitude was infectious for her, although it always seemed as if there were something he was hiding behind that smile.

Marie focused on the positive vibe she picked up on though as that is what she needed. The past four or five months of her life had been nothing short of crazy. First, she had lost her house and a good portion of all of her belongings in the hurricane. Then she got out of a stressful and toxic relationship. She had been in and out of about four different roommate situations in that short four-month amount of time and almost just as many jobs. She could not hold her life together anymore for whatever reason.

She wanted to give Andy a chance but she had other problems. There was this guy she had been dating for the past two months and he was okay. The problem was that he had a crazy ex-girlfriend that was not letting the relationship go so easily. It was a situation where the two had broken up but only one of them got the memo. This girl would call Marie's phone and leave threatening voicemails. How she got Marie's number she had no idea. This girl would stalk Marie and even went as far as to vandalize her car. Marie seriously was at her breaking point. Then there was this text Andy had about a week earlier. It was weird. It was a picture of a handwritten poem for her. It was something about patience and understanding. It included what appeared to be his feelings for her. She did not know the details. She did not read the whole thing. She thought, "Who does that anymore? Writing poems? What are we? In third grade?" Marie could not take it anymore. Since the day Andy had sent that weird text with the poem she had decided to ghost him and do her best to avoid him. She decided it was time for a change. In the middle of the night, she packed what belongings she did have into her car. She disappeared, never to be heard from again.

STEVE'S DAY OFF (WINTER 2017)

Steve opened his eyes and felt immediate pain in his right leg. There were aches and pains all over his body, but the worst was in his leg. Lying on his back, he propped his head up to access his situation. The pain in his leg felt worse when he noticed the way it twisted around and the bone sticking out. He let out a yell of frustration, as he knew he could not move from his position. His vision was blurred and his mind was still foggy as he tilted his head to the left. He saw another man lying next to him. He was in jeans and a black T-Shirt. His neck was contorted, his face swollen, and his head was lying in a puddle of blood. Steve let out another scream of frustration as memories of the day that led him here started to fill his clouded head.

Steve stood at the bottom of the Centro de la Isla Mountain on Isla de Cabeza Martillo. It was the highest mountain on the island chain. It was Steve's day off. It was his first day off in what seemed like a very long time. Being it the nature of his work, he had to stay on the island during the wrath of hurricane Tonya. Whether it was to help those in need or arrest those putting others in need, he was there. The aftermath of the storm was not easy. The island would need a lot of rebuilding. This would be both physical and mental. Everyone had been through much turmoil and tensions were high. Steve was no different. This was his first day off in probably six weeks. He needed a release. Steve was an adventurist. He sought after high adventure. Whether it was climbing around on rope challenge courses, zip-lining, or white water rafting, Steve had a heart for thrills. Those are things he would do on vacation. Climbing this mountain he did on every day off. It was a place to challenge his body. When he got to the top he could reward his mind by looking out over the Atlantic Ocean or turning around and looking over the entire island chain he was responsible for. It was his way to recharge.

Steve parked his car in the parking lot of the Our Lady of the Lake Church and organized his gear in front of him. He went over a quick inventory checklist in his head. He had a climbing harness, a few carabiners, a belay device, a rope that was nine millimeters, a helmet, a chalk bag, his hiking shoes that were down-turned with a pointed toe. He had four bottles of water, fresh fruit, and a granola bar. That was all he needed for a basic trip. He repacked his bag quickly and tossed it over his shoulder as he walked toward the mountain thinking that he forgot something. As he walked he could not shake the feeling that he was missing something. He just could not figure out what. He went through his inventory again in his mind. At about three hundred paces away from the car he was at the base of the mountain. He took a look up to the sky then to his wrist to check the time. He sighed heavily as he looked at his bare wrist. He forgot his watch. Visually in his mind, he could see it sitting on the dash of his car. He thought a minute about whether or not he needed to know what time it was. This was his time away. So therefore, time is not of the mind. But it would keep him aware of his heart rate and that was important. He let out a long grunt as he went back to his car, retrieved his watch, and put it on.

For the second time, Steve stood at the base of Centro de la Isla Mountain. There was a sign that made two offerings. To the left was a trail that twisted around and through the mountain range. It was a beautifully scenic trail that would take those that don't want to climb to the top. With much to look at on the way, it was no doubt an awesome way to the top. Steve did not come here to hike. He came to climb. He heard a voice call out to him. It said, "Hey officer Steube!" Steve looked behind him and said, "Hi Father Murchandha!" Father Murchandha was the pastor of Our Lady of the Lake. He had some kids with him and they all greeted Steve. He said back, "Hi kids! How are you all today?" One of the kids said, "Great! We are doing Catechism class outdoors today"

Father Murchandha approached Steve and with a laugh asked, "You still remember your Catechisms, Stephan?"

"Of course, Father," Steve said praying he did not ask for one since he really did not.

Father Murchandha asked Steve if he was planning on hiking to the top today. Steve spoke with an affirmative. The pastor then looked over his shoulder to make sure the kids did not follow him. "Listen, I know this is your day off, but if you could keep an eye out for three guys up there.

Yesterday afternoon three guys took the trail and I have not seen them come back since. They did not look as if they were prepared for a night of camping. I'm worried that maybe something happened to them. Would you keep an eye out for me please?"

Steven told the pastor he would look out for them at the top and if he did not see them, he would take the trail back down.

"All right, Stephan. Thank you. You're a good man. God Bless" the pastor said as he patted Steve on the shoulder.

"God Bless you father."

The pastor went back to the kids and Steve could hear him loudly say, "All right kids, say goodbye to Officer Steube."

The kids all once said, "Goodbye, Officer Steube!"

Steve feigned a laugh and waved as he said back, "Bye kids." He turned around to face the mountain and mumbled to himself, "Ya, miserable little cocksuckers." Steve did not think those specific kids were miserable little cocksuckers. It was more of a generalized statement about all kids.

It was time to climb. Time to clear the mind. With that, Steve started his ascent from the base and made his way to the actual climbing part. It was not a super big challenge for him. This was a climb he had completed numerous times before. He could probably do it in his sleep. There were even anchors on this mountain he had left behind himself. Still, that did not make him appreciate the climb any less. It was a time away from the stress of his job and the stress of his life. With each inch further up the mountain he made, was another shimmy up and away from his life on the ground.

It was not that he did not enjoy his life on the ground. Steve had a pretty good life the way he saw it. He was not attached to anyone holding him down. He had a decent job. It is not what he dreamt of doing as a kid. He never would have thought the day would come that he would be a cop. It was a job. He had good pay and benefits. In his experience, Steve thought there were two types of cops. There were the ones who did it for the power and then there were the ones that did it for the paycheck. In his mind, he did it for the paycheck. He was not out to ruin anyone's day. He was not out setting speed traps and pushing his badge in people's faces. He was there to protect and serve. Should someone break the law, then he was there to enforce the law. He knew he did not write the laws. He only enforced them. Even with that, he was pretty lenient with people. He was willing to give anyone the benefit of the doubt as long as they did not set off his bullshit detector. There may have been times he used his badge in ways that it was not meant to be used, like scoring with the ladies. But overall, he thought of himself as one of the good guys.

Steve was at the top of the mountain. He had completed the climb. He took off his gear and stood near the edge overlooking the Peeking Islands. From this view, it seemed so peaceful. He could see every bit of the islands from where he stood and every inch of those islands had a memory to offer him. He loved it here. He was born here, raised here, and knew he would die here. He had no reason to live anywhere else. The channels between the islands had boats upon boats. Some were destination bound while others sat in place as people fished off of them. He looked to his right and saw the tip of Martillo. Aullando Calla Lobo, where he went to military school. Looking to his left he saw the marshlands of Shady'tn. Looking straight ahead he saw Isla Sirena and Manta just beyond that. If he looked a little bit to the right of those two he saw Bear Island and the Vista Bahia mountains and beyond that was Isla Fantasma. From this spot, he could see how all these islands got their names. Isla Fantasma looked like a ghost! It had mountains at the north making hair, two little lakes just below those mountains forming eyes and everything south of that was woodland surrounded by beach. He had many good camping memories there. Bear Island kind of looked like a bear. He guessed. He did not see it, but he'd buy it. Isla Sirena looked like a manatee, or mermaid as the old-time sailors thought they were. The island he was on, Isla de la Martillo was shaped like a hammerhead shark. This was a special place. Not just the mountain he was on, but the island chain itself. This was home.

His thoughts were interrupted when he heard a voice say, "Steve-OH". Shocked, he turned around. He saw three men before him. His thoughts went back to what Father Murchandha had told him about three men going up the trails. They were big men, all of them were at least six feet tall and packing some good weight. They all had beards. They wore jeans, boots, and flannel shirts over T-shirts. Steve noticed they all carried pocketknives attached to their belts.

Steve's cop instinct took over and assessed the situation in his mind. Realizing that he was near the edge of a cliff and had three men in front of him, he was in a bad spot. He asked, "Can I help you, gentlemen? Are you lost?

The man in the middle spoke up. "Are you Steve Steube?"

Steve was trying to put this man's face with a memory. "I'm sorry, who are you?"

The man spoke up again, "Just answer the question, stupid. Are you Steve Steube?"

Out of habit, Steve reached to his shoulder where there was no radio to call. He did have a VHF radio, but it was in his bag.

"I am Officer Steve Steube, now who are you?"

The man spoke up again while the other two remained silent with their arms at their sides. "I'm Jillian's husband."

Steve tried to access his memory again for someone named Jillian that he would have either arrested, given a ticket to, anything. Nothing was coming to mind.

The man on the left spoke as he said, "Jillian Heizer, dipshit. The woman you slept with. This man's husband!"

A light went off in Steve's head. He had slept with many different girls. He had many hash marks on his bedpost, figuratively speaking. He did remember Jillian though. She was quite the number if this is whom they were speaking of. "Whoa, now listen up. She wasn't wearing a ring when I was with her. And if she was your wife, then you need to be talking to her and working on whatever is wrong at home."

The man in the middle yelled, "IS. She IS my wife, not was. IS. And son, you are no place to be telling me how to run my house."
Steve's heart rate was starting to race. He knew this because his watch vibrated a message telling him to sit down and take a break.

Steve was in a really bad spot. He had three men in front of him who probably were not here for a social call, a cliff behind him and he had no way to call for backup. Steve said, "Now hold on gentlemen. We can talk this out."
The man on the right said, "Time for talkn' is done. Come on Jeb, let's get this done."
Putting his hands out in front of himself in protest Steve told the men, "Now, I don't know what you are thinking, but you don't want to do this. I'm on an officer of the law."

The man in the center, who was presumably named, Jeb said, "Which will make this all the more worthwhile. Grab him."

The men on each side of Jeb rushed Steve and there was a tussle as Steve tried to break any hold they could get on him. He fought as well as he could and he may have gotten in a good swing or two but he could not hold off the two men indefinitely. In a matter of seconds, they had won and were each holding onto Steve's arms. They were holding him in place. Jeb walked right up to Steve as he took off his flannel shirt. He had a tattoo of a woman on his right forearm. Steve said. "Now come on. If you got a beef with me, let's be fair. Three on one? How about just you and me go round for round?"

Jeb did not answer. He wound up and took a swing. Hitting him right in the jaw. It was followed by another hit from the other hand. Again, right to the face. Steve forced a laugh as he spat blood out right on Jeb and asked, "That's the best you got, boy? Your wife can smack my ass harder than that." Steve was trying to get into Jeb's head. He knew that if he could get this stupid redneck flustered enough, he might make a mistake and give Steve an opening.

Jeb took a few more swings. Some were to the face and some were to the stomach. In between punches, Steve would gasp for air and spit out more blood on the ground in Jeb's direction. Jeb took a step back and made a motion with his head to the two men holding him. In one single motion, they threw Steve on the ground and were both kicking him in his sides repeatedly. All Steve could do at this point was play defense and try to cover his head. As he was taking a beating Steve could hear Jeb yell, "All right boys. Hold up, hold up. Pick him up." The two men hoisted Steve up and before he could even get his bearings Jeb had already taken a few more jabs to Steve's face. Steve was starting to get a little dizzy and felt himself fall to the ground. He was trying to catch his breath and block out the pain. He could hear Jeb talking as he hovered above Steve. "Boy, I hope your learning somethin' today. Don't mess with a man's woman."

One of the men said, "He ain't going to be messn' with any woman now. Look at his face."

Another man said, "No more ladies for you pretty boy, you done messed up."

Steve went to spit again and this time spit out a couple of teeth."

Jeb said to his friends, "I have half a mind to chop this boy up and use him for chum."

One of the other men basically repeated that statement when he laughed and said, "Yeah, Let's chop him up and use him for chum."

Steve was digging deep in his mind trying to grab on to some bit of spirit that had not been beaten out of him. He had been through much worse than this when he was a kid in military school. He closed his eyes and remembered how they taught him that the mind is very strong and can make one go on when they think there is no more gas in the tank.

Jeb was still yammering on about his wife when Steve came out of his reflective state. He continued to lie on the ground as he scanned the ground surrounding him with his eyes. He saw it. The golden ticket. It was a rock. It was kind of oval and jagged all around the edges. It was the perfect size to knock someone out and small enough to get a good grip on. It was about the size of a potato.

Steve slowly and with a bit of stealth, grabbed the rock and held it tightly in his hand. He closed his eyes and took himself back to his military school days. He could hear his cadre yelling at him. The voice in his head said, "Get up, private!

Dig Deep! Get up. You have so much more left in you! What if you were really a POW right now? Are you going to just lay here and die? Get up, son! Get up!"

Steve took a deep breath and in one fluid motion jumped to his feet. With his arm high in the air, he flung himself in the direction of Jeb, ready to bring the rock in his hand down hard on the temple of Jeb's head with a vengeance. He was up. One step. Almost there. Two steps. Only one more to go. Three steps. He gripped the rock with all his might and clenched his teeth as he started to bring the rock down. He felt himself get tripped as one of the other men had stuck his leg out.

Steve fell toward Jeb and in an automatic muscle response he could not even control, Jeb caught Steve in his arms. The two men were now wrestling in a standing position. The momentum of Steve's fall had sent them twisting, both fighting for balance and neither letting go of the other for fear of giving up an advantageous hold on the other. One twist in a circle of fury. Both men held on to the other with one arm and with one free arm took short jabs in the side of one another. Two twists around in a circle of fury. Jeb could hear his friends cheering him on. Three twists around in a circle of fury. Jeb felt a sharp pain in his side as he felt himself get stabbed repeatedly in a fast and repetitive motion by his own pocketknife now in Steve's hand. Four unbalanced circles of fury. Both men felt weightless as they fell over the edge of the cliff. They only felt that way for a millisecond as gravity did its job.

Both of Jeb's friends stood in stunned silence as they had just watched both men fall off the edge of the cliff. They both looked at each other and back to the cliff again without saying a word. As if using the same brain, they both slowly walked to the edge of the cliff and peered down to the ground twenty feet below. Their friend Jeb lay motionless. A pool of blood surrounded his head. Steve lay motionless as well. One of the men picked up a small rock and tossed it over the edge. Hitting Steve directly in the gut, it had hit its target. From above it appeared Steve did not make a sound.

One man looked to the other and asked, "Huh. Now, what do you suppose happened there?" The other man stood silent for a few seconds before answering and said, "I don't know. I've been out on my boat all morning."

The other man nodded his head up and down and said, "Yeah, me too. Come on, let's skedaddle." Both men scurried away off of the mountain.

LOVE LITE AT NIGHT
(SPRING 2018)

Larissa was laying on her bed in her candlelit room with a glass of wine that sat on her nightstand next to her bed. She stared into a corner of her room that was as dark as her current love, listening to the radio. A slow song faded out and a warm, friendly, slow speaking voice said, "102.7 WVCX. It is Love Lite at night and I'm your host, J. J. Reinhold. Hello, caller, you're on the air"

It was a male voice on the phone that said, "Hey J.J., love your show, listen to you all the time"

"Thank you, who is this I am speaking with?"

"My name is Simon and I just want to send a shout-out to my girl. Her name is Kerry."

J.J. asked, "Anything special you want to say to Kerry, Simon?"

"Yeah, man. She is so special. She could have chosen from so many different men, but she chose me. I just want to say, Kerry, you are well worth the fight, and I would do anything to keep you near me forever. You bring feeling and meaning to my life. You totally inspire me. I love you, baby."

As a song stated that exemplified the words Simon had just spoke J.J. said, "It is Love Lite at night, with me, J.J. Reinhold on 102.7 WVCX

It was the perfect day in late May. Which meant a few things. The weather could not have been better. Every day was picture perfect and the temperature was amazing. It was the wedding season. Because of the near-perfect weather, this time of year is when many couples would travel to the island chain to exchange vows for life. Rebirth was abundant everywhere that one would look. The flowers and trees broke out in the most vibrant colors they could. Every day at approximately 3:35 in the afternoon the island would get a fifteen minute rain shower that would recharge the island life for the night to come. Then there was the new birth of life being created in the ocean with the sea turtles.

Mating was slightly more of a daunting task for the sea turtles than it would be the newlywed couples in human form on the island. For starters, it was all done in the water.

A male sea turtle had approached his mate. Whether she was accepting to him or she was just going with the flow really did not appear to matter. While swimming through the water, the male approached his chosen mate and mounted her from above her shell.

His long tail helped to hold the female to him, as he would fertilize the eggs. His front flippers had long claws that he was using to clench onto his mate by the front of her shell and hold himself in place. Her front flippers moved graciously up and down as it was up to her to keep them moving through the open water. Occasionally she would take them both to the surface for a breath of fresh air. This was no time to relax, however. Their frolicking of passion was attracting other males to the area. The male-to-female ratio was not a fair one. There were far more males in the sea than females. Competition could be fierce.

As the lovers swam bound together to create new life, other males in the area noticed a voluptuous female giving away her virtue. Each of them thinking they were more entitled than the next, made their way to the couple that had drifted off of the reef. They attacked the male, trying to knock him off of his mate so they could take his place. They knew he could not fight back as his front flippers were currently in use to hold on with all of his might. There was no way he was going to give up this opportunity. He had won this one over and was not going to give her up. Not at this point in the game anyway. The other males did not give up. They would try and try to find other ways to dislodge this suitor that had preyed upon what they thought belonged to them. As one would try to knock him off of his lover another approached from the other side and bit one of his flippers. Another went below the couple and tried using a blast of air bubbles. When that did not work another male hungry for some love wedged his head between the two and tried to wedge them apart.

The mating male wanted so badly to be left alone. He wanted so much, to fight off these other rival males. He could not though. He knew this. He knew that fighting back would mean losing his grip. He knew that is just what his rivals wanted. He was bound and determined to clench on for his dear life. He was a good boy. He had worked too hard. Waited too long for this match to happen. The future of his name depended on this one moment of passion under the waves of the open water.

The female put her head up, as she once again took them to the surface for a breath of air. She then took her, and her lover, into a deep dive straight down away from the flocking males. But four more new males showed up, fresh and ready to place their bid. They were all trying the same techniques as if it had been bred into the mind of all-male turtles. The male, on top of his mate, was starting to get worn down. He was determined to hold on with everything he had. He was prepared to dig deep. Deeper and deeper he went, into his mind to hold on to this moment of life recreating life. The deeper that they went, the deeper he went into a trance-like state to finish what he had started.

As exhausted as he was, it was nothing compared to what his lover was feeling. For, he was only struggling to hold on. The female had spent this entire time struggling if for no other reason, to survive. She had the weight of her lover on top of her the whole time. It was as if she were being held down. She was swimming for two. Other males in the area, rather than come to her rescue only seemed interested in taking his place. It was hours later that the coupling had come to an end. Without the courtesy of even an after cuddle, the two went about their separate way. Regardless, the seed for a new life had been planted. With a little luck, there would be a new life on the island in about forty-five days.

It was starting to look like a hot mid-June day as Andy sat on Looking Man beach. As the sun started to rise above the horizon his feet were buried in the sand. Despite the sand still being cool from the darkness of night, he could already feel the heat from the sun starting to awaken over the horizon. It felt soothing to his face but harsh on his eyes. He reached into his pocket and put on his sunglasses. Sitting on a beach anywhere was always good medicine for the soul at any time of the day. Andy loved the beach and enjoyed looking at the sea. If he believed in reincarnation he would have been sure that he had been a sailor at one point in the history of life. Looking out to the sea was inspiring for him. His best ideas always came from moments like this. A slight chill was still in the air soon to be replaced by the heat from the bright shining sun. There was not a cloud in the sky to be seen. Today was going to be a good day.

A good day was exactly what Andy needed. Those were few and far between recently. There was the unexpected passing of Nina. Adding that loss was the unfortunate death of Tino. Not to mention of course hurricane Tonya. All of those had left some residual recovery that was still occurring. It was not only in the physical sense but the mental sense as well. Hurricane Tonya had left her mark on many islanders. This small chain of blissful islands hid an ugly secret which was many of the locals had been given a dose of PTSD from the storm leading to their self-inflicted demise.

Andy felt at one with the island and could feel that as of lately, the heartbeat of the island had not been the same. This island needed a hit of positivity. Andy needed a hit of positivity. Over the past few years, Andy had sunken into a pit of darkness. He had felt so alone. He felt that no one cared about him, not in the way Nina had anyway. She was special. She was different and there would never be a person that could come close to taking her place. He felt he would no longer have a muse to inspire and push him to follow through with his ideas. He tried to fill that hole with Marie. As it turned out Marie was a rebound from the loss of Nina, which, his mind, tried to subconsciously push away. Recently he had concluded that he had to accept Nina's death and move on. His choices were to wallow in self-pity and depression or get his head back up in the air. It was time to turn the page and flip the script.

FLIP THE SCRIPT! (SPRING 2018)

Andy scanned the beach and could see areas of it had been taped off into squares. These areas are where turtles had laid their eggs. Every year the state would seek out these future places of birth and cordon them off to would-be passerby. They would be born soon. There was a rebirth about to hit the island.

He stood up and kicked most of the sand from his feet. He felt the weight of the sand come off his feet as well as the weight of grief on his soul. The sun had completely risen over the horizon and a new day had begun. It was time to leave yesterday exactly where it was, in the past.

He reached into his backpack and took out a single rose that earlier he had put some of Nina's ashes on. He held it and looked at it briefly. He took in all the fond memories he had of her at once. Andy reached into his pocket and took out a poem that he had scribbled onto a piece of paper. He read it out loud, knowing that somehow Nina was listening and smiling, as she loved his writing. It would have been about this time of day that she would be reading anything he had emailed to her in the middle of the night before. When he was done he placed the rose into the outgoing tide and watched it go out to sea. He smiled as thoughts of a seed he had planted in his mind only a couple months of ago were about to blossom.

He heard a voice behind him that gave him a startle, as he was lost in thought thinking he was alone on this quiet beach at sunrise.

"Mr. Chelios?"

Andy jumped and turned around as a smile hit his face. "Oh hey. How are you?"

It was Pete Barrios. He was the contractor Andy hired for a project he was working on.

The two men shook hands as Pete said, "Thanks for meeting me out here this morning. We are just about done at the job site and I wanted to give you a walkthrough and hand you the keys."

Andy felt a sudden wave wash over him. This is something he had implemented after Nina's death. It was an idea that came to him, out of nowhere, while sitting on this same beach. It was an epiphany. He knew it was an idea that had been sent to him from Nina and Tino. Thinking about it and planning it was one thing. This was different. It was actually going to happen. Now was the time for Andy to step to the plate and swing.

The two walked up the beach to a large structure. The building that had formally sat on this property was known as Sunrise Pet Care. It was a kennel for pet owners to have their pets watched over if they away from the island. It was a pet sitting home. That building had been mostly destroyed by hurricane Tonya. Pete looked at Andy, and asked, "You nervous?"

Andy clapped his hands together and said, "Yeah. I feel like one of those people on TV that have a completely revamped house or business revealed to them. But I'm excited. Let's do this."

Pete handed the keys to Andy and said, "Your place. Lead the way."

Andy put the key in the door and closed his eyes. After opening the door, he took a deep breath and an elated smile hit his face.

"Holy shit! Wow. Look at this place!"

Pete said to Andy, "We took your desire of keeping it alive with an island vibe and synergized it with making it look also like the 'in' place in a large city."

Pete gave Andy the tour. "This is where your guests queue up to get their ID checked. Now we added something unique so that your bouncers can control the flow of the patrons entering the club. After checking into the club the bouncers will have two options to send people. They can send them straight ahead"

Andy looked to where Pete pointed and it was a boardwalk bridge that twisted over a Koi pond filled with tropical foliage. This led to a large frosted glass automatic door.

"Now you see all those rocks in the water? Those are speakers that will play music. You can play music straight from the deejay booth or you can have anything else programmed to play on its own channel. Those frosted glass doors lead directly to the dance floor and open automatically. The other way the bouncers can send people to control the flow is by sending them in that direction."

Andy looked to his right and there was a metallic silver automatic door. He asked, "Where does that go?"

"That is an elevator that takes people to a balcony to the second floor. As I explained, it will help control the flow. Your bouncers send one group over the Koi pond and through the doors, which lead straight to the dance floor. Then they can send the next group to the elevator.

"There is a second floor now, What happened to the balcony idea?"

Pete said, "It is more of a balcony that wraps around and overlooks the entire dance floor. We'll get to that in a bit. You ready for more?"

Andy told him, "Um, yeah. So wait. You said the bouncers control the flow by sending people one way or the other. How do they decide who goes where?"

Pete shrugged his shoulders, "Hey man. I just build the stuff. This is your bar. That's up to you. Now before we move on look over to your left."

Being that Andy was the person who designed this club, none of what Pete was showing him should have come as a surprise. However, since Andy was not completely sure what he was doing, all he had given Pete was a basic idea of what he wanted. Plus, the ideas that Andy did expect, he was not expecting it to look this amazing. This looked like a real nightclub!

Andy looked to the left, just before the boardwalk leading over the Koi pond leading to the dance floor. He noticed a fairly large area that looked like it was outdoors but was actually indoors. Along the far wall was a bar about twenty feet long. Behind the bar, and above the area that display bottles would go was a large aquarium that had small sharks swimming in it. In the middle of the floor, there were about eight tall tables with no chairs. Wrapping around the other three walls were areas that had sand and trees. Those were blocked off by a wooden fence to prevent people from going in them. Andy was in awe as all he could say was, "Wow."

Pete told him, "Think of this as an area where people can chill, get away from the dance floor, while still being able to drink and mingle. Just like with all the rocks in that Koi pond, there are many things you see that are really speakers and you can do with those what you choose."

Again, all Andy could say was, "Wow."

Pete laughed and told him, "You haven't even seen your main floor yet."

"So, wait", Andy interjected. "Those sharks, are they going to get big and outgrow the tank?"

"No. Those are freshwater captivity-bred sharks, Andy. They don't grow any bigger than the space allows. In an aquarium such as this one, they will probably never get longer than eight inches. Come on, follow me."

They walked over the boardwalk bridge and to the large, frosted glass automatic doors. As the door opened a sudden blast of fog rushed from above to the ground. Pete said, "That is as much for comfort as it is for looks."

Andy said, "yeah, it helps cool off people coming off the hot dance floor."

Andy looked around the dance floor. It was a very large empty space, as any dance floor should be. Along the two walls to the left and right, were bars almost the length of the wall it was adjacent to. The far wall ahead of them had a small stage. In the middle of the giant dance floor was the deejay booth that was on a pedestal. Pete and Andy climbed into the deejay booth. It was fifteen feet above the dance floor. The booth had eight decks in it that filled three of the four sides to the booth. This way the D.J. could be facing multiple parts of the crowd he or she was playing to. On one side of the booth was a lighting control board. Pete said, "Now I didn't install this, so I don't know much about it. But I had the lighting tech show me a few tricks so I can show you something since I knew you specifically wanted it." Pete hit a button and the entire dance floor dimmed to barely a candlelight level. He hit another button and on the far wall that had nothing but a stage were two large and animated blue cat eyes. Andy laughed and said how awesome he thought that looked. Pete hit the button again and the cat lights disappeared. He touched another button and the house lights came back on. "Now you said you wanted to also host sporting events. Watch this." With the flip of a switch, a large screen came down from the ceiling now covering the wall. "You can use this for the big games if you choose. Behind that wall, by the way, is a hidden storage area for tables and chairs."

Andy asked, "So that is my only way to show sports? I didn't see any TVs out in the front room."

Pete told him, "Oh wait, we'll get to that later. Come on, follow me."

They climbed down a ladder out of the deejay booth and walked to the right side of the bar on the right side of the dance floor. "Now you said you wanted both a VIP room and another room with a special bar that gave a speakeasy feel. We did not have the space for two separate rooms so we consolidated those two ideas into one." Pete gestured with his open hand towards a phone booth. The booth was a red London-style booth and was solid and frosted glass all the way around so one had privacy if they were in it. Andy looked at him confused and asked, "What?"

Pete told him to go inside the phone booth. As he did Andy asked, "Now what? I'm in a phone booth. I don't get it." All he saw is what looked like a normal phone booth. Inside was a payphone that only someone who grew up in the eighties or before would recognize and nothing else.

Pete said, "Pick up the phone and enter the numbers; one, nine, three, three." Andy did and a hidden back door clicked open slightly on its own. He pushed it open all the way and was looking at a hidden room. It had one small bar. There were a few tables that were knee-high and were surrounded by lush love seats. The feel and look of the room was that of a late 1920's vibe Andy thought. It was clearly a place where people could chill but at the same time had a very classy feel to it. "Wow, Pete! This room is fucking cool! Man, if I were a guest, I would spend all my time here!"

Pete added, "If you had the code. But I guess you'll decide who gets that and how. By the way, do you know the significance of the code you used to open the secret door?"

"What was it again?", Andy asked.

"It was; one, nine, three, three."

Andy had no clue and knew that he would not but pretended to think before saying, "I give up."

"It was the year probation ended."

"Huh. Who knew? That's cool. I think I'll keep it."

"Are you ready to go up and see the balcony? Do you want to take the stairs or the elevator?" Pete asked. Andy told him, "I've been on an elevator. Unless there is some special surprise you did with it, I'm good with the stairs." The two walked up the stairs. The balcony wrapped all the way around the dance floor and had plenty of walking space. The tops of the guard railings were flat and wide so that patrons could rest their drinks on them. There was a mini guardrail on top that would prevent drinks from falling onto the dance floor. Up against the walls and spaced out evenly were small lounge couches that wrapped halfway around knee-high glass tables. Andy pointed out those and asked, "So those are for my table service. I can rent them out and people can purchase bottles of wine or champagne?"

Pete shrugged his shoulders and said, "Hey man, once again, I just build the place. But now come in here." Andy asked, "You're showing me the ladies' restroom?"

"Yeah, I want to show you something that was an idea my wife had."

Andy walked into the restroom and it looked like a typical nightclub restroom: Stalls, a row of sinks, and an area for a bathroom valet to hand out perfumes for gratuity. Andy asked, "What am a missing?" Pete pointed at numerous signs around the bathroom. They were signs that gave women getting unwanted attention from another bar patron instructions to order a specific drink from any bartender and they would be taken care of. Andy read one of the signs and asked, "So it's like a secret code for a woman to feel safe?" Pete nodded his head up and down as Andy told him his wife was a genius.

"Finally, Andy I want to show you my personal favorite part of the club." The two walked back downstairs and to the back of the main dance floor. From there they went through a door that led to a large porch area. The floor was one giant wooden deck. Tables and chairs were covering it. A tall privacy wall surrounded the whole outdoor area. Along the far wall was a long bar. Andy did not count but he guessed there were at least fourteen large screen TVs. Andy looked to Pete and said, "I noticed you were able to acquire sails to use as a ceiling. I got that idea from a restaurant over on Manta at the seaport. I think it is so cool." "Yes, Andy, and notice the large privacy fence we put all the way around. It's tall enough that no light escapes onto the beach. This way you don't have to shut this part of the bar down during turtle hatching season."

"Right, because we can't have lights visible from the beach during that time. Good thinking Pete." Pete said, "So that's it. What do you think?"

Andy smiled and said, "I love it. It goes beyond my expectations. So, what's this going to cost me?"

"I'll have the office send you your invoice. We were able to come in under the quote and we will work out a deal for you. This is a good thing, Andy. You're giving people a place to hang out that we don't have here and you're providing a lot of jobs. I'm curious. Why didn't you do this at the seaport on Manta? You could have gotten a lot more tourists in."

"For that exact reason, Pete. I wanted a place that belonged to the locals. I will still get tourists here, no doubt about that. Just not as many. It's not them I am after anyway. I want the locals to have a place they can call their own. "

"You've done a great thing, Andy."

Andy nodded his head up and down and thanked Pete as they walked to their cars.

As a song had faded there was the sound of a clown laugh followed by a very hyper voice that said, "It is 102.7 WVCX and the Morning Zoo!" There was the sound of applause. "I am your host, Dave Archellia, along with the rest of the Zoo Crew; Wheezy, Mutt, Diane, Bubba, and Britta!" All the other co-hosts chimed in with their own hello. Dave continued, "Now tell me, Wheezy and Bubba, where can our listeners find you tonight?"

Wheezy spoke up, "Tonight we are going to be at the all-new Club Valentino at Looking Man beach on Isla de Cabeza Martillo!"

Dave asked, "Now that is the brand-new club opening up tonight, owned by former WVCX staffer, Andy Chelios?"

Bubba said, "That's right, sir. This place is on the beach and they have it all. Even a sports bar, I'll tell you what."

"Well, tell us about it" Dianne interjected with intrigue. Wheezy said, "Oh man, Andy created a place just for the people of this island. Bubba's not kidding. Andy gave us a tour the other day and let me tell you- man, this place is super dope! They have a massive dance floor, and two smaller dance floors to check out."

"And they have a sports bar", Bubba added

Wheezy continued, "There is a wrap-around balcony to view the whole main floor from, a special VIP room, Koi ponds, shark tanks, and so many separate bars to get your drink on!"

Dave asked, "Now tell me, Bubba, you saw it all, what was your favorite bar at the all-new Club Valentino at Looking Man?"

"I liked the sports bar," Bubba said slowly as his statement was followed with laughter from the rest of the crew."

"Uh-huh. I see. You mentioned a VIP room. Tell me more about that. That sounds more like my speed since I am a V-V-V-VIP myself."

Wheezy said, "Well that is just the thing Dave, we can't tell you about it. It is a secret. All I can say is first you have to find it. Then after you find it you need a special code to get in. We don't know the code. Andy took us inside it on the tour but did not show us the code to open the hidden door."

Dave asked, "So you know how to at least get there, you just can't get in?"

Both Wheezy and Bubba confirmed.

The morning Zoo host continued. "Well now see, that proves my point about me being a very, very...very important person. In my hand, I have six envelopes that Andy Chelios personally gave me. In these envelopes is the secret code to get in the VIP room. Be listening all day to 102.7 WVCX for your chance to win the code. Six chances all day to win one of these envelopes and your first chance is in the next half hour with Stacy Davis and the midday brunch. My name is Dave Archellia and before we leave you with one more song let me say this. On behalf of myself, and the rest of the Zoo crew here, thank you so much for joining us this morning! We truly appreciate you giving us your time!" There was the sound of clapping in the background, "Stacy Davis is up next on your radio! I am Dave Archellia and this is my Morning Zoo!" The sound of laughter, cheering, and clapping could be heard as it mixed into a stream of laser effects and a voice that said, "It's the Morning Zoo on the station that plays your hottest hits and favorite old school retro, 102.7 WVCX!" An upbeat pop song began to play.

Somewhere in a hallway in the Peeking Broadcasting building, Bob Overwrite could be heard yelling from his office, "What the fuck was that? Was that five minutes of free advertising I just heard?"

ALIVE (SPRING 2018)

The dance floor was packed. It was almost completely dark except for two luminescent blue cat eyes on a far wall that appeared to watch over the floor. A beat with a low, ear-numbing frequency played over the sound system that sounded more like a vibrating hum. It caused a feeling of warmth and anticipated arousal in the heart of every single person on the dance floor. The crowd on the floor all looked up to a deejay booth that they surrounded. From the balcony above a crowd gathered watching in excitement for the crowd below to explode in a fury of crazed madness.

A bright spotlight from the center of the ceiling lit up and pointed straight down on the deejay booth as the crowd cheered. Three men were standing in the booth. A lighting technician, a deejay, and Andy. With a microphone in his hand, Andy looked out over the crowd and yelled, "What's up Peeking?" The crowd answered back with yells and screams. "My name is Andy Chelios, and let me be the FIRST to welcome you to Valentino's! This is your club, Peeking! This is your night, and this is your deejay, Deejay Finz!" The crowd continued to go wild. "Deejay Finz! Spin that shit!" The spotlight went out. The cat's eyes disappeared from the wall. It was completely dark black in the entire club. A slow and low bass line played. It had two tones. It was reminiscent of something that would make one think twice about swimming in the ocean at night. Animated dorsal fins appeared to swim around on the walls surrounding the dance floor. A deep and loud overly modulated voice said, "Deee Jayyyy" It went even lower as it said, "Finzzzz" The letter Z stretched out and had a choppy sound to it. The ominous two-tone bass line that had started slow and creepy picked up its pace without the assistance of a beat. It was its own beat. It picked up its pace till it was at 186 beats per minute. Strobe lights flashing made everything appear to move in a slow stop motion animation. There was an explosion of sound. The floor went dark and silent for what was probably only three seconds. The overly modulated voice once again said, "DEEJAY FINZ!"

A blast of cool feeling fog hit the crowd and brightly colored lights filled every inch of the main room. At the same time, an EDM song started with a heavy bass beat accented by a four-chord progression on piano that made the urge to feel happy irresistible. Confetti dropped down onto the crowd and the floor exploded with energy as vocals sang about the joys of being alive.

Andy looked to the deejay next to him and said, "We did it, brother! We fucking did it!" The deejay looked to Andy and with a hand holding a headset to one ear nodded his head up and down. Andy did not know if he was nodding in agreement or bopping his head to the song he was cueing up. It did not matter. Andy knew he did it and that was all the confirmation he needed.

Andy looked back to the deejay and asked, "You good? You got this?"
Deejay Finz looked to Andy and said, "I totally got this shit, dude! You go do you!"
Andy climbed down the ladder to the floor and was in the mix of it all. He could feel the energy of the crowd. Every single person surrounding him had a big cheesing perma-grin on his or her face. This is exactly the way he had seen it in his dreams.

Andy made his way through the crowd to automatic doors. He walked over the Koi pond to the door. He saw his head of security and asked, "Don! We good?"

Don said, "We are great Andy, a full house." He put his finger to his ear as he appeared to be listening to someone speak into it. He took the small microphone off his collar and quickly said something back. He looked back to Andy and said, "We're good brother!" and turned his attention back to his security team and the guest in front of them. Andy went over to the bar off to the side of the Koi pond where, Amanda, his head bartender was. She handed a drink to a customer, took some money, and looked at Andy as she said, "You need anything, Andy, what can I getcha'?"

Andy smiled and said, "I was about to ask you the same. You need anything? You good?"

She smiled and said, "It's all good in the neighborhood, Andy! Go enjoy your club!"

As he turned around, Andy saw his friend Steve. He was on crutches and had two very good-looking women next to him. He had one on each side. Andy smiled big and greeted his friend that he was very much happy to see alive. "Steve-OH! Bro, it is so good to see you, man! How the fuck are you even alive?"

Steve smiled back to Andy and said, "Dude, it's me. Come on."

"Yeah, but dude, I heard you fell out in the middle of Centro Mountain. How did they even know to look for you there, not only that but how did they know they should even be looking for you?"

With the forefinger of his right hand, he pointed to the watch on his left wrist and said, "This little thing that you make fun of me for wearing? Turns out these little puppies are smarter than we realize. It detected I had a quick elevation change and was not moving after that. It contacted 911 and they were able to find me with GPS."

Andy just nodded his head up and down and said, "Wow. So they took good care of you at the hospital? You didn't harass the nurses too much did you?"

Steve gave Andy a look and said, "Andy, this is Nadia and this is Natalie." Andy was just now noticing the two girls by Steve were twins. "They are the nurses that brought me back to life and now we're celebrating that." Steve leaned into Andy as he said with a wicked smile, "Always room for one more."

Andy smiled back as he disappeared into his mind for a brief second. 'Dude almost dies. Ends up in the hospital, gets two female nurses…that just happen to be twins. And now he is out drinking with them. This would only happen to Steve. '

Andy snapped out of his thoughts and said, "I appreciate the offer, bro, but I'm kind of occupied tonight. You know, opening my club and all. But you enjoy your night."

As Andy started to walk away Steve said, "You too, man. Awesome place you have here bro. You did well."

Andy thanked him and started to walk toward the main room he heard Steve call his name. He turned back around and Steve said, "What about this VIP room I've heard all about? You gonna hook a brother up?" Andy pointed to his right and mouthed, "Phonebooth." Steve said, "Okay, how do I get in once I'm there? What's the secret password?"

Andy said, "It's the last year of prohibition."

Looking confused Steve asked, "What?"

Andy smiled and told him, "Figure it out, Mr. Ness."

One of the twins whispered something in Steve's ear and he smiled with a thumb up as he said, "Got it! Thanks, dude. Have a good night"

Andy said, "You too. Be safe."

Andy went back into the main room, through the dancing crowd, and ran up the stairs. A security man put his hand out toward Andy as he reached the top of the stairs and said, "No running sir." Andy just stopped and looked at him. With a smile, the man said, "Just kidding, Andy. Enjoy your night." Rolling his eyes Andy saw his table service manager. He approached her and yelled out, "Veronica! Everything good? You need anything?" She said, "We are all good, sir. Tables are full and people are ordering."

"Awesome! Do you need anything? Need me to get you any bottles?"

Veronica looked at him with the service smile he hired her for and said, "No sir, we got this. Go enjoy your club!" She turned around and was immediately talking to one of her servers appearing to give some sort of direction. Andy turned and saw an empty space at a railing. He walked up to it and admired the dance floor of the club he had created. He felt a tap on his shoulder as a guy next to him said, "Hey man, my girl was there. She just went to the bathroom. She'll be back."

Andy looked to the stranger and said, "Sorry." As he started to walk away he could hear the guy say, "No worries, man."

Andy laughed to himself as he walked away and toward the elevator. He walked in and was followed by a girl as the doors closed behind them. Andy hit the button that had a large number one on it. The girl was dressed in a tight black leather skirt and wore a sparkly top that had nothing but strings on the back and some sparkly material covering only the chest area in the front. A lot of girls wore these and Andy referred to them as wonder shields, as they made him think of a shield. He looked at the girl and nervously said, "Hi." She said, "Hi. I'm Shelly. Are you enjoying yourself tonight?" The elevator started to move, as Andy was about to introduce himself, Shelly interrupted and said, "Yeah, this place is the shit! It's owned by a local radio deejay."

Andy looked at her and said, "Oh, really. Yeah, I think—" Shelly interrupted again as she said, "Uh-huh. Andy Chelios on 102.7. Him and me are good friends. We go way back. Uh-huh. Way back."

Andy asked, "Oh really? That's cool."

The doors opened and Shelly walked out first. Andy saw her greet what must have been her friends. As she walked to them she could be heard yelling, "What's up, bitches!" She then stumbled and waved her hands high up in the air. Andy gave a half-smile, as he had no idea who that girl was. He had never met her in his life. He gave himself a shrug as he walked out onto the sports patio. There were no sports on tonight. It was a designated chill-out zone tonight. The bar served a variety of IPA's and this area had another deejay playing music. It was more of an ambient chill music as was the attitude on the patio. It was a place for people to get a break from the loud thumping music, grab a smoke, talk, or just chill. Andy made his way to the bar and got the bartender's attention. He came right over and asked, "What can I get you, Andy?"

Andy smiled and said, "I left a black backpack behind your bar earlier, Zach. May I get that please?" As Zach handed the backpack over Andy said, "Thanks Zack, can I get you anything, need any help?"

"We are all good here, sir. You enjoy your night!" Zach gave Andy two thumbs up and went back to conversing with his patrons at the bar.

Andy turned around and was facing the patio again. He admired it. At night it looked so awesome. It was dimly lit and tiki torches were placed all over the area. There was a fire pit with people around it engaged in conversation. If he were not so awkward and afraid of conversation with strangers, this area most likely would have been his favorite part of the entire club. It was chill.

The past three hours rushed through his mind. It had been such an adrenaline rush. Now that he was out in the 'chill-out zone' as he called it in his mind he felt it all coming down. The rush was leaving his body. He placed his hands on his hips and said out loud to himself, "Huh. Nobody needs me. They're all good." He let out a big sigh. A tear rolled down Andy's cheek. He was a man of the people, for the people and now he could physically see it. He hated that phrase with a passion, but now that he could physically attach it to something he did not mind it so much.

Andy walked to the back corner of the patio to a door marked, "private". He looked over his shoulder and pushed on the door. Andy walked out of the club and was on sand. He was surrounded in darkness as the door closed behind him. Andy looked to his left and about jumped out of his skin as he saw a large shadow standing next to him. It spoke and said, "Hi Andy. Everything all right?"

Breathing quickly and putting his hand on his chest said, "Yeah, Carl. Thanks, how are you?"

Carl's voice was deep and could move mountains. Yet, it was calming at the same time. "I'm good sir. Can I get you anything?"

"No, Carl. I'm good. Listen, you cannot sneak up on me like that. You almost gave me a heart attack. What are you doing out here?" Carl said, "Protecting your fortress, sir, and of course making sure there are not any shenanigans going on back here."

"Shenanigans. Right. I just wanted to come out for some fresh air. I want to go and sit on the beach for a little bit. Is that okay? You need me to get you anything? Do you need water, bell around your neck? Anything?"

"No sir. You said you are going to the beach? Do you have a radio?"

Andy felt his pockets. "Yeah, I'm good Carl. Thanks."

"I'll be on channel six if you need me, sir. Enjoy your night."

Andy walked out onto the beach. He tossed his backpack on the ground and sat down next to it. He sat in the sand and looked up at stars as he thought about Nina and Tino.

He reached into the backpack and pulled out a pistol. Holding the pistol in his hand across his lap he checked the chamber. He looked out towards the dark sea. He heard the sound of the waves coming in and the muffled beats from the club behind him. Andy took a deep breath and put the pistol to his head. With a big breath, he pulled the trigger and there was a click. Andy put his hand down and was once again holding the pistol in his lap. The waves continued to crash in on the shore as he said out loud, "Huh. It's just that easy."

He reached back into his bag and pulled out a clip for the pistol and loaded it in. He then set the weapon on the sand next to him.
Andy sat on the beach looking at the loaded gun in the sand by his side. He thought about the reasons he should not do this. The pain of those left behind, but really would there be anyone left behind? Isn't this why he was here? Because there was nobody who cared? Nobody seemed to listen. What about the mess? He did not want to leave a

mess for paramedics to clean up any more than he wanted to leave an unmade bed for housekeeping. More importantly, what if he failed? What if he only injured himself drastically and survived. Not only would he suffer the embarrassment of a suicide attempt, but he'd also be disfigured or brain-damaged. All the what ifs played in his head. But they could not play louder than the voice that told him this is the only way out.

He once again reached into his backpack and pulled out a rose. He tossed it down in front of him at his feet. He had bought it earlier from a street busker over on Manta.
It was the last rose in her basket and he had haggled with her to get it. The color had faded and it had a broken stem. It was her last rose. He looked at the rose by his feet and felt himself like the last rose on the ground. This was no way to feel. There had to be another way out. Then Andy felt an urge come on to him. It was almost irresistible. It was as if he had to sneeze.

From the backdoor of Valentino's, Carl stood at guard. The darkness he looked into was interrupted as he saw a bright flash in the distance followed by a loud boom.

As the lightning in the distance painted the sky and the rolling thunder answered in reply, suddenly, it occurred to Andy this was no way to end this. A sneeze that otherwise would be a clever and crafty symbolic undertone that had been foreshadowed to signify the end of his own life? Is that really how it all ends? No. That was no way to end this. He had flipped the script. From his place in the sand on the beach, Andy looked up to the stars. In his head, he could hear the sound of Nina's crazy laughter. She was watching down on him. She was happy for him. The happy memories of her smile made him feel warm. It took him to a place where the streets are made of gold and the walls of jasper. He could hear the music pulsating from his club behind him a short distance away. He knew he had created something special. It was a place for the people to come together and act as if their personal pains did not matter. He had found what he had been chasing after, and that was a beat in his heart that he promised himself would now beat with a cheerful purpose. A tear of joy rolled down his cheek as two stars twinkled at him from the sky. He knew it was Nina and Tino giving their approval. Andy was alive.

Hatchlings
By Andy Chelios

The last wave from the high tide came up with one final grasp on the beach before switching to low tide. With it, it grabbed the last rose and took it out to sea for a never-ending ride. Baby sea turtles hatched out of their eggs and scurried along the sand. The hatchlings scurried in the soft beach sand in the direction of the full moon. This path would take them out to the ocean where a new life awaited them. Some would make it, some would not. For each a different life, they would live. Nothing was written or set in stone. There would be no room for hate. There would always be a chance to appreciate. They would each reach a fork where they must choose the path to take. At the end of the day, no matter what, they could flip the script and create their own fate.

AUTHOR'S NOTE

A topic in this book that is very real and needs to be discussed is suicide. It is very important to realize that understanding the issues concerning suicide is a way to take part in prevention.

Suicide does not know race, class, or gender. It can get the best of anyone, even when they seem to be in what may appear to be the best of situations. There will still be signs. Please learn how to look for the warnings. Evidence shows that learning to be aware, talking about suicide, removing means of self-harm, and following up with loved ones are just some of the actions we can take to help others.

If you are someone who has or is currently contemplating this route, please know that there are people who care and are willing to listen. Most importantly, you should know that tomorrow would not be the same without you.

The national suicide prevention lifeline is a toll-free number that is staffed twenty-four hours a day and seven days a week.

1-800-273-TALK (8255)

The lifeline does feature TTY services for the hearing impaired.

1-800-799-4TTY (4889)

The lifeline provides Spanish speakers as well as Tele-interpreters to service the crisis centers.

1-800-628-9454

For more information on how you may become more aware of suicide prevention visit:

www.suicideprevention.org

ABOUT THE AUTHOR

Ted Messimer was raised in Naples, Florida and now resides in the Florida Keys. He got his start in writing by documenting paranormal activity and history. He decided to make a switch to fiction as it allowed him more freedom to speak with creativity. Ted enjoys kayaking, hiking, cooking, sports, and horseback riding.